TAKING ANOTHER Chance

A PRIDE AND PREJUDICE VARIATION

TAKING ANOTHER *Chance*

A PRIDE AND PREJUDICE VARIATION

BRENDA J. WEBB

Taking Another Chance is a work of fiction. All characters are either from the author's imagination, or from Jane Austen's novel, Pride and Prejudice.

DarcyandLizzy@earthlink.net
www.darcyandlizzy.com/forum
ISBN-9781070263618

Cover design and formatting by Roseanna White

*I dedicate this book, as always, to those who
helped me create this story.
My friend and editor, Debbie Styne,
whose expertise and encouragement are invaluable.
My betas: Kathryn Begley, Janet Foster,
Tracy Brown, Terri Merz and Wendy Delzell,
who do everything within their power to make the story error free
and, lastly, to those who enjoy my books.
Thank you for promoting them by word of mouth and review.
Without your help and support, I would not be writing.
Thank you all for being a part of my team.*

Chapter 1

Weymouth
Claxton Hall
June 2, 1826

In the eight years she had resided at Claxton Hall, Elizabeth Bennet had grown to love the estate and its occupants, especially the children she served as governess. She had come to know the family after Lord Claxton's maiden aunt, who had resided in Wales, hired her as a companion. She had held that position for six years until Lady Edith's death. Afterwards, Lady Claxton had approached her about becoming the governess for their four children, and Elizabeth had eagerly accepted.

As was customary for the last day of the week, she prepared to meet with the mistress in her personal study to report on the children's progress with their lessons; however, when Elizabeth entered the room, she was taken aback to see Lord Claxton standing by the window.

"Come in, Miss Bennet," Lady Claxton said as she motioned to a chair. "Please be seated."

As soon as Elizabeth had complied, she added, "I hope you do not mind if my husband joins us today, for he and I have something important to discuss with you."

Though a large lump had suddenly formed in her throat, Elizabeth heard herself reply, "Of course not, my lady."

"First, I wish to state we both agree that you have done an excellent job as our children's governess. We could not have asked for anyone better suited for the position," Lady Claxton said, looking to her husband for confirmation. He nodded.

Have done? Elizabeth tried to swallow but found her throat was too dry.

"However, now that Julia is thirteen, we believe the time has come..."

Elizabeth could see Lady Claxton's mouth moving but she could no longer follow her words. Her mind was reeling. She knew the time would come when her services would not be needed, but she had never dreamed it would come this soon.

"Next Friday will be your last day as governess, and we assume you will want to begin looking for another position straightaway. Of course, we will provide you with a glowing letter of recommendation and an extra month's pay."

Elizabeth found herself smiling wanly, though her heart was beating like a drum. She had become attached to all four of the Claxton daughters, especially the youngest. Steeling herself not to cry when it came time to reply, she waited patiently for Lady Claxton to finish.

"Howard and I think of you as almost a member of the family, and it is our hope that you will keep in touch. I know the girls will want to know how you are. Moreover, if you are ever in the area, we want you to visit us."

Elizabeth stood, smoothing her skirts awkwardly as she willed her voice not to break. "I thank you for the kindness you have shown me during my employment. It has been my privilege to serve as governess for your daughters, and I should like to write to the girls often."

"We intend to provide a private coach to take you anywhere you like," Lord Claxton said.

"That will not be necessary."

"It will be our pleasure," Lady Claxton insisted. "We are determined to see you safely to your family. Which of your relations will you choose to visit?"

The question stirred old wounds as Elizabeth recalled that her mother and father were no longer at Longbourn, having died within months of each other the year after Lydia ran off with Mr. Wickham. Mary was married to a vicar, Charles Logan, had three children, and lived just outside London in Richmond. Kitty had married one of Uncle Phillips' law clerks, David Miller, borne four children and still resided in Meryton. It was Jane, however, whom Elizabeth was closest to and with whom she would stay until she found new employment. Moreover, Jane's house was large enough to accommodate all the sisters and their families, so they could reunite whilst she was there.

"I shall go to Jane's home in Cheapside. After all, London is the best place to begin a search for another position."

"If you like, we should be glad to spread the word among our friends that the finest governess in all of England is now available," Lady Claxton said, smiling.

"I should appreciate that very much."

"Excellent," Lord Claxton continued. "Just leave an address where they may contact you."

"I thank you."

Elizabeth was able to reach her room before collapsing on the bed in tears. She found the prospect of being without employment disturbing, not only because she needed a means of support, but because being busy caring for the children had helped to keep her mind off her greatest regret. It had been easier not to think of Mr. Darcy whilst living in Wales, and later Weymouth, because it was unlikely she would ever be thrown into his company there; however, should she be employed by a family that lived in London, or spent a great deal of time there, the odds of running into him could increase dramatically.

What would I do if I met him by chance? Pretend indifference? She shook her head. To dwell on that prospect now would drive her mad. *Perhaps if I am fortunate, I can secure another position far from London or Derbyshire.*

London
Cheapside
Nine days later

The closer she got to London, the more apprehensive Elizabeth felt. If she believed the tales of her friends in service, the fact that she had excellent employers for the past fourteen years was not something of which most companions or governesses could boast. Fortunately, Lord and Lady Claxton had been generous with her separation pay, and it would be some time before she would have to seek another position.

Elizabeth glanced out the window of the coach. Instantly recognising that the bridge they were soon to cross was the one nearest Jane's residence in Cheapside, she clutched her bag in anticipation of disembarking. Soon, the coach skidded to a stop, and the door was opened. Whilst her trunk was being set on the ground, she stepped out of the vehicle to see Jane and her family waiting patiently beside the mercantile building where she had instructed them to meet her, which would leave the Claxton's coach free to return to Weymouth.

"Lizzy!" Jane cried rushing towards her, and immediately Elizabeth was caught in her sister's embrace.

"How did you know when to be here? We arrived earlier than I said we would."

"Jonathan, the children and I have been waiting here since morning," Jane said. "We did not want to miss you, so we spent the day in town. The children loved having a picnic in the park."

Ignoring the fact that *town* was no more than a few buildings, Elizabeth glanced to where Jane's husband, Jonathan Cowan, stood with their four sandy-haired children: Thomas, age twelve, David, age eight, Betsy, who was six, and Susanna, who was almost four. When she smiled and headed in their direction, Betsy broke from the others and ran to her.

Throwing her arms around Elizabeth's legs, she said, "Aunt Lizzy, I have missed you so much."

That paved the way for all the children to surround her, and Elizabeth struggled not to cry as she embraced them all in turn. Over their heads, she smiled at Jonathan, who motioned to a footman to take her trunk and then spoke to the Claxtons' driver. As that vehicle rolled away, he walked towards her.

"It is good to see you again, Brother."

Jane's handsome, blond-haired husband smiled and bowed. Elizabeth had always thought this tall, quiet fellow more handsome than Mr. Bingley, though she never mentioned the man who once broke Jane's heart.

"It is always nice to see you, Lizzy."

Suddenly, Jane declared, "We had best return to the house as soon as possible. I left our new cook instructions on how to stew a chicken, and Lord knows what we will find when we return. I shall be glad if the house has not burned down."

Elizabeth laughed. "Is she that awful?"

"She is a sweet girl, and her mother was a cook for many years for our neighbour; however, despite the fact that she answered my advertisement for a cook, I do not think she learned a thing from her mother."

As the footman followed them down the street with her trunk, Elizabeth teased, "Jane, how do you always manage to hire people for positions they cannot perform? First the lady's maid who was never a lady's maid and now—"

"Do not start with me, Lizzy," Jane cautioned kindly, threading her arm through her sister's. "The woman had excellent references. How was I to know they were forged? And you know I cannot be stern if someone starts to cry."

"It is one of her weaknesses," Jonathan quipped over his shoulder. "And one of the things I love most about her."

Jane blushed whilst Elizabeth beamed. Leaning close to her sister, Elizabeth whispered, "You may not have an eye for servants, but you certainly picked a prize for a husband."

"I did, did I not?" Jane replied, glancing dreamily at her husband. "Oh, Lizzy, I would give anything if you could find someone like Jonathan to marry. You were not made for spinster-hood."

"I beg your pardon! I have made an excellent spinster!" Forcing a smile, she added, "I am content."

"You can fool others, Lizzy, but not me. Your words ring hollow, and I see the loneliness in your eyes."

"If I am lonely, I have no one to blame but myself. I had the chance to marry a man I could have esteemed, but pride blinded me to his true character, and I do not believe someone of my station gets more than one chance like that in a lifetime."

"Please do not say that. We both know when you visited Pemberley with our aunt and uncle that Mr. Darcy acted as though he still cared for you. I believe he wanted to give you another chance."

"That was before Lydia ran away with Mr. Wickham. Mr. Darcy could never have accepted that villain as a brother, which was evident when he did not return to Meryton. Besides, why speak now of him caring for me when he has long since been married?"

"There are plenty of good, eligible men, if only you would give one a chance. Whilst they may not be the men we fantasized about marrying when we were young, I dare say you could find contentment just as I have."

"In truth, you married the last good man in all of England," Elizabeth teased, "and I flatly refuse to spend what little time I have with you discussing men who do not exist."

Resignedly, Jane changed the subject. "I dare not say anything to Jonathan about Lydia, but I often find myself wondering how she is or if she is even alive."

"As do I; however, since she sailed to the Americas, I doubt we shall ever know."

By then, they had reached the carriage where, with the help of the driver, the footman placed Elizabeth's trunk on board. Jonathan helped the children inside, so Jane and Elizabeth grew quiet. As they always had, they would discuss their family once they were alone, for it was too painful to recall some of the events that had befallen them in front of anyone else.

London
That same day

"Where is Emily?" The Grande Dame of London society, Lady Gordon, questioned upon reaching the landing halfway down the central staircase of her townhouse.

Hearing her exclamation, the housekeeper, Mrs. James, rushed into the foyer in time to see her mistress waving a handkerchief, as was her wont when she was upset. "I thought she was upstairs with you, my lady."

"I swear that child is a magician! Here one second, gone the next!" Lady Gordon declared as she leaned over first one side of the railing and then the other, scanning every inch of the room below as though expecting the three-year-old to appear from thin air. "I was just speaking to her in my sitting room, and I looked up to find she had disappeared. Do you suppose she slipped into the garden to join her sisters?"

"I shall send a maid to find out," the housekeeper replied.

One wave of her hand towards a maid who had come into the foyer at the sound of the mistress' distress sent that woman flying towards the back of the house. It was not unusual for Lady Gordon's grandchildren to go missing when they visited, so the servants had grown used to searching for them.

Lady Gordon, not a small woman by any stretch of the imagination, fanned herself with her hand. "I am too weary to chase after those little scamps, and God knows the maids cannot seem to keep track of them. If my daughter cannot retain a suitable governess to teach them some manners, I shall just have to hire one myself. How dare Richard and Isabelle relax by the sea whilst my patience is tested by their offspring!"

She started back up the stairs only to stop halfway. "I shall be in my study. Notify me the minute you find Emily." She stopped. "And let me know if Evelyn and Ellen are still in the garden. I would not be surprised if they have slipped out the back gate again."

Mrs. James watched her mistress murmur to herself until she disappeared above stairs.

Her ladyship certainly has a point! Lady Matlock seems to have let the children get completely out of hand since the last governess left. Whilst her pregnancy is likely the reason, one can only imagine how unruly the children will be by the time the baby arrives.

Upon recalling her pledge to report back to the mistress concerning Lady Emily, Mrs. James quit her contemplations and hurried towards the back of the house.

Gracechurch Street
The Cowan residence

Upon entering her sister's spacious old home, Elizabeth abruptly stopped. "Jane, you have changed this room entirely since I was last here."

Jane laughed. "You have not visited in over two years. Carpets wear out, especially when you have children, and the curtains were here when we purchased the house, so they were due for a change."

"But you have a new mantle and wallpaper, too."

"One benefit of having a husband who owns a warehouse is that you get bargains on fine materials," Jane teased. "And what Jonathan does not stock, our uncle does."

"I have missed Aunt and Uncle Gardiner and our cousins so much since they were in Lambton when I was here last. Tell me about them. I cannot imagine how the children must have grown since last I saw them."

"Uncle Edward still works long hours, and Aunt Madeline has her hands full now that their oldest is married. His Maddie is already one year old and our aunt loves to keep her."

"I cannot imagine Randall a father. I still think of him as a child," Elizabeth said. "I am anxious to meet his wife and little Maddie."

"They cannot wait to meet you, either. Randall has taken his place in the warehouse. His assistance was much needed since our uncle has expanded to the next building. Martha is seventeen now, so she thinks she is grown. Abigail is quite the seamstress for a fifteen-year-old and Rebecca, being the youngest, is spoiled."

"Is she ten or eleven? I cannot remember."

"She is ten. I told them we would visit tomorrow." Jane pulled Elizabeth into an embrace. "I wanted you all to myself today."

Tears sprang to Elizabeth's eyes as she returned Jane's hug. "I love you, too."

The next day included a joyful reunion with the Gardiners and an introduction to Randall's wife, Margaret, and their child. As she had predicted, all Elizabeth's cousins had grown so much that she might not have recognised them in a different setting. Moreover, to her surprise she discovered her aunt's hair was now almost entirely grey, as was Uncle Edward's. The sight brought tears to her eyes, but she blinked them away so as not to show how affected she was by the knowledge that life was passing too fast.

Since the Gardiners knew all her favourite activities, they insisted they would escort Elizabeth to several dinner parties to be given by their acquaintances, as well as two exhibits at the British Museum and a play at Drury Lane whilst she was in London. Though her dread of encountering Mr. Darcy was never far from her mind, Elizabeth's worry lessened after Jane reminded her of that gentleman's propensity to keep to Derbyshire—something Mr. Bingley had often mentioned when Jane was ill at Netherfield.

After all, Jane had said, *a man who avoided dancing like the plague is not likely to be attending soirées in Town.*

Reassured by this truth, when Elizabeth was left alone the next afternoon to peruse the stack of newspapers Jane had saved for her, she was confident Mr. Darcy's name would not appear in them. After a time, she had finished reading all but the section she dreaded most—the advertisements. Aware that if she saw a position that looked suitable, she would feel obligated to investigate, she debated whether to wait until the following week to begin reading them. Curiosity got the better of her, however, and she relented. On the second column of the first page, one advertisement in particular caught her eye, for it was written in such a way as to make Elizabeth laugh out loud.

> *In need of a governess to take three young ladies ages nine, six and three under her wing and domesticate them in a matter of weeks. Faint of heart need not apply. Excellent wages. Benefits include furnished uniforms, Sundays off and two weeks of your choice each year. Apply at 20 Grosvenor Square this Thursday morning at eight o'clock sharp. Bring a list of your previous positions and letters of recommendation.*

Jane walked into the sitting room just as she laughed. "What is so amusing?" she asked.

Elizabeth read the advertisement to her. "I am of a mind to answer the advertisement as the benefits are extraordinary. No governess I know has Sundays off, not to mention two weeks of their choice every year. I could see you more often."

"But you promised not to seek another position straight off!" Jane lamented. "Our aunt and uncle have so many plans for you."

"I doubt I shall get the position."

"Furthermore, Jonathan has written to Markus, and I understand he is planning to be in Town next week."

Elizabeth had met Jonathan's brother once before. Though he owned a large farm outside of Birmingham and was pleasant company, he was the exact opposite of his brother. Whilst Jonathan was tall, blond and handsome, Markus was short, brown-haired and unremarkable.

Elizabeth sighed. "You do know that, whilst I like Markus, I am not *interested* in him. I am not interested in any man."

"But Lizzy! He is stable and kind, and according to Jonathan, the only reason he put off marrying was to grow his farm until he had a decent income to support a wife and children. At least you would not have to support yourself for the rest of your life, and you know that some employers do not have the best interest of their employees at heart. I fear what could happen to you in some of those grand homes."

Elizabeth took Jane's hand. "I appreciate your concern... and Jonathan's. Truly I do! But I can take care of myself. And, as I have said since you and I were girls, only the deepest love will persuade me to marry, and I missed that opportunity years ago."

"Oh, Lizzy, will you ever listen to me?"

Elizabeth laughed. "I fear it is too late for me to start!"

The Gordon townhouse
The following Thursday

After Mrs. James showed the prospective governess out of the house, she returned to find her mistress' spirits low.

"I fear I may have shown more confidence than sense, believing I could do better than Isabelle in hiring a suitable governess. We have had a good response, but none so far are what I had in mind. Several are entirely too old and set in their ways, two were simply not qualified and, if I am correct, the blonde-haired one is looking for a man, not a position." She laughed. "Isabelle would not put up with her flirtatious ways for one second!"

Though she agreed with her mistress, Mrs. James was not one for stating her opinion.

When she remained silent, Lady Gordon said, "Tell me about the remaining candidate?"

"She is a Miss Bennet," the housekeeper said. She pulled Elizabeth's paperwork from the folder where she kept all the information received from the applicants and handed it to her mistress.

Lady Gordon scanned it. "Her letter of recommendation

does her credit. Let us hope she will be willing to take on my grandchildren. Show her in."

Waiting in a drawing room at the front of the house, Elizabeth was drawn from the sofa where she had initially sat down towards the windows overlooking Hyde Park. Knowing that Mr. Darcy had a townhouse on one of the streets nearby, having heard Caroline Bingley mention it frequently, she wondered if she might see him if she were to walk in the park. Shaking her head at the absurdity, she reminded herself that, in all likelihood, he was in Derbyshire. Besides, Mr. Darcy preferred riding whilst she preferred walking.

"Lady Gordon will see you now!"

Jumping at the sound of the housekeeper's voice, Elizabeth turned and straightened her skirts before following the servant from the room. Once they reached the parlour, Mrs. James stopped at the door to announce, "Miss Elizabeth Bennet."

"Come forward, Miss Bennet," a voice demanded.

Elizabeth obeyed, and halfway across the room, she caught sight of Lady Gordon. The imposing matron was seated to her right in a large chair situated in front of floor-to-ceiling windows that overlooked a garden. Elizabeth thought she bore a strong resemblance to Fitzwilliam Darcy's aunt, Lady Catherine, though her clothes were more fashionable and she wore no wig. In fact, it appeared to Elizabeth that the thick, brown hair piled atop Lady Gordon's head was natural.

Suddenly recalling her manners, Elizabeth dropped a curtsey. "Thank you for seeing me, Lady Gordon."

"If you do not mind, I should like to get straight to the point. I have interviewed several women already, and I am growing tired."

"Certainly." She did not instruct her to sit, so Elizabeth took that as a sign the interview would be brief.

"Tell me, how would you handle a three-year-old who refuses to learn her numbers?"

18

"In my experience, small children learn best when they do not feel as though you are forcing them. I like to start by having them help me count familiar objects—the number of pieces of chalk in a box, or biscuits on a plate, the steps on stairs, or even the steps of a folk dance. Meanwhile, when we paint, I help them to create the numbers they are learning."

"You allow children that young to paint? I would think that would be terribly untidy. Why not use chalk on slates?"

"I find chalk boring. Besides, any disorder is a part of learning and painting is an excellent way to keep their attention whilst memorising numbers and colours."

"You state in your correspondence that you speak and read French and Italian. How do you propose to teach the children these languages?"

"I would begin by teaching all of the children French and Italian folk songs. Once they know them well, we will learn to sing them in English. In addition, I introduce the French and Italian name of a familiar object every day, incorporating it into our lessons. As they progress in reading, I introduce appropriate stories written in those languages."

"Where do you find such books? Most of the foreign language books in my library were not written for children."

"I found that to be the case as well. That is why I wrote two short stories, one in French and one in Italian. The children I previously worked with seemed to enjoy reading them."

Elizabeth watched the corners of Lady Gordon's lips lift in a smile. "Can you be firm?"

"If the situation calls for it, madam."

Lady Gordon tilted her head and studied Elizabeth. "Something makes me think you just may be the answer to my prayers. Would you be willing to accept the position for one month?"

"Only a month?"

"By then my daughter and her husband will have returned from their trip to the sea, and you will know if you wish to continue. You see, my philosophy is that if you truly enjoy teaching the girls, they will sense it and try harder to please you. At month's end, if we both are satisfied, I shall inform my daughter that you are the girls' new governess."

Elizabeth's brows furrowed. "Are you certain your daughter will not mind that you hired me?"

Lady Gordon dismissed the idea with a wave of her hand. "When the last one quit, I told Isabelle that I was going to hire her replacement. I do not know if my daughter believed me; however, I have no doubt that her husband will be pleased. He has been after her to find a governess promptly, since she is with child again and has little energy."

Elizabeth was intrigued. "How many governesses have the children had?"

"You will be the fourth this year." At Elizabeth's stunned expression, Lady Gordon quickly added, "The advertisement warned that the faint of heart need not apply. That is the reason for the excellent pay and benefits."

"I see."

"Miss Bennet, I hope I am not wrong when I say that you do not impress me as someone who would let anything frighten you, especially not anything as insignificant as following several unqualified governesses."

"As I have always said, my courage rises with every attempt to intimidate me."

"Well said! Then, you will accept the position?"

"Yes, my lady."

"Excellent! A carriage will collect you on Monday morning at seven at the address listed on your letter. I will send a footman along to handle your luggage."

Elizabeth smiled. "Monday it is." As she turned to leave, however, another question came to mind. "Excuse me, Lady Gordon, but you never said who the children's parents are."

"I completely forgot!" Lady Gordon replied. "I should have mentioned that, for it is another advantage to this position. As governess to my grandchildren, you will be exposed to the highest echelons of society, for my daughter Isabelle is married to Lord Matlock." At Elizabeth's stunned expression, she asked, "Are you acquainted with the name?"

"Years ago, I had the fortune of meeting Lord Matlock's son, Colonel Fitzwilliam, whilst staying in Hunsford."

"Oh, Colonel Fitzwilliam's father died years ago! The title then passed to Richard's brother, Viscount Sele, who unfortunately was killed in a riding accident last year. So now the title belongs to my son."

Too full of conflicting emotions to speak, shakily Elizabeth nodded.

"Good day, Miss Bennet. I shall expect you on Monday."

Numb with the knowledge that she had agreed to work for Mr. Darcy's cousin, Elizabeth bobbed a curtsey before hurrying from the room. By the time she was on the portico, her heart was racing as one thought played repeatedly through her head.

What a muddle I have got myself into.

The Cowan residence

By the time Elizabeth returned to her sister's home in the carriage Jonathan had provided for her use, she had come to a decision. All that was left was to convince Jane she was not mad. After the children were in bed and Jonathan had excused himself to work on the warehouse accounts in his study, Jane brought up the interview.

Elizabeth related all that had happened, but Jane was still perplexed. "Let me see if I understand correctly. Lady Gordon's intention in placing the advertisement was to hire a governess for Colonel Fitz – I mean the Earl of Matlock's children?"

"Exactly. She hoped to have someone familiar with the children in place by the time he and his wife returned from their trip to the seashore."

"That seems presumptuous."

"Apparently, Lady Gordon had threatened to hire a governess, and she believes her daughter and son will be relieved that she has."

"But Lizzy, you always said you never wanted to have to

face Mr. Darcy again. Certainly, you would be thrown into his company quite often if you work for his cousin."

"Not if I quit the position the minute Lord and Lady Matlock return to London. It is simply too good an offer to decline, Jane. The pay is double what I was paid at Claxton Hall, so one month there will provide enough money to allow me to look for a better job instead of taking whatever comes along."

"Would you not feel regret at deceiving Lady Gordon in that way?"

"Perhaps a bit; still, I know she will have no problem filling the position given the salary and benefits, and frankly, I need the money. Besides," Elizabeth said with a shrug of her shoulders, "by her own definition, the month is only a trial and those children must be incorrigible if they have driven away three governesses this year!"

Jane shook her head. "I hope you know what you are doing."

"I do! I look forward to the challenge. Now, if I am to start on Monday morning, I shall need your help to decide what to take to Lady Gordon's home. They will provide uniforms, so I will only need gowns when I visit you on Sundays. The rest of my things I will leave here, if you do not mind."

"You know I do not. You also know that Jonathan and I wish you would stay here and look for a husband instead of seeking a new job."

Elizabeth reached for her sister's hand and brought it to her lips for a kiss. "And I love that you do, but I refuse to live off charity or to settle for a man I do not love just to have a roof over my head."

"But—"

"Hush, Jane. My mind is set."

"If you insist."

"I do."

Chapter 2

The Cowan residence

Fortunately, Mary and Kitty and their families arrived the next morning and Elizabeth was able to learn all their news and to reintroduce herself to some of her nieces and nephews. It was especially painful to see that the youngest children had no recollection of her. Of all the things she hated about being in service, missing her nieces and nephews was at the top of the list. Still, she had done her best to write them letters and send presents, so only the smallest were truly unfamiliar with her.

The Gordon townhouse

Monday arrived faster than Elizabeth would have liked, and after saying her farewells to her family, she entered the carriage Lady Gordon had sent to fetch her. Since Mary, Kitty and their families would be returning to their homes that day, as she waved out the window of the vehicle Elizabeth tried to memorize all the faces she loved and carry them in her heart to her new position. The thought of how much the children would change before she saw them again weighed heavily on her heart, though, and it was not until the carriage arrived at

Gordon House that she had recovered enough to paste a smile on her face that would fool even the keenest observer.

Elizabeth waited in the foyer until Lady Gordon walked out of the parlour to greet her. "How good to see you again, Miss Bennet." Motioning to a nearby footman she said, "Fetch Miss Bennet's luggage and take it upstairs." As he hurried to do so, Lady Gordon began walking up the grand staircase and Elizabeth followed. "You, of course, will be on the hall with the children, the nanny and their maids."

"The children have maids?"

"Emily still has a nanny, whilst Evelyn and Ellen have maids. All you are responsible for is their education. As soon as they have finished breaking their fast each day, they will assemble in the room I had converted into a classroom. It is quite spacious, and I believe you will find everything you need inside: a chalkboard, desks, books, pencils, a globe, and paints and paper. If you think of anything else you need, just make a list and it will be provided."

"Thank you."

By then they had progressed down a long hall and were standing at an open bedroom door. A maid stood just inside.

"Miss Bennet, this is Daisy. She will be your maid. If you need anything, you have only to ask her."

"I... I did not expect—"

"As governess to the earl's children, you will have many privileges other governesses may not."

"I see."

Lady Gordon walked into the room. "Come in and see your bed chamber."

Elizabeth walked in and looked about the exquisite space decorated in shades of lavender, green and coral. She almost felt like a trespasser. "It is... beautiful."

Daisy crossed the bedroom to open a door and stepped back for Elizabeth to see beyond her.

"That is your private sitting room," Lady Gordon declared.

Crossing the bedroom quickly, the maid opened an identical

door on the opposite side of the room. "And that is your dressing room," Lady Gordon added.

Without another word, the matron went back into the hall. As Elizabeth followed her, a footman came down the hall with her bags. "Daisy will unpack for you. Come! I will introduce you to my grandchildren."

Several doors down, on the opposite side of the hall, she opened another door and motioned for Elizabeth to follow her inside. The huge room was filled with all the things Lady Gordon had mentioned... except the children.

"Where are my grandchildren?" She asked a maid who had suddenly jumped to her feet upon their entrance.

"Lady Ellen said that you wanted them to assemble in your sitting room directly after they finished eating, ma'am."

"I certainly did not! I told them to wait in here, just as I explained to you yesterday."

"I... I am sorry, Lady Gordon," the flustered servant replied. "I understood that you had changed your mind."

"If I change my mind, Clara, I will inform *you*—not my grandchildren! Now, go find them and bring them back here immediately!"

"Yes, ma'am!"

As the anxious maid rushed from the room, Lady Gordon slowly shook her head. Then she recovered and turned to address Elizabeth. "Let us sit down. I dare say it may take a few minutes for my grandchildren to be located."

Lady Gordon took the large chair meant for the governess, so Elizabeth sat in the largest of the chairs provided for the children. As they waited, her employer continued to give her guidance.

"I hope you will discover that, whilst they often do not follow orders, they are not meanspirited. As I told my daughter, they have been allowed far too much freedom for far too long, and it has taken its toll."

Though Elizabeth offered her employer a sympathetic smile, she could not agree with Lady Gordon until she got to know the girls better.

In any case, she told herself, *I shall not be here long enough to mind if they are scamps.*

It had taken twenty minutes to locate the children in the attic. They had only recently discovered that the stairs to the attic were behind a door on the floor above, and every so often they occupied themselves by digging through generations of items stored there in large trunks. By the time they were found, they were covered in dust. Marched into the classroom just as they were, they looked more like ragamuffins than the daughters of an earl, and Elizabeth bit her bottom lip to keep from smiling as Lady Gordon took charge.

"Elinor, come here!"

The eldest child, nine and already a beauty with reddish-blonde hair and blue eyes, lackadaisically walked forward, in spite of knowing that the use of her proper name meant she was in trouble.

"I am disappointed in you the most. You should be setting an example for your sisters."

"Yes, Grandmama."

Lady Gordon tilted her head towards Elizabeth. "Please greet your new governess, Miss Bennet."

"Pleased to make your acquaintance, Miss Bennet," Ellen said, executing a perfect curtesy.

Elizabeth smiled. "I am pleased to meet you."

"Evelyn, come forward. You, too, Emily."

Two angels with white-blonde curls and the same blue eyes as their eldest sister held hands and did as they were told. Without prompting, they performed imperfect curtseys. "Pleased to meet you, Miss Bennet," was said in chorus.

Trying not to smile, Elizabeth replied, "Likewise."

Lady Gordon was not amused when next she spoke. "Why do both of you insist on following Ellen, even when you know I will not approve of what she does?"

The smallest child looked at the middle one. Evelyn did not answer, so Emily cried, "Cause Ellen is smarter than us!"

"It is not very smart to disobey your Grandmama," Lady Gordon replied. "In fact, for not obeying me and going into the attic when you have been told not to, you shall wear those nasty clothes all day and be confined to this room so as not to spread the dust. Moreover, you will all go to bed tonight without any supper."

Emily started to whine, but Evelyn shushed her. "Do not cry, Emily. You know what Ellen said!"

Lady Gordon glanced to her eldest grandchild, who rolled her eyes. "What did Ellen say?" she asked her middle grandchild.

For a moment, Evelyn looked as though she was not going to confess; however, under Lady Gordon's steady glare she relented. "Ellen said not to act like babies. We should take our punishment and pretend it does not bother us."

"Oh, she did, did she?" Lady Gordon said, giving Ellen a frown before addressing Elizabeth. "Do you see what I deal with daily?"

"I shall try my best to address the problem," Elizabeth whispered low enough that the girls could not hear.

Lady Gordon nodded. "I shall leave you to it then."

In seconds the door closed, and Elizabeth was left staring at three pairs of cautious eyes.

That same day in Brighton

At two and forty, Lord Matlock still cut a fine figure with his slim build, reddish-blond hair tinged with grey, and brown eyes. He caused quite a stir as he strolled down the boardwalk towards his rented cottage on the beach. Several women tried to engage him in conversation, but leery of their motives, he offered no more than a tip of his hat and a cursory greeting. Still madly in love with his wife, Isabelle, who at forty still sported dark-blonde hair, green eyes, and skin as unlined as a debutante's, he paid no attention to the other women.

Upon reaching the cottage, he entered to find his cousin having tea with his wife. "Darcy! Fancy seeing you here!"

"Why do I think my presence is no surprise?" William asked, standing to hold out a hand. "It became obvious that I would not get a minute's peace until I agreed to bring Marianne to Brighton, and I have you to blame for that!"

Shaking his hand, Richard said, "Can I help it if Marjorie confided in her cousin that we intended to visit Brighton?"

"Yes. Next time do not tell Marjorie your plans until the day you are to leave. In that way, she may not have time to write Marianne and have her pester me until we join you."

"You had better enjoy what little time you have left with your daughter," Isabelle interjected. "She will make her debut before you know it. In fact, I planned to ask you if she can stay with us after Michaelmas, so that I may begin instructing her and Marjorie for their debuts."

William's brows knitted. "I had thought that could wait until Marianne was older."

"Oh, no. Our Marjorie is seventeen, and it will take until her next birthday to prepare her. At sixteen, Marianne will follow right behind, and it would be less stressful to prepare her at the same time." Then she sighed. "My, how I miss Richard's mother, God rest her soul. Evelyn would have been such a help with all of this."

William said sombrely, "I suppose that if Marianne wishes—"

Suddenly, his daughter rushed into the room, pulling Marjorie behind her. It never failed to amaze him how much the two favoured each other, having the same red hair and blue eyes. These thoughts ended, however, the second Marianne spoke.

"I want to go, Papa! It would be so much easier to learn everything with Marjorie."

"Ever the eavesdropper, my dear?" William said. "If that is your desire, I see no reason why you cannot."

"Thank you, Papa."

Then, just as quickly as she and Marjorie had entered, they rushed from the room in a flurry of delighted squeals. After Isabelle followed the girls from the room, William sat down.

Noting that his cousin's smile no longer reached his eyes, Richard took the seat across from him. "Tell me what you are thinking, Darcy."

William took a deep breath and let it go slowly. "I knew this day would come, but I was not expecting it to come so soon. It is sad to consider that Marianne is no longer the little girl who delighted in riding across Pemberley with me, counting the new lambs, or seeing how many fish we could pull from the lake."

"I had to face the same thing with Marjorie. Though she was three years of age when I married Isabelle, she is my child in every way, and it has been hard to accept the fact I am no longer her whole world."

"How strange that you and I both married widows with children," William replied.

Left unsaid was that he and Richard had married under very dissimilar circumstances. The widow Darcy married, Lady Cornelia, had been an unscrupulous fraud. Pregnant with another man's child when they wed, she and the baby had died during childbirth not six months later, leaving him to raise her child, two-year-old Marianne, alone.

"Darcy, do you not think it time you considered marriage again?" Richard asked. "After all, raising Marianne has been your excuse for remaining single all these years, and that will come to an end soon. Some lucky man will make her his wife, and you will be left all alone in that mausoleum you call a home."

Annoyed, William stood as though to leave. "I happen to love that mausoleum, thank you. And from the way you speak, I can only assume that you have joined Isabelle in promoting Lady Parker."

"I have not joined Isabelle's scheme to match you with her sister. Still, I have to say that you could do much worse than Amy. She is not only beautiful, but at thirty, she is still young enough to bear children. Moreover, her daughter proves she is not barren."

Recalling Amy's light-blonde hair and green eyes, William said, "Beautiful she may be, but she is too silly to suit me. Besides, I am too old to start worrying about producing an heir. Georgiana can inherit Pemberley."

"Listen to yourself! From the way you talk, one would think you were five and sixty instead of forty!"

Richard walked over to pour himself a glass of brandy. Then, he held the bottle up in a question. When William shook his head, he set it down. Taking a sip from his glass, he sat back down to continue.

"See here, Cousin, I realise that life has not been kind to you. First, Miss Bennet broke your heart, and then Lady Cornelia stabbed you in the back—"

William whirled around. "I told you I never wanted to hear Miss Bennet's name again! If I had not been out of my mind with fever after the accident, you would never have known about her in the first place!"

Richard held up his free hand. "I apologise." At his cousin's stiff nod, he added, "It bothers me to think of you being alone for the rest of your life. You deserve more than that."

"I will not be alone. Marianne will no doubt have a family, and Georgiana's children—"

"Live in Edinburgh, for God's sake!" Richard finished. "You are fortunate to see her and the children once a year at Christmas, and who knows where Marianne will settle once she marries."

"I appreciate your concern, but please accept the fact I know what is best for me."

Richard shrugged. "I cannot help it. I care deeply about your happiness."

William walked over to grasp Richard's shoulder and give it a squeeze. "I know."

Isabelle returned at that very second. "Marianne wishes to stay here tonight, Darcy. Will you stay as well?"

"No, thank you. The cottage I rented is only eight houses away, and after listening to Marianne chatter the entire trip, I shall welcome the quiet."

"Might I stay with you?" Richard teased. "I could use some peace and quiet, too."

A pillow stolen from the sofa by Isabelle flew across the room. It hit Richard in the back of the head, prompting him to let go a long whistle whilst rubbing his head. "See what you are missing by not being married, Cousin?"

With a glance to make certain Isabelle could not hear, William replied with a smile, "I fear you have just hardened my resolve to remain single."

The Gordon townhouse
Later that day

The children were on a strict schedule, which included being under Elizabeth's tutelage from after breaking their fast until their nap in the late afternoon. Elizabeth was so exhausted by that time that she decided to have a nap as well. The minute she lay down, however, she found she could not keep the conversations she had that day with her charges from running through her mind.

As soon as she was left alone with the girls, each had walked over to her own personalised chair and table and glumly sat down. They looked so petulant it was all Elizabeth could do not to laugh. She sat behind her own desk which faced theirs and opened the drawers to see what was inside. Finding some chalk and a slate, she laid them atop her desk and watched as the girls opened the drawers on their desks and did likewise. It was then that inspiration struck.

She stood. "Leave the chalk and slates on your desks and push them and the chairs to the side. We are going to sit on the floor."

The girls looked shocked, the youngest two glancing to Ellen for direction. When she lifted her shoulders in a shrug and stood to move her chair, Evelyn and Emily followed suit. Once the centre of the room was cleared, Elizabeth sat down on the carpet and motioned for the children to join her.

Once everyone was settled, she said, "I think we should take time today to get to know one another. I have found the best way to do that is by asking questions. I will start. What is your favourite colour, Ellen?"

"Blue."

"There are many shades of blue. Can you describe which blue you like best, for instance, sky blue?"

"Dark blue—like my mother's eyes."

"What a lovely answer. Evelyn, what is your favourite colour?"

"Yellow—like the daisies in the garden."

"I like green!" Emily declared proudly with no prompting. "Because I like playing on the lawn."

"I like green, too, but my favourite colour is lavender, just like the walls of my bedroom."

"I want to ask a question!" Emily cried, raising her hand at the same time. Ellen rolled her eyes, but that did not deter her youngest sister. "What is your favourite dessert?"

"Hmm. I would have to choose apple tart," Elizabeth replied. "And yours?"

"Christmas cake with dates."

"And your favourites, Evelyn... Ellen?"

"I love ginger cookies," Evelyn replied softly.

"Baked apples," Ellen pronounced as though bored. "However, I fail to see how these questions will help us get to know one another."

"Then you should ask a question," Elizabeth said.

"I will! Why is every governess an old maid?"

"If a governess were married, it would be hard to be away from her husband and children the majority of her time."

"Well, I think it is because most of them are too ugly to receive an offer of marriage," Ellen declared.

"Miss Bennet is not ugly!" Emily cried, making Elizabeth smile.

"Well, the last three were!" Ellen retorted. "And they were mean, too."

"Why do you say they were mean?" Elizabeth asked.

"They were always cross about something, and they never smiled."

Evelyn's hand went up. "Yes, Evelyn?"

"Do you like to play games?" the six-year-old asked. "Only one of our governesses let us play games."

"And that was to keep us occupied whilst she read novels," Ellen added.

"I like games very much. In fact, one way we are going to learn is by playing games together."

Emily nodded excitedly, whilst Ellen folded her arms across her chest. "I am too old for games. Moreover, I already know my letters, numbers, colours, some French and Italian, and I can read. I expect you to bore me to death just like the others."

"Boredom is a sign of a very intelligent person," Elizabeth said. She was pleased to see Ellen look confused. "And intelligent people make excellent teachers. Perhaps you will consider helping me teach Evelyn and Emily everything you already know."

Ellen looked as though she was considering the possibility, so Elizabeth addressed three-year-old Emily. "Do you have a question, Emily?"

The child nodded. "Do you have sisters?"

"I have four."

Her eyes lit up. "What are their names?"

"Jane is the oldest, and I am next in line. Then there are Mary, Kitty and Lydia, in that order."

"No brothers?" Ellen asked, her eyes narrowing as though she had stumbled upon something interesting.

"Unfortunately, no."

"And your parents, are they still alive?" Ellen persisted.

"No, they are not."

"Mama says that women with no connections, no fortune, and no dowries end up in service or on the streets, which is why she wants us to study very hard. As part of our education, we are to learn foreign languages, draw, embroider and play the pianoforte, so we can make advantageous marriages."

Elizabeth pasted on a smile. "Your mother is correct."

Even now, the wound inflicted by the oldest child's remarks hurt deeply.

I cannot blame her for stirring up old regrets. And it is my fault that those regrets still rule my heart.

Grabbing a pillow, Elizabeth pulled it over her head in an effort to blot out the memories that usually kept sleep at bay.

Chapter 3

London

Two weeks later

As soon as the coach came to a stop at the rear of Darcy House, a blur of red hair, blue eyes and fiery indignation rushed from the vehicle. Waving away a footman who tried to assist her, Marianne stomped towards the back door of the house in a huff. The daughter of his late wife and her first husband, Lord Dudley, William had loved and protected Marianne during the fourteen years since her mother's death, and as far as he was concerned, she was his child in every sense of the word... every sense except by birth. That did not mean, however, that at times his love for her was not tested by her pig-headedness.

As William exited the coach, his eyes met the footman's, and he shook his head as though silently apologising for Marianne's behaviour. He walked towards the house, and immediately upon entering the door, encountered the butler.

"We were not expecting you until next week, sir," Mr. Barnes remarked.

"A stomach ailment is quickly spreading throughout Brighton, which prompted my decision to return early."

"I have seen nothing about it in the papers. Is it serious?" Barnes asked.

"Not thus far, although I assume it could be for the elderly or the very young. I was told it takes four to five days to recover from it, and one is bedridden the entire time. That was not something I wanted to test first-hand."

"Certainly not! What of Lord Matlock? I understood he and his family were in Brighton, too."

"Not wishing to take any chances since Lady Matlock is with child, they returned to London as well."

"Pardon me for being so bold, sir, but Lady Marianne did not seem herself when she entered the house. She did not greet anyone, and that is not like her."

"She is not ill, if that is what you mean. She is only displeased with my decision to return early."

As he talked, William continued towards the front of the house. "I intend to change clothes, then disappear into my study and go through the last two weeks of correspondence. Please do not put the knocker on the door until the day after tomorrow. I hope to get most of my business out of the way before I am interrupted. Will you ask the steward to meet me there in half an hour?"

"Mr. Perry was not expecting you this soon, either, sir. He is out at present, but the moment he returns, I shall inform him."

"Thank you."

"Certainly. Might I ask when you plan to leave for Pemberley?"

"As soon as possible. Take no offense, Barnes, but I detest London. The second the *ton* realises I am in residence this year's crop of debutantes and their mothers will descend upon the house like vultures. The matrons will feign interest in Marianne or Georgiana before inviting me to a ball with the refrain that one can never have too many men to partner the ladies. One would think that after all this time, they would have noticed that I do not dance and would stop asking me to balls."

Though accustomed to William's slight limp, Barnes was once more reminded of the coach accident that nearly claimed his employer's life.

"I could not agree more. I sent a maid to inform Mr. Martin of your arrival. He would be upset had I not."

William smiled at the mention of the old valet who had spent his entire life in service to the Darcys—first to his father and then to him. Though retired, he resided at Darcy House and still insisted on caring for William whenever he was in Town.

"I do not mind, but tell me, does his back still pain him?"

"The last time I asked, he said it was much improved."

"That is good to hear."

By then William was standing at the bottom of the grand staircase. "If Marianne asks, she is welcome to interrupt me in my study." Having said that, he ascended the steps.

As Mr. Barnes watched William leave, he could not help but admire him.

Still quite a force to be reckoned with!

Darcy House
The next day

William and his steward, Mr. Perry, were in the study with the door open when Richard entered the room.

"I know you have the knocker off the door, Darcy, but could you spare me a few minutes of your time?"

"I always have time for you, Lord Matlock!" William said, smiling wryly.

Mr. Perry stood, acknowledging Richard with a quick bow. "Lord Matlock." Then addressing William, he said, "I shall be in my office, sir."

Richard waited until the steward left. "You know I hate it when you call me that. If you feel you must use a title, I prefer Colonel Fitzwilliam."

"We both know that Isabelle would not appreciate hearing me call you that. She loves the idea of being married to an earl... being a countess."

"Not long ago, she was satisfied being married to a colonel, and I dare say she could get used to it again."

"I do not know about that. Whilst your wife has many admirable qualities, she is as loyal a member of the *ton* as was your mother and a stickler for decorum—maybe even more so than Aunt Evelyn."

"I cannot disagree. Although I love Isabelle dearly, she is certainly a product of her upbringing. Still, whilst she may be entirely wrong to parrot the rules of the *ton*, she is sincere in her beliefs."

"I will allow her that," William said, putting his pen in the ink stand and leaning back in his chair. "How can I be of service?"

"I am on my way to retrieve the children from Isabelle's mother and—"

"You left them there last night?"

"Isabelle was so weary after the trip from Brighton I decided another night with their grandmother would be best."

"Hearing you speak of Lady Gordon's ill-tempered disposition, I would not wager on it."

Richard barked a laugh. "Isabelle's mother is a tough old bird! She can handle those silly girls without any real harm. Now, back to my purpose in coming here. Marianne sent a note to Isabelle yesterday asking to ride back to Derbyshire with us."

William pinched his forehead as though he was developing a headache.

"Before you get upset, keep in mind that she and Marjorie are less of a problem when they travel together. In that way, they keep each other company. Moreover, Marjorie was so disappointed they did not get to spend more time together in Brighton that Isabelle promised she would ask if you would consent to allow Marianne to stay with us for several weeks after the ball."

"Who am I to say no when I know she will be bored to tears once we reach Pemberley? Yes, she may stay."

"Now, *I* have a favour to ask you." William's brows lifted in question. "I want you to join us at Matlock Manor and stay part of the month. Now that her year of mourning is over, Isabelle is planning a ball to reintroduce her sister to society and—"

Sitting up straight again, William rolled his eyes. "How many times must I—"

"Hear me out, Cousin!" Richard insisted. "This not about my sister; this is about our daughters. You and I both know that Marjorie and Marianne think themselves old enough to be out, and I will need your help to quash their pleas when they beg to attend the ball. Isabelle always places me in the position of being the ogre who will not allow it, and I will need reinforcements."

"I am quite certain my daughter will not be happy to have me come."

"You know as well as I that girls of that age never want their parents around. Do not take it to heart. Just come so I will not be the only tyrant telling them what they may not do."

The corners of William's mouth curled upwards. "Coward."

Richard smirked. "This from a man debating whether to come because his daughter may not approve."

"I will come for the ball, but I reserve the right not to linger a day longer."

"That is all I ask."

"When do you return to Derbyshire?"

"Isabelle must rest before attempting another trip, so we will be in London until the end of the week at least. What is more, according to a note awaiting us at our townhouse, Lady Gordon hired a new governess whilst we were away. Therefore, staying in Town a while longer will give us time to decide whether to keep her on. I pray she is suitable, for Isabelle is not able to chase after the little ones now that she is with child."

"Pray tell me how Lady Gordon came to hire a governess for your children?"

"She threatened to do so when the second one quit... and the third. I imagine she sought help as soon as we left the children. They can be a handful."

"Hopefully she had better luck selecting a governess than you had."

"Hopefully." Then he added, "Darcy, you do not know how much I appreciate your willingness to attend the ball."

"Why do I feel as though your sole purpose in coming here today was to talk me into that?"

"Because you are becoming overly distrustful in your old age."

"My old age? What happened to your argument that I am not too old to marry again?"

"If one goes merely by years, you are not; however, nothing ages a man's spirit like cynicism."

"I will not be drawn into another analysis of my faults. Will you take Marianne with you now?"

"No. I will stop by here on my way back," Richard proclaimed. "That will give her maid enough time to begin packing her things."

"An excellent idea."

Gordon townhouse
The library

Lady Gordon had just sat down to enjoy the peace and quiet of her library and to finish reading the book she began yesterday when her housekeeper appeared in the doorway.

"Lord Matlock, madam," Mrs. James announced.

Barely had the words left her mouth than Richard walked past her into the room. Seeing his wife's mother rise from her position on the sofa nearest the windows, he walked in that direction. Lady Gordon's face had gone pale, and her hand was now over her heart.

"Has something happened to my Isabelle?"

"No. No. Nothing of the sort, Mother Gordon. I apologise for frightening you," Richard said, grasping her hands and placing a gentle kiss on her forehead. "We had to return from Brighton sooner than expected, and I have come for the children." He went on to explain what had precipitated their early return.

"My heavens! I am so pleased you brought Isabelle and Marjorie back to London so swiftly. One can never be too cautious in regard to these diseases, especially a woman in Isabelle's delicate condition."

"I am in complete agreement," he said, motioning to the sofa. "Please sit down."

After she had done so, Richard took a seat across from her on the matching chair. He smiled. "Now. What is this you wrote about a new governess?"

"Oh, my boy, you will never believe how fortunate I was to find this young woman. She took the children under her wing the very first day, and by the end of the week, they were hurrying through breakfast to get to the classroom. Seldom have I seen them so eager to learn."

"Even Ellen?"

"We both know that Ellen is not one to show her approval; she had rather show disapproval. Still, she has not once led her sisters to hide since the new governess took charge."

"Pray tell, who is this paragon of virtue."

"Miss Elizabeth Bennet."

Richard's face reflected his shock, causing Lady Gordon to recall what Elizabeth said. "Oh, I forgot! Miss Bennet mentioned that you and she had met before."

The matron began to explain what Elizabeth had said, and as she droned on and on, a picture of Darcy lying in bed, delirious with fever and calling that woman's name came to mind. Quickly determining he would shield his cousin from any more heartbreak from that source, Richard was preparing to reject Elizabeth when a still, small voice stopped him cold.

What if Elizabeth Bennet holds the key to repairing your cousin's heart?

"Richard?"

Jarred from his reverie, he murmured, "I was thinking how odd it is that we should meet again after all these years."

"As I always like to say," Lady Gordon replied, "there are no accidents. All things happen for a reason." She walked over to pull a cord. "I shall ask Miss Bennet to join us. I am certain you will be just as impressed with her as I am."

As he and Lady Gordon awaited Elizabeth, Richard walked over to a wall of books, leaving his wife's mother seated in the centre of the room. Pretending to search for titles, he kept one eye on the door. Fortunately, when Elizabeth entered the room, she walked to where Lady Gordon sat and curtseyed, giving Richard time to study her. He noted that she had changed very little in appearance.

"Miss Bennet. I know you will be just as surprised as I am to learn that my children have returned to Town early."

Immediately, thoughts of how to resign before the Matlocks arrived for the children popped into Elizabeth's head.

"I believe you have already met my son," Lady Gordon continued, waving a hand towards the wall of books on the left. The instant her eyes drifted in that direction, she caught sight of Richard.

Numbly, she curtseyed. "Yes. I have. Good morning, Colonel—forgive me—Lord Matlock."

Appearing to sense her unease, Richard said. "We met so long ago that I am certain Miss Bennet would not have recognised me had we passed on the street."

"On the contrary, you have hardly changed at all," Elizabeth managed to say.

Suddenly Mrs. James rushed into the room. "Excuse me, my lady, but we are packing the children's things, and Lady Emily cannot find her doll. She insists you put it away, and she refuses to leave without it."

"I shall handle the matter," Lady Gordon said. "Richard, I will leave you and Miss Bennet to discuss the particulars of her employment, though I insist you honour the benefits I listed in my advertisement."

After Lady Gordon departed, Elizabeth stared uncomfortably at the carpet, so Richard said, "Please be seated, Miss Bennet." Once she complied, he tried to lighten the mood by saying,

"Why do I have the impression that you would rather be anywhere but here?"

Surprised at his perception, Elizabeth smiled wanly. "My circumstances are so altered from when last we met, I hardly know how to act."

"Being a governess is no disgrace, Miss Bennet."

"No, but it is a far cry from being a gentleman's daughter."

"Forgive me if I overstep, but may I ask *why* you are in service?"

"It is simple. I decided that a life of servitude was preferable to marrying just to have a roof over my head."

Richard chuckled. "I recall you saying something of that nature once in Hunsford."

Elizabeth relaxed, and a genuine smile graced her face. "And I recall you saying that you could not marry for love."

"I was very lucky in that regard. I fell in love with Isabelle, who happened to be a very wealthy woman."

"Then count yourself fortunate. In my limited experience, such happiness in marriage is not common." There was an awkward silence before Elizabeth ventured, "May I speak frankly?"

"Please do."

"I had no idea that you would be my employer until after I had accepted the position; however, since Lady Gordon suggested I try it for the month you were away, I agreed. I am aware that I should have turned it down the instant I knew you were involved, but to be honest, I need the money. My plan was to resign just before you returned."

Richard smiled. "I see."

"Now, if you will excuse me, I will pack my things and return to my sister's home in Cheapside."

As she turned to go, Richard said, "Miss Bennet, I beg you to reconsider. Lady Gordon tells me you have done wonders with the children, and I really need your help. You see, Isabelle is expecting our fourth child, and is not capable of handling our very active daughters. She believes she is, but I see how much of a strain it is on her. And, as you have no doubt heard, we have had no luck with governesses."

"Even if you do not mind, I fear my presence might—" Elizabeth's expression fell, and she turned to stare out the windows. "Some of your family may be uncomfortable with my presence, and I would never want to cause them discomfort."

"You speak of Darcy."

She nodded.

"Miss Bennet, I have no idea what happened between my cousin and you, other than the fact that when we left Hunsford, you and he were not on good terms. Rest assured that he is not one to share his feelings, even with me. Still, I have faith that should you and he meet again, both of you will be civil. After all, it has been fourteen years. Moreover, Darcy spends most of his time at Pemberley, not with me."

"I... I do not know—"

"Consider this! In addition to what Lady Gordon promised, I will pay you one hundred pounds if you will stay for at least six months."

"Why would you do that?"

"Because the babe is due in late November. If in December you still wish to leave, you may go with my blessing."

It seemed forever until Elizabeth replied. "I will take the position on the condition that should my presence begin to cause discord, I will leave at once. Of course, if less than six months has passed, I will forfeit the bonus."

"You drive a hard bargain," Richard teased, "but I agree."

"I do not work on Sunday. May I return first thing on Monday?"

"You may."

As she exited the room, a single thought came to Richard's mind.

When all is said and done, Darcy, either you will hate me, or you will thank your lucky stars that I was clever enough not to let her get away. I pray it is the latter.

Matlock townhouse

When Richard entered the house with the children, Marjorie flew down the grand staircase to greet her sisters and cousin. After kissing each of her siblings, she grabbed Marianne's hand and started back up the stairs.

Before they got completely out of sight, Richard called, "Where is your mother?"

"In her sitting room!" Marjorie replied, quickly disappearing from the landing.

The children's nanny and maids had returned with them and were busy removing the girls' bonnets and gloves.

"Their mother will want to see them right away, so take them to her sitting room. Meanwhile, have someone lay out paints and paper in the classroom. I understand their new governess allowed them to practice their numbers and letters with paint. Hopefully, that will keep them occupied until she joins us."

"When is Miss Bennet coming, Papa?" Emily asked.

"Monday," he replied. "Ellen, you are in charge of helping your sisters with their lessons until then."

Ellen's brows wrinkled. "You want me to teach them?"

"Yes. Miss Bennet told your grandmother that you are a natural teacher."

Ellen's chin rose proudly. "I shall do my best, Papa."

She looked so much like him in that moment that a lump formed in Richard's throat. As he brushed a blonde lock of hair behind one ear, he said, "That is all I ask, Poppet."

"I am Poppet!" Emily declared, stamping a foot.

Richard pulled his daughters into one hug, declaring, "All of you are my Poppets!"

They were still giggling when they followed the servants upstairs.

Lady Matlock's sitting room

Once they were alone, Isabelle asked Richard about the governess, and he related all that Lady Gordon had said about Elizabeth's abilities. He also explained that she had asked to begin her employment with them on Monday.

"You forgot to mention her name."

"I did?"

Richard's courtship of Isabelle began directly after William's accident, so she was aware that her husband's cousin was hurt in the service of a friend, whose sister, Lydia, had eloped with a cad who grew up at Pemberley—thus explaining William's reason for getting involved in the matter.

Richard hoped against hope she would not recall Lydia's last name. "Miss Elizabeth Bennet."

"Bennet? Bennet? Where have I heard that name before?"

"I have met many Bennets in my lifetime, so I could not say. Rest assured, however, that this Bennet has been able to impress your mother in a short period of time, and that is no small feat."

"Indeed, it is not."

"According to your mother, Miss Bennet has breathed new life into our girls' thirst for education."

"I cannot fathom anything so grand, but I am willing to be proven wrong."

"All I know is that our girls talked of nothing save their new governess on the way home. So much so, that Marianne asked them to find another subject."

"Speaking of Marianne, I am pleased she agreed to come. I do not think I could stand another day of watching Marjorie sulk."

Richard was relieved that Isabelle had changed the subject. "Then you will also be pleased to know that Darcy agreed to let her travel to Derbyshire with us and stay for several weeks."

"It does please me, but I have to ask—what about the ball? If he does not attend, Amy will be devastated."

"He agreed to attend the ball, but I feel I must warn you again that my cousin is not interested in your sister."

"I know that Amy can be a bit giddy, but that can be reined in. Moreover, she is still young enough to give him an heir, and she is wealthy. What else could he ask for?"

"Darcy was never drawn to beauty alone; he values intelligence. Besides, he told me that he is not worried about producing an heir since Georgiana can inherit Pemberley."

"Nonsense! Darcy is still young enough for children. He may be forty, but he does not look a day over thirty."

"What about the silver in his hair?"

"It only serves to make him more devastatingly handsome."

"If I did not know you so well, I believe I would be jealous of my cousin."

Isabelle grabbed her husband's hand, pulling him down beside her on the sofa. Framing Richard's face with her hands, she kissed him soundly.

"I am not blind to Darcy's attributes, but I only have eyes for you."

A more passionate kiss followed before Richard pulled back. "You always know just what to say to make me love you even more, my sweet."

"I am glad, for rest assured you are the love of my life, Richard Fitzwilliam."

Consequently, the Matlocks were not in communication with the rest of the house until dinner was announced hours later.

Chapter 4

Matlock Manor
Derbyshire
Two weeks later

As Elizabeth stepped out of the impressive coach she had shared with the three youngest children, her stomach filled with knots. Richard had boasted that Matlock Manor was not only older than Pemberley, but it was just as magnificent. Moreover, he said it strongly favoured Darcy's home. Given the long front drive, the colour of stone used to construct the manor, and the way the house was laid out, Elizabeth could see a strong resemblance. This served to bring back memories of being at Pemberley before receiving Jane's letter regarding Lydia's folly.

Tamping down the emotions that threatened to overwhelm her, Elizabeth turned to help her charges from the coach, and they followed Lord and Lady Matlock up the steps and into the manor. The instant she stepped in the foyer, however, she was struck by the realisation that the furnishings more closely resembled those of Rosings Park than Pemberley. She breathed a sigh of relief.

At least I will not be reminded of Pemberley every time I come down the stairs.

Her attention was drawn to Lady Matlock, who was introducing her to the housekeeper.

"Mrs. Perkins, this is Miss Elizabeth Bennet, the new governess I wrote to you about."

Elizabeth turned to face an older, ruddy-faced woman whose mop of grey hair was doing its best to escape from beneath an elaborate lace cap. Her smile was sincere, as was her greeting, welcoming her to Matlock Manor.

Lady Matlock then turned to a stout, middle-aged maid with light brown hair and plain features standing nearby. "Essie, this is Miss Bennet." To Elizabeth she added, "Essie will show you to your room and will serve as your maid at Matlock Manor."

The maid stepped forwards and bobbed a quick curtsey. "Pleased to meet you, Miss Bennet. Pray follow me."

As Elizabeth followed Essie up the grand staircase, nine-year-old Ellen caught up with them.

"Miss Bennet, I hope you like your rooms. I helped Mama pick out the colours and the wallpaper last year."

Elizabeth reached for the child's hand, holding it as they continued to ascend the stairs. "I am certain I shall, for you have excellent taste."

Ellen's face was beaming as they reached the landing and vanished from sight.

After all the ladies had gone upstairs, Richard turned to converse with the butler, Mr. Goings. When that man left to deliver a message to the steward, Mrs. Perkins seized the opportunity to speak to Richard. With the Matlock family since he was a boy, she was like a second mother to him, and she had always spoken frankly.

"Compared to the others, the new governess seems very young."

"She may be young, but I believe time will prove we were fortunate to have found her," Richard replied. "She definitely has a way with children. Emily, Evelyn and Ellen have not hidden once since she has been employed, which is almost a month now."

"That could be a record," Mrs. Perkins said with a wry smile.

"Since your sister is her housekeeper, you know Lady Gordon well. And we both know that she does not suffer fools gladly."

"This is true."

"Well, it was she who hired Miss Bennet, and she was positively ecstatic about her abilities by the time I retrieved the children after our trip. Moreover, after less than two weeks with us, my wife is convinced she is a saint."

"A saint? That appellation will be hard to live up to."

"Whilst I do not think her a saint, I am convinced that Miss Bennet can handle any challenge. That is why I cannot wait to see what she accomplishes with Marjorie."

"Lady Marjorie? I thought she had declared herself too old for a governess when she managed to bring about Miss Kennedy's resignation last year."

"It is not her decision. Marjorie's conversational Italian is very poor, and Isabelle hopes Miss Bennet can improve it."

"Lady Marjorie seemed delighted to be home, so may I assume she has no idea about your plans?"

"As always, you are very observant, Mrs. Perkins," Richard said, giving the housekeeper a smile. "Lady Matlock and I wished the trip home to be pleasant, so Marjorie has not been told."

"I pray that she does not take her frustrations out on Miss Bennet once she finds out."

"I intend to make certain Marjorie treats Miss Bennet with civility," Richard said. "Now, I need to wash and change clothes before I meet with my steward."

As Richard took the stairs two at the time, Mrs. Perkins watched. *You may not keep this governess either if you do not check Lady Marjorie's behaviour. She has a way of causing trouble whenever she is unhappy.*

Then she turned to go back to the kitchen to consult with the cook about dinner.

One week later

"If my friends learn that my baby sisters' governess is tutoring me, I shall become a laughing stock," Lady Marjorie cried. "Even though my Italian may not flow as well as you would like, it is passable! Besides, what of Marianne? It would be impolite to leave her alone for hours on end whilst I sit through lessons."

"Marianne will take part in the lessons," Isabelle said. "One should be fluent in foreign languages. In fact, I think Miss Bennet could improve your French, as well."

"Miss Bennet! Miss Bennet!" Marjorie wailed. "I am sick of hearing that name! First, my sisters talk of nothing else, and now I am to be humiliated by having her tutor me!"

"You have said quite enough!" Richard declared. "Your mother and I will not be dissuaded. You are acting far worse than Emily when she cannot have her way. In fact, this tantrum proves you could benefit from a full-time governess, if merely to improve your manners."

"Oh, Papa!" Marjorie cried. "Must you always make threats you do not intend to carry out?"

As Richard's face reddened with anger, his wife said, "I would hold my tongue were I you, young lady. You have no idea how many times I had to convince your father to lessen one punishment or another that you fully deserved."

Uneasily, Marjorie dropped her head to stare at her feet.

"I will brook no more protests," Richard stated. "When your sisters take their nap in the afternoon, you and Marianne will have an hour lesson in Italian. You will start tomorrow. Is that understood?" Marjorie nodded. "Then, you are dismissed."

As Marjorie fled from the room crying, her mother said, "I hope we are not putting too much on Miss Bennet. I would not want her to despair and leave."

"I shall make certain she knows that if Marjorie or Marianne are not respectful and attentive, she has only to inform me."

"Thank you, dear. I pray our daughter will let Miss Bennet be of help."

"As do I."

Four days later

Elizabeth had determined almost immediately that whilst Lady Marianne had good conversational skills in Italian, Lady Marjorie did not. Marjorie knew how to read Italian but was not confident when trying to pronounce it. Consequently, Elizabeth decided that her pupil would benefit most if they read aloud from books written in the language for half the hour—so she could correct any mispronunciations as they occurred—and converse in Italian for the balance. In addition, she proposed to conduct the lessons in one of the gazebos in the garden instead of the classroom.

Marianne had taken instantly to Elizabeth's style of instruction, which made it difficult for Marjorie to oppose her. By the end of the fourth day, even she was taking part in the lessons without her usual detachment.

After Elizabeth announced that the lesson was over for the day and began to gather her supplies, Marjorie joined her cousin on the swing that hung from the centre of the gazebo. Immediately they began discussing the upcoming ball.

Elizabeth had walked several feet towards the house when she heard a name that stopped her in her tracks: Darcy. Hidden from view by shrubs and trees, she held her breath to listen.

"I cannot wait," Marjorie enthused. "I hope Papa will reward my cooperation in these lessons by allowing me to attend the ball."

"Surely you do not believe he will let you dance."

"No, but if I can watch, I shall be satisfied."

Marianne sighed. "I have no hope. My father will never let me attend."

"Your father may not even come! You know how he hates hobnobbing with society."

"Oh, he will. I asked him to."

"Why would you do that? He is even more protective of you than my parents are of me."

"At times I think I shall scream if I cannot escape from under his thumb, but when I think of all he has done for me, I am ashamed. I am not his child, but he has never treated me as anything less than a daughter since Mother died. In any case, even if *he* does not attend, *your* parents would not let me attend."

Marjorie patted her hand. "I fear you are right. After all, you are a year younger than I."

When Marianne had been introduced to Elizabeth, it was as Lady Marianne Dudley, so she had never associated that young lady with Mr. Darcy. She was not surprised to hear that gentleman had married a widow with a daughter, but Elizabeth was astonished to learn that Marianne's mother was dead. The sound of a door slamming made her realise she was risking discovery if she stayed hidden, so she hurried on to the manor house. Once inside her room, Elizabeth lay on her bed, willing her heart to stop racing whilst she considered the prospect of meeting Mr. Darcy again.

Will he be shocked to discover I am the children's governess, or has Lord Matlock informed him already?

She envisioned being introduced and answering his bow with a curtsey. Then, suddenly, she sat up and turned so that her legs hung off the bed.

What utter nonsense! Mr. Darcy is no longer interested in you, foolish woman.

Rising, she went to the window-seat and sat down. Pulling aside the curtain, she surveyed the tranquil garden below. Then, closing her eyes, she imagined walking through it. This exercise had always brought her peace, but today it seemed useless.

If he should come, I shall make certain our paths never cross.

Pemberley
Mr. Darcy's study
A few days later

After reading the last entry logged by his steward for the third time, William realised he still could not recall what it said.

Closing the ledger, he laid it aside, propped his elbows on the desk and dropped his head in his hands.

He began to massage his forehead. Sleep had evaded him since his return to Pemberley, and for that he placed the blame squarely at Richard's feet. Had his cousin not reminded him that Marianne could soon be married, he might have put off tormenting himself about that eventuality for a good while longer. Richard's words had stung more than he was willing to admit... even to himself.

Marianne's mother, Lady Cornelia, had used him cruelly, but he had never faulted the child for her mother's treachery. No, she was an innocent, and if truth be told, she was all that had saved him from despair after he learned what most of London already knew: Lady Cornelia was an unscrupulous strumpet who had taken a second son with no fortune as a lover, only to leave him and pursue William once she discovered she was with child. The worst part was knowing that Lady Matlock, who had pushed the alliance, knew about her deceit. After all, his aunt and Cornelia's mother were old friends.

The day of his wedding ran through his mind as though he were watching a play at Drury Lane. Cornelia had fainted just before the wedding breakfast began, so William summoned his physician. He would never forget the look on Dr. Graham's face when he announced that the new bride was several months with child. Naturally, Graham had assumed they had anticipated their vows, and he was as shocked as William once he realised the groom was not the father.

As it happened, fate intervened, and six months later Lady Cornelia died whilst giving birth, as did the child. Though William felt sympathy for Marianne in the loss of her mother and sister, he was too numb to feel grief for Cornelia then or now.

A knock on the door disturbed his reflections, and he called, "Come."

The housekeeper entered, holding a silver salver piled high with letters. "You asked to see the post as soon as it arrived."

It had been six years since Mrs. Reynolds' death, but William was still not used to her niece, Mrs. Brown, acting as housekeeper. Though she filled the position admirably, having worked under Mrs. Reynolds during her last two years, he missed the servant who had been like a second mother to him. Shaking off the remembrance, he asked, "Did you happen to notice if any were from Matlock Manor?"

"There were so many that I did not sort through them, sir."

"Thank you, Mrs. Brown."

Instead of leaving, the housekeeper waited.

At last he looked up. "Is there something I can do for you?"

"Yes, there is. I would like to see you eat what Mrs. Lantrip has taken the time to cook for your dinner."

"My appetite is not—" William began, only to be interrupted.

"You always stop eating when Lady Marianne is not here. Have you any idea how much that worries those of us who care for you? After all, there will come a day when she will marry and reside elsewhere, and you will be alone more often than not."

Must YOU remind me of that, too? William wanted to scream. Thankfully, he recalled that he should be grateful for her concern.

"If it will make you happy, I shall attempt to eat most, if not all, of my dinner."

"It will. Thank you."

As Mrs. Brown exited the room and closed the door, William found a thick letter from Matlock Manor and broke the seal. Instantly, a smaller letter fell to the desk. Recognising his daughter's hand, he read it first.

Dear Papa,

I do not have much time to write, but I did want to send a note to say I am having a wonderful time here with Marjorie. Not only do we swim in the lake every day, we have played lawn bowling so much that I am quite the proficient. Moreover, the new governess hired for my youngest cousins is working with us on our Italian and French.

She is unlike any governess I have ever seen; by that, I mean she is young, witty and entertaining. Why could you

not have hired someone like her when I was being bom-
barded with letters, numbers and all things educational?
I can see your frown from here, Papa. Smile. It was
only a joke.
Cousin Richard said you are coming for the ball. Please
come a few days early, for I miss you terribly.
Love,
Marianne

That Marianne would say she missed him was more than
William had hoped for, and to be truthful, Pemberley had been
far too lonely without her. Her absence and the recent death
of Zeus, the stallion he had owned for three and twenty years,
had engendered something inside that he had yet to understand,
much less conquer. Though he dared not give voice to it, it was
as though he was standing on the side, watching his life pass by,
and God help him, he did not care. As usual, when thoughts like
these began to plague him, William forced himself to focus on
what must be done.

Picking up the letter from Richard, he noted that his cousin
started his missive by mentioning the new governess, too, although he spoke of how impressed he was with how she handled his youngest girls. Pleased that his cousin had apparently
found someone intelligent to manage them, he read on. Richard
asked if he had received his invitation to the ball, which Isabelle
had sent earlier, so William stopped to shuffle through the stack.
Finding the invitation, he opened it to note the date before re-
suming Richard's letter. The letter contained his usual com-
plaints—the crops would die if it did not rain soon and the market for lambs was down, as well as questions about which crops
to plant next. Having been master of Matlock Manor for only
a short time, Richard relied on William's strategies for managing an estate, since both his property and Pemberley shared the
same climate and type of soil.

After repeating that he wanted William to come sooner
rather than later, Richard ended his letter in his usual abrupt
manner. Leaning back in his chair to contemplate which day

to leave, William recalled the drawbacks of getting to Matlock Manor from Pemberley. Thought it was only fifteen miles to the west, the road between them was narrow and not well kept in certain areas. Moreover, when heavy rains fell, it often proved impossible to navigate by coach until after the mud had fully dried.

William sat up again and began writing a list of what to discuss with Richard regarding crops. When he finished, he decided it was time to take Orion, Zeus' offspring, on his evening run. Whilst Orion could never take his father's place, he seemed eager to please, and that went a long way towards carving out his own niche in his master's heart.

The Cowan residence
Cheapside
That same day

Whilst the children played in the yard, Jane and her Aunt Gardiner sat under the shade of a large oak tree, fanning themselves against the summer heat.

"Have you heard from Lizzy?" Mrs. Gardiner asked.

"I have received only two letters since she left for Matlock Manor. The last came yesterday. I was planning to share it with you on my next visit, but you saved me the trouble by coming here. Would you like me to fetch it?"

"There is no need. Just tell me what she had to say. Does she regret her decision yet?"

"From what she writes, no. She allows that she loves the estate, for there are miles of trails to walk. In addition, numerous gravel paths crisscross the gardens surrounding the manor. She told me to tell you that Matlock Manor reminds her greatly of Pemberley and that you would understand."

"Oh, my! Pemberley's gardens are magnificent, so I can imagine how pleased Lizzy must be to have found its equal."

"She also mentioned that she is now helping the Fitzwilliams' oldest child, Lady Marjorie, as well as her cousin, Lady Marianne Dudley, with Italian."

"Dudley? I seem to recall that name, though I cannot place it right now. Perhaps it will come to me later."

"In any case, Lizzy said she enjoys teaching languages more than numbers and letters. That is nothing new. She and Papa loved conversing in Italian or French. It was as though they had a language all their own."

"He would have taught you, had you shown any interest."

"I know, but it held no attraction for me." Jane laughed. "Or, more to the point, I was too lazy."

Having overheard that much of their conversation, her youngest child, Susanna, said, "We are not supposed to be lazy. You said so, Mama."

Jane laughed, turning to her aunt. "My words come back to haunt me." To Susanna she said, "You are right, my sweet. We are not supposed to be lazy, and your mother suffered by not learning her lessons as well as your Aunt Lizzy."

"I miss Aunt Lizzy," Susanna said, her expression settling into a frown. "When will she come back?"

Jane pulled her child into a quick embrace and gave her a kiss. "Very soon, I hope."

"I hope so, too!" Susanna declared, breaking free of Jane to sprint across the yard and join her siblings in a game of chase.

"I pray Lizzy knows what she is about," Madeline Gardiner said. "For years whenever I mentioned Lambton, Pemberley or Mr. Darcy, she would change the subject. To see her act indifferently at being employed by Lord Matlock is disconcerting. Whilst I would like her to confront her fears, I do not want to see her hurt again."

Jane reached for her aunt's hand. "I feel the same way."

Suddenly, Jonathan walked out of the back door, his brother following right behind. He greeted his wife with a kiss atop her head. "Markus has to return to Birmingham."

Jane rose. "We have enjoyed having you with us. I only regret that Lizzy took another position so swiftly that you did not get to see her again."

Markus twisted the well-worn hat in his hands. "Perhaps the next time she visits, my crops will not have to be harvested before I can get away. Will you let me know if Elizabeth writes that she is coming to visit?"

"I will," Jane said.

As Jane's husband and his brother walked back to the house, Mrs. Gardiner whispered, "Markus seems to be a fine young man. It is a pity Lizzy vowed not to marry but for the deepest love. That kind of inflexibility does not bode well for her future prospects."

"I tried to tell her the same thing before she left, but she refused to listen."

"When Lizzy sets her mind to something, there is no turning back."

"I fear she will go to her grave in love with Mr. Darcy."

"In love, but too fearful to speak to him again."

"That is so unlike the sister I grew up with," Jane said, sighing. "Lizzy used to be so bold that I feared what would come out of her mouth whenever she spoke."

"All of you were affected by Lydia's foolishness, but I think our Lizzy lost the most."

"I had never thought of it that way, but you are right. My poor, poor sister!"

Chapter 5

Matlock Manor
One week later

On the Wednesday before Saturday's ball, the coach carrying Lady Matlock's mother and sister arrived at Matlock Manor. Isabelle had expected her family's arrival earlier that week, and as soon as her sister, Lady Amy, followed a maid up the stairs, Isabelle pulled her mother into the parlour to ask about the delay.

"You have me to thank for that, Isabelle," Lady Gordon said. "Your sister has talked of nothing save Mr. Darcy since she learned he would attend the ball. Should that gentleman have come early, I did not wish her to wear his patience thin before the ball had even begun. Therefore, I made certain we did not come too early."

"Darcy has yet to arrive, but when he does, you must help me to caution Amy not to press too hard for his attention. She always acts foolishly whenever she is in his company."

"Foolish does not begin to describe her conduct," Lady Gordon huffed. "I have no idea how I raised such a silly daughter. I can only blame it on your father. Harold spoiled her; God rest his soul."

"As did Lord Parker before his death," Isabelle added, mentioning her sister's late husband. "He was far too old for her, and he doted on her as though she were a child. I worry no one else will be willing to offer for her."

"Lord Parker was certainly too indulgent," Lady Gordon agreed. "I do not know why your father approved of the marriage, other than he knew Parker would carry on where he left off."

"In any case," Isabelle said, "Amy will push Darcy away unless we restrain her."

"I will do all that I can, but you know her temperament."

"I noticed Rose did not come," Isabelle said, mentioning her niece. "Where is she?"

"We left her in London with her godmother, Lady Sinclair. Amy felt she would appeal more to Mr. Darcy if she did not have a child clinging to her skirts."

"I am not so certain. Darcy loves children. Having Rose here may have made my sister more appealing."

"Please do not mention that to Amy, or she will insist on having the child brought here immediately."

"I agree."

"Is anyone else here?" Lady Gordon asked.

"Lord and Lady Blakely, David's cousins," Isabelle said, mentioning her first husband. "Richard saw them in London, and when they mentioned they were about to leave for home, he invited them to the ball."

"I have not seen them in ages. Their daughter is about the same age as Marjorie, is she not?"

"Clarissa will be seventeen in just over a week. She is visiting her grandmother in Bath but is to return to Locklear Manor in time for her birthday celebration. In fact, Lady Blakely specifically requested that Marjorie and Marianne attend that event. They have invited several girls in Clarissa's circle to the party and to spend the night afterwards."

"Refresh my memory. Where is Locklear Manor?"

"Approximately ten miles north of here."

"Now I remember. Your father and I stayed there once when

we were newly married. Of course, that was before the Grant-leys died and it was put on the market."

"Lord and Lady Mandeville of Mandeville Manor in Liverpool have arrived; however, I do not expect the majority of our guests until Friday or early on Saturday."

Just then, Lady Amy walked into the room. "There you are! I wondered where you had got to, Mother," she proclaimed. Then, eyeing her sister and mother suspiciously, she added, "I suppose you were discussing me, since you quieted the instant I came in."

"On the contrary, we were discussing Mr. Darcy," Lady Gordon replied, telling a half-truth.

"That reminds me of why I came down," Amy replied, addressing Isabelle. "The maid said Mr. Darcy is not here. I do hope he has not reneged on his promise to come."

Rolling her eyes so only her mother could see, Isabelle replied, "Barring something unforeseen happening, I expect him to attend."

Always melodramatic, Lady Amy sighed heavily. "It would be just my luck for something terrible to happen that would keep him away."

"In that case, I would think it would be poor Mr. Darcy's misfortune, not yours," Lady Gordon suggested.

"Oh, Mother! Why can you never take my side?"

With that, her daughter swept from the room in an impressive display of ill temper and swaying skirts.

"Why do I feel Mr. Darcy will never consider offering for Amy?" Lady Gordon asked.

"Perhaps because we both know Darcy will never again be fooled by a cunning woman."

Her mother sighed. "Precisely."

The next day

Despite his best intentions, William was unable to leave Pemberley until the Thursday before the ball because an unexplained fire had burned several acres of pasture on the eastern border with Parkleigh Manor. Pemberley's tenants and servants had managed to keep the fire contained, and fortuitously, no people or animals were harmed. Still, a sizable shed was lost, taking half of the hay for the winter months along with it. This prevented William from leaving until he had calculated and ordered the lumber to rebuild the shed and hired men to do the job.

Arriving at Matlock Manor in the late afternoon, an hour or so after tea had been served, William was told that Richard was playing billiards, and the butler escorted him to the billiards room. At the door, Mr. Goings stopped to announce him.

"Mr. Darcy is here, sir."

Richard lay down his cue stick just as William walked past the butler. "Darcy! I was about to give up on you!"

"I apologise for not arriving sooner, as I had promised. There was a fire at Pemberley, and I could not leave until the matter was handled."

"Good Lord! What happened?"

As William explained the situation, Richard's stance relaxed. "At least it was not worse."

"I agree. It could have been disastrous had the fire started nearer the stables."

"Speaking of escaping disaster," Richard said, lowering his voice, "you must be living right, for all the ladies just now retired to their rooms to do whatever ladies do in the afternoon. That means Isabelle's sister will have no idea you have arrived."

"If you do not mind, I would like to keep it that way for a while."

"Of course."

"I assume my usual room has been set aside."

"It has, and if you go up the back staircase, you will stay hidden. I shall have Mr. Goings send up hot water so you may wash and hide away until dinner... or even tomorrow, if you like."

"I want to see Marianne, so until dinner will suffice."

"So be it!" Richard declared. As William turned to leave, he added, "I hope you will play some billiards whilst you are here. I need to win back what I lost the last time we played."

William smiled wryly. "It would be easier if you just paid the pound you owe me."

"That is easy for you to say! I am the one in debt!"

Shaking his head, William went through the door, chuckling softly.

At dinner

Everyone was seated when William entered the room and walked straight to his daughter.

Marianne jumped up, crying, "Papa!" as he embraced her and placed a kiss on her forehead.

Some at the table remarked that they were glad he had arrived, whilst others expressed how worried they had been, so Richard explained about the fire whilst William took the seat next to Marianne. The fire at Pemberley occupied the dinner conversation, with the men weighing in on what might have caused it and speculating on whether it might have been set intentionally.

Being tired and hungry, William let the others theorise about the matter whilst he concentrated on eating, something he knew would make Mrs. Brown proud. The thought allowed a smile to escape, but as he looked up, Lady Amy smiled in return. Quickly, his expression changed to his usual frown.

After dinner, Lady Isabelle asked the men to forego cigars and join them in the music room where Marjorie was going to exhibit on the pianoforte whilst Marianne accompanied her on the harp. Once everyone was seated, those young ladies began searching through a stack of music to select a song.

Whilst they did, Lady Gordon leaned in to quietly talk to her daughter. "How are my grandchildren faring under the new governess?"

"Very well, Mother. Miss Bennet has the ability to bring out the best in the girls," Lady Isabelle replied, equally quietly. "They practice the pianoforte without complaining and sing songs in French, and—" She stopped. "In fact, I shall have a servant fetch Miss Bennet and the children now, so everyone can hear them."

"Do you not think it too late?" Lady Gordon asked.

As her daughter summoned a nearby footman, she said, "If I know my children, Miss Bennet is reading them yet another story before they will agree to go to sleep."

Half an hour later, just after Marjorie and Marianne finished performing two pieces, Elizabeth shuffled her charges into the music room via the side door. Though already in nightgowns and robes, the girls were wide awake and excited to be asked to exhibit. Already prepared for bed, Elizabeth had taken the long plait she wore whilst sleeping and fashioned it into a bun before changing back into her uniform.

"Miss Bennet, I would like you and Ellen to perform the duet I overheard you practicing this week," Lady Isabelle said.

Forcing a smile, Elizabeth led Ellen to the pianoforte, whilst Emily and Evelyn took places beside their mother on the sofa. Ellen sat on the right side of the bench, whilst Elizabeth took the left. After playing four lines or so, Elizabeth slipped off the seat and hurried to take Ellen's place on the right, whilst the girl played chords that took her to the lower keys as she slid in that direction. This exchange occurred twice more during the song, and by the time they had finished, their performance was met with laughter and a strong round of applause.

The moment Elizabeth and her protégée stood, she caught sight of William sitting beside Richard, behind Lord and Lady Mandeville, and her heart stood still. Other than the fact that his dark hair was now interspersed with silver, he looked so much as he had the last time they were together that she was astounded. Moreover, to her mortification, she found that when their eyes locked, she could not look away. The longer she stood immobile, the more awkward the situation became. Lady Amy and Lady Gordon both turned to follow her line of sight.

"Now, would you please have the children perform the folk

song that you taught them in three languages?" said Lady Isabelle.

Her request broke through Elizabeth's trance, and with no choice but to comply, Elizabeth motioned for Emily and Evelyn to join her and Ellen at the pianoforte. After helping Emily to sit beside her sisters on the bench, Elizabeth leaned over to hit the right key, and they began to sing.[1]

Frère Jacques, Frère Jacques,
Dormez-vous? Dormez-vous?
Sonnez les matines! Sonnez les matines!
Ding, dang, dong. Ding, dang, dong.
Fra Giovanni, Fra Giovanni,
Dormi tu, dormi tu?
Suona la campana, suona la campana,
Ding-dang-dong, ding-dang-dong.
Are you sleeping, are you sleeping
Brother John, brother John?
Morning bells are ringing, morning bells are ringing
Ding, ding, dong. Ding, ding, dong.

When the song ended, applause filled the air once more. Naturally, the children were proud, and they beamed as they received hugs from their mother, grandmother and aunt. Elizabeth then began herding her charges from the room and, once in the hallway, she, Marjorie and Marianne guided the youngest girls back to their rooms.

Whilst immensely proud of his children's accomplishments, Richard could not properly celebrate because he was being held prisoner by a steely glare. After William stood and murmured, "A word with you, Cousin," Richard knew there was no way to avoid the confrontation to follow.

Standing, he replied, "Of course."

---

1   * *Please note that I do not speak French or Italian, so I consulted several people regarding these versions of the song who do speak the language. There are so many dialects and differing opinions that it would be impossible to please everyone, so I chose the versions most often indicated as correct. Please do not let the translations ruin your enjoyment of the story. After all, this is fiction.*

As he and William headed towards the main door, Lady Isabelle said, "Where are you going, Richard? My sister is about to exhibit."

"I suggest she start without us, my dear," Richard stated solemnly.

Frustrated that Mr. Darcy was not going to witness her performance, Lady Amy huffed, "I should have known this would happen!"

"Now, Amy," Lady Gordon chided through clenched teeth, accompanied by a glower that shouted *act your age*. "I am certain the rest of our company would be delighted to hear you play."

Reluctantly, her daughter walked to the pianoforte.

Richard's study

William had got no more than halfway inside the study when he whirled around to confront Richard. "What is the meaning of this?"

Knowing he must tread carefully, or William might suspect his true motive in hiring Elizabeth, Richard replied, "I am not certain to what you are referring. If you are asking why I hired Miss Bennet as a governess, the answer is simple. She has proven an excellent teacher to my children."

He walked over to the liquor cabinet and poured two glasses of brandy. Handing one to William, Richard sat down behind his desk with the other. "If, however, you are asking why I did not mention her employment to you before now, that is more complicated."

"I have found that truth is not complicated, only lying is."

"I did not lie. I weighed the benefits of telling you ahead of time and having you refuse to come to the ball, or letting you discover she was here. I chose the latter."

"These last fourteen years I asked only one thing of you, and that was never to mention Elizabeth Bennet to me again. How could you possibly conclude it would benefit me to be thrown into her company without warning?"

"That was not remotely my conclusion. In fact, I knew that seeing her would be the last thing you would want." William started to interrupt, but Richard said, "Please, hear what I have to say."

After his cousin quieted, Richard explained how Elizabeth came to be his children's governess. Then, he added, "I almost dismissed the idea of hiring her, but I thought it would be cruel not to when she is perfect for the job. In other words, I did not want to make *your* problem *her* problem."

"You sound like my mother," William retorted.

"Your mother was a very wise woman, and she would be heartbroken to see how you have allowed this *issue* to cloud your judgement all these years."

"I suggest you write that down," William said cynically. "You could put it in one of those sappy novels and make a fortune."

"If it makes you feel any better, Miss Bennet was just as reluctant to be in your company."

"Frankly, I would be surprised if she were not."

"Tell me. What troubles you the most about her presence here?"

William looked away, as though carefully considering his answer. Then, he murmured, "Whenever Elizabeth came to mind over the years, I convinced myself that she had married some country squire and birthed a house full of children. Seeing her today forces me to admit that did not happen. Because of my actions, she was reduced to spinsterhood, teaching other people's children."

"Darcy, you are not God! Everything that happens in life is not your doing."

"Had I exposed Wickham when I should have, her family would not have been ruined."

"You were merely trying to keep Georgiana's mistake hidden."

"I should have been honest with Mr. Bennet. He would have kept my sister's secret, and Lydia would never have gone to

Brighton with the militia. Moreover, I have absolutely no excuse for taking Caroline Bingley's side regarding Charles' attachment to Jane Bennet."

"No excuse except that you thought you were advising a friend against an unequal marriage."

When William did not respond, Richard said, "So, what would you have me do? Dismiss her?"

"It is I who should go, not Elizabeth. I will simply stay away as much as possible whilst she is your children's governess."

"Emily is three, for heaven's sake! It follows that Miss Bennet could be with us for at least another ten years."

"That will be my problem."

"After the way you glared at her tonight, perhaps it will not."

"I did not glare. What is your point?"

"One of Miss Bennet's conditions for accepting the job was that if her presence made anyone uncomfortable—meaning *you*—she would leave."

"Immediately after the ball, I shall assure her that I could not be more pleased that she is your governess. Then I shall find an excuse to return to Pemberley."

"Why not stay long enough to have a rational conversation with her? Tell her how you tried to retrieve Lydia, and about your accident. Who knows? You could become friends again."

"What right have I to step back into her life? All my interference ever meant for Elizabeth was heartache!" William said, his temper flaring. Tossing the rest of the brandy down, he grimaced as he set the glass on the table. "She deserves better than that."

Having said that, he exited the room.

Right or wrong, the heart chooses whom it will love. I pray that you, and she, realise that before tossing away a second chance.

William's bedroom

Unable to sleep, William sat on the balcony in the moonlight with his feet propped on a table. He was having no luck trying to identify the different constellations—an occupation which usually made him drowsy.

That was because Elizabeth kept appearing before him looking just as beautiful as she had this evening. If she had any grey in her hair, from where he sat, he could not tell. However, one thing he knew for certain—her eyes were just as dark and luminous as they had been when last he saw her in Lambton. Back then, those ebony orbs had been filled with unshed tears as she recounted the contents of Jane's letter. Even now, whenever he wished, he could recall that memory as though it were yesterday.

Going back inside his bedroom, he headed to the closet to retrieve an item from his trunk. In a pocket hidden in the lining, he kept a reminder that called to him whenever melancholy won out over prudence. Taking the journal from its place, he ran his fingers over the gilded numbers on the cover: 1812. Though he kept a record of every year, due to the accident that year was never finished. Now it served as a reminder of all that he had lost.

Opening the book, he flipped the pages to the last entry.

August 18, 1812
Tuesday
Mr. Gardiner seemed very pleased with the size of the fish we caught and is looking forward to having them for dinner tomorrow. Mrs. Lantrip has an excellent recipe and often laments that I do not fish as much as I should. She will be very happy with the number we left in the kitchen when we were done today.

From what Georgiana said, after showing our guests around the manor, she and Elizabeth had a splendid time playing duets on the pianoforte whilst Mrs. Gardiner cheered them on. Oh, how I wish Elizabeth could be her sister in truth. Dare I ask too much?

I had hoped they would stay at Pemberley tonight, but I could not convince Elizabeth it would be no imposition. Therefore, I left her and her relations at the Crown Inn in

Lambton. Perhaps I shall have better luck tomorrow when they come for dinner.

Closing the journal, he stared into space, reliving every aspect of that day. All these years later, he still recalled it as the last time he had been completely happy, for the next day the letter revealing Lydia's foolishness arrived. Of course, Elizabeth and the Gardiners had left straightaway for Longbourn, with Edward Gardiner vowing to find the couple and make them marry; however, William knew his old nemesis, George Wickham, would not be coerced easily into doing the honourable thing. No, that would take a goodly amount of persuasion and money.

Consequently, by the time the Gardiners' coach rolled out of Lambton, he had devised a plan to find Wickham and force him to marry Lydia Bennet. And he would have succeeded, had not fate intervened. Near Leicester, in a blinding rainstorm, his coach had gone off the road and rolled down an embankment. Only he had survived, and with a limp as a constant reminder of his failure.

Several months had passed before he was able to think clearly, and by then his sources told him that Lydia had sailed to the Americas with Wickham. Moreover, Charles Bingley had visited during his recovery to share the news that he had married an angel he met after leaving Netherfield—a Lady Tipton. William knew the woman well, though he did not say as much to Bingley. She was one of those women who always hurried to hang on his own arm whenever Lady Matlock insisted he attend one of her soirées.

Crushed that he had not been able to undo the damage for which he felt responsible, William had gone into a deep melancholy that was capped off by agreeing to marry Lady Matlock's choice for his wife, the widowed Lady Cornelia.

After Cornelia died, other than being left with a child he loved, everything else he once desired in life had been pushed to the recesses of his mind. And there they had stayed... until tonight.

Chapter 6

Matlock Manor
The ball

As William made his way down the magnificent grand staircase, it occurred to him that under Isabelle's watch nothing at Matlock Manor was done conservatively, especially soirées such as this one. The ball was scheduled to begin in less than an hour, and not only were pots and vases of flowers and greenery occupying every available space, vines and cut flowers had been woven through the rails of the staircase and placed atop every doorway. In addition, the candles in every chandelier in the house were lit, whilst numerous candelabra had been scattered throughout the house, lighting all the recesses not reached by the chandeliers.

Though pleased for his cousin, William was secretly glad Pemberley's furnishings were less ostentatious, for Matlock Manor reminded him too much of Rosings Park under Lady Catherine's reign. That woman had died three years to the day after his marriage to Lady Cornelia, with the estate passing to his cousin Anne.

Anne had survived her mother by a mere two years, during which time Lord Matlock helped her run Rosings Park with the aid of a steward. After Anne died there were no de Bourghs alive to inherit, so the estate passed to Lord Matlock. After his death it became part of the family holdings and the steward continued to manage it under William's watchful eye because Viscount Sele, the new Lord Matlock, showed no interest in doing so. William hoped that once Richard became more comfortable managing Matlock Manor, he could pass part of that responsibility on to his cousin.

As these thoughts were going through his head, William was oblivious to the fact that Lady Parker was waiting to accost him in the foyer. The minute she heard his boots on the marble floor, she swept out of the nearest parlour as though she had no idea he was there.

"Mr. Darcy," the blonde-haired beauty purred as she floated towards him. "It seems we are the only ones dressed for the ball. And how handsome you look, too!"

William could not deny that Lady Parker was beautiful, and tonight she looked even more so, wearing a teal-coloured, silk damask gown with a delicate, gold-sequined net overlay. The gown's sleeves were fashioned off-the-shoulder, and the bodice was cut so low that, for a brief moment, William found himself pondering what could be holding it up.

He quickly recovered. "That is not true. I was just talking with your sister and Richard, and they are both fully dressed."

Ignoring his curt reply, Lady Parker walked over to weave her arm through his, lifted her chin and batted her eyelashes. "What a shame you cannot dance. I would love to be your partner tonight."

"It is not that I cannot; it is that I choose not to. I will not chance ruining an unsuspecting partner's foot should I misstep."

"I am willing to take my chances," she said brazenly.

"I am sorry, but I am resolute on the matter."

"I could refuse to dance and keep you company."

"Since my cousin is hosting this ball for your benefit, do you not think that would be inconsiderate?"

Suddenly, Lady Matlock called from the landing, "Darcy, Richard needs to speak with you right away. He is in his dressing room."

Whilst Isabelle disappeared as quickly as she had come, William feigned disappointment. "Duty calls. Please excuse me."

Cursing under her breath as William started back up the stairs, Lady Parker walked on to the ballroom.

Elizabeth had come downstairs to fetch flowers from the conservatory in the hope that having flowers for their hair might coax a smile from Lady Marianne and Lady Marjorie, who were disappointed at not being allowed to attend the ball. Instead, they were to stand in the receiving line to greet the guests and then retire. Having found the perfect rose buds, Elizabeth was unable to go up the rear stairs because footmen were carrying a table down them; thus, she hurried towards the grand staircase. Stumbling upon Lady Parker's ambush of William, she barely managed to stop before rounding the corner into the foyer. Holding her breath, she listened as he successfully parried each of Lady Parker's advances, which reminded her of a similar scene involving Caroline Bingley years ago.

Covering her mouth to keep from laughing, she thought, *Poor man! After all this time, you are still being pursued by the ladies.*

As soon as the foyer emptied, Elizabeth rushed up the stairs, praying that she could present the flowers to the girls without encountering William. That was not to be, however, for the instant she pinned two white rosebuds at the back of Marianne's head, William knocked on his daughter's dressing room door.

"Come!" Marianne called and William walked in. Elizabeth froze.

"Would you excuse us, please?" he asked.

"Of course," Elizabeth replied.

Picking up the pink rosebuds she had selected for Marjorie, she hurried into the hall and proceeded straight to that young woman's dressing room. Cautiously laying her ear against the door and hearing nothing, Elizabeth tried the handle. The door opened, and she slipped inside to find Marjorie alone and weeping.

"Whatever is the matter, my dear?"

"Papa treats me like a child!"

"You may feel that way now, but once you have a daughter of your own, you will understand."

Whilst drying her eyes on a lace-trimmed handkerchief, Marjorie retorted, "How can you possibly know that? You have no children."

Elizabeth's expression became wistful. "I once witnessed the downfall of a young lady who followed her own counsel. Believe me, the outcome was dreadful, not only for her but for her family as well. You should thank God every day that your father cares enough to limit what you do until you are mature enough to handle the responsibility that comes with making your own decisions."

Marjorie's brows furrowed. "Is this woman the reason you are in service?"

Surprised at Marjorie's intuition, Elizabeth replied, "I am in service because I chose to be." Changing the subject, she held up the pink rosebuds. "I found these in the conservatory and thought they would look beautiful in your hair tonight."

Marjorie's face brightened. "They are lovely. Will you pin them in?"

"Of course."

Marianne's dressing room

"Why was Miss Bennet in here?" William asked.

"She brought flowers for my hair," Marianne said, picking up a hand mirror and turning to admire the delicate white roses in her hair by looking in the dressing room mirror. "I think she hoped to make me feel better."

"Feel better about what?"

"Cousin Richard told Marjorie she cannot attend the ball, and I know if Marjorie cannot, I have not a prayer."

"Do you understand why?"

She cocked her head as though contemplating his question. "For myself I do, but I do not understand why Marjorie cannot. After all, she is almost eighteen."

"Almost is not entirely."

"Oh, Papa! You are such a stickler for the details! I cannot imagine you were once young or ever foolish."

Thoughts of Elizabeth flashed through his mind. "Believe me, at one time I was both."

"Tell me."

William shook his head. "No father worth his salt admits his faults to his children."

"Why not?"

"How can he enforce a rule he admits to breaking?"

"That does not seem fair."

"Fair or not, that is how it is." William stepped back to admire her. "You look lovely."

Marianne threw her arms around him. "I am glad that you came for the ball. I love you very much, Papa."

"I love you, too."

Halfway through the ball

Tired of repeatedly explaining why he was not dancing, and of fending off Lady Parker between her sets, William was ready for a respite. As was his habit, he made his way out of the ballroom and walked down the hallway towards the library. There, he intended to pour himself a brandy, sit down and prop his aching knee on a cushioned footstool.

Just before opening the library door, however, he heard someone say, "Psst! Cousin Darcy!"

Glancing to the end of the hall, he saw Ellen peering around the corner. Hurrying in that direction before someone else spied her, he discovered his cousin's child was already dressed in nightclothes. Amused, William squatted down to speak to her.

"You are supposed to be in bed, young lady."

"So are Marianne and Marjorie, but they are not! And I cannot go to bed until I know Miss Bennet will not get blamed for what they have planned."

William's brows furrowed. "What have they planned?"

"I will explain everything, but you must follow me whilst I do. There is no time to waste!"

Taking Ellen's outstretched hand, he allowed her to lead him to the back stairs that led to the floor above. Once upstairs, she headed straight to the door that led into the balcony high over the ballroom where the band sat. His aunt had converted an alcove next to the musicians to a private box, much like those in a theatre, when she had grown too ill to attend the events hosted by her son and his wife. Lady Matlock would sit there unnoticed, watching the scene below until she grew weary and retired. Since her death, the box had remained empty.

Once in the balcony, Ellen opened the door to the theatre box and led him in. The only light came from the candles in a chandelier over the musicians, and it took a moment for their eyes to adjust. Then Ellen whispered, "Follow me."

As she led him to the darkest corner, the musicians took a break, and William leaned down to whisper, "Now, what are Marianne and Marjorie planning?"

"Mama asked Miss Bennet to make certain Marjorie and Marianne went straight to bed once the ball began. Only I know that Marjorie always slips out of her room to watch the balls from up here. Moreover, I heard her tell Marianne not to don her bedclothes, which makes me think both are going to slip out of their beds tonight."

"Why not just tell Miss Bennet and let her handle it?"

"I tried, but Emily cannot sleep because of the music, and she insisted our governess read to her. The nanny would not let me interrupt them, so I wrote a note and slipped it under Miss Bennet's bedroom door."

"Then, why are you so worried? Miss Bennet will find the note and make them return to bed, and no one will be the wiser."

"Not if Aunt Amy has her way."

"How would you know what your—"

Ellen let go an exasperated breath as she interrupted. "If you must know, I was hiding in her closet!"

"What did your father say about eavesdropping?"

"But that is how I discovered Aunt Amy wants my governess to get in trouble! I know she does not like her because she wrinkles her nose whenever she says *Miss Bennet*."

"What did you hear?"

"Aunt Amy's maid bragged that a maid told her my sister slips out of her room and comes here to watch the balls and that Marianne intends to join her tonight. Aunt Amy said that Mama should dismiss Miss Bennet if she cannot be relied upon to make certain they go to bed."

William looked as though he was considering what to do, so Ellen continued. "Cousin Darcy, you were the only person I could think of who could convince Mama that Miss Bennet is not at fault should my sister and Marianne be discovered. No one will listen to me."

Abruptly the door to the box opened, so they went silent. The dim light of candles in the hall sconces was enough to reveal the interlopers: Marianne and Marjorie. Taking no notice of William and Ellen in the corner, they sat down and began whispering animatedly. Alas, the musicians had begun to play again, drowning out their conversation. Just when William was about to confront Marianne, the door opened, and Elizabeth stole inside. For a second time, the music kept him from hearing what was said, though judging by her comportment, it was obvious Elizabeth was upset.

Without warning, the door flew open once more, and this time Lady Parker and Lady Isabelle were outlined by the dim hall lights. Isabelle ordered the girls from the box so forcefully that had the band not been in the middle of a rousing song, the guests below might have heard. Instead, blissfully unaware of what was happening above their heads, they continued to dance.

Elizabeth followed Marianne and Marjorie into the hall, where Lady Matlock ordered, "Go to your rooms immediately!" When Elizabeth started to follow, her employer added, "Not you, Miss Bennet."

They waited until the cousins were out of sight before Lady Parker exclaimed, "It is just as I said, Isabelle!"

Lady Matlock addressed Elizabeth, "Please explain why you encouraged my daughter and my niece to disobey their parents."

Patting Ellen's hand, William whispered, "Stay hidden." Then, he stepped from his hiding place into the light before Elizabeth had time to reply. The shocked look on the sisters' faces and a barely audible "*Mr. Darcy*" uttered by Lady Parker almost drew a smile from him.

"You are wrong to think Miss Bennet played any part in our daughters' prank, Isabelle. She had just arrived and was chiding Marjorie and Marianne for disobeying."

Lady Parker's face flushed red with anger, whilst Lady Matlock's face paled. "I apologise, Miss Bennet. I should have known you played no part in this. Please, take your leave."

As Elizabeth walked away, Isabelle addressed William. "What were you about, hiding up here?"

"I felt the need to rest my knee, and I recalled that my aunt often occupied this box in her later years, watching the falderal that passes for entertainment below. When my daughter and Marjorie entered the box, I kept silent to see what they would do."

"I suppose this is yet another place I must search when next you disappear."

"When I disappear, it is because I wish to be left alone; it follows, therefore, I had rather you *not* search for me."

Suddenly, Richard came rushing towards them, a worried look on his face. "I wondered what became of you. What has happened?"

"I will explain later," Isabelle said. "For now, I suggest we all return to the ballroom as inconspicuously as possible before our guests begin to wonder why their hosts have deserted them. Richard, you and Darcy go down the grand staircase, Amy and I will take the back stairs."

"You may return," William replied. "I believe I shall rest a while longer."

After everyone left, William entered the box again, and Ellen came out of hiding to sit beside him.

"Are you not concerned they will discover you are missing?" he asked.

"No," Ellen said. "I arranged my pillows as I usually do. They will just think I am in bed and not bother to check."

William chuckled. "Sometimes I think you are much older than nine."

Ellen smiled before saying, "May I ask you a question?"

"Of course."

"This morning I also heard my aunt tell Grandmama that you are *in crawled* with Miss Bennet. What does that mean?"

"I believe what you heard was *enthralled*."

"Then, what does *that* mean?"

"It means your aunt suspects that I like Miss Bennet."

"Do you like her?"

"Of course. I think she is a very nice person."

"I like her, too. She does not treat me like a baby."

"She is very wise in that regard. By the way, we need to keep the fact that I am *enthralled* with Miss Bennet between us. Some women become jealous of other women, even if there is no reason, and it makes them act uncivilly."

"Like Aunt Amy acted towards Miss Bennet tonight?"

"Exactly."

Ellen held out one small finger. "You know what that means."

William linked his little finger with hers.

"I swear!" they pledged simultaneously.[2]

---

2   *Pinky Swear was not referred to until the 1860's, but for the purpose of this story I have chosen to use it. https://en.wikipedia.org/wiki/Pinky_swear

Lady Matlock's bedroom
That night

"I do not know what to make of your cousin," Isabelle said as she undressed for bed. "At times I think Darcy is rude to me on purpose."

"As I have said often enough, Darcy is not like the men of the *ton*," Richard replied as he donned the nightshirt his valet had laid out. "If you try to force him into that mold, you will fail miserably."

"You make it sound as though he is an animal that cannot be tamed."

"In many ways, he is."

"My sister has decided he has feelings for Miss Bennet. Furthermore, she worries that our governess may return those feelings."

"And, pray tell, on what does Amy base that assumption?"

"Simply by the way they stared at one another in the music room when the children came in to exhibit." Isabelle stopped braiding her hair to consider the matter more fully. "Do you think I should be worried?"

Richard knew it was time to confess everything or risk his wife making a bigger issue of William and Elizabeth's shared past once she found out—and he was certain she would.

"Do you recall when my cousin was involved in that horrific coach accident?"

"How could I forget? We had just begun to court, and you were upset for months, especially after the infection set in, and they thought he might die."

"It was an awful time," Richard said, his expression growing sombre. "Whilst I was thrilled by our courtship, I was fearful of losing my best friend."

Isabelle crossed the room to embrace him. "I know, dearest." Then, she pulled back to look into his eyes. "But why do you bring that up now?"

"The young woman my cousin was trying to rescue was Miss Bennet's sister."

When Isabelle grew quiet, Richard knew she had realised

there was more to William's involvement in the rescue than the fact that the perpetrator grew up at Pemberley.

"You knew," she said at last. "Why did you not mention her connection to Darcy when you recommended that we hire her?"

"I did not think it should be an issue after all these years. Your mother thought her the perfect governess, and we needed one. Moreover, I have always had confidence in Miss Bennet's ability to do whatever she sets her mind to, and I thought her the perfect person for the job."

"Oh?" Isabelle replied, her tone suggestive of jealousy. "How long *have* you known her?"

"I met her just after Darcy had fourteen years ago. She was a country gentleman's daughter, and whilst Darcy and I were at Rosings, she was visiting her friend who had married the vicar at Hunsford. At the time, Darcy was impressed with Miss Bennet's intellect. Mr. Bennet had no sons, you see, so he taught her everything he would have taught his heir. In Hunsford, she discussed crop rotation as easily as the merits of muslin versus gingham."

After considering Richard's explanation, Isabelle shrugged. "Miss Bennet is pretty; I will give her that. Surely, she could have married. Why would anyone *choose* service over being a wife and mother?"

"I do not claim to understand why women do anything."

"Perhaps we were too quick to hire her."

"You are jealous!"

"I am not! It is only that I worry her presence here may make it difficult for your cousin."

"I hope it does. Darcy needs to face his fears, not continue to run from them."

"His fears?"

"I speak of his reluctance to give his name to another woman after the disaster with Cornelia."

"And you think Miss Bennet's presence can help?"

"I do."

Though Isabelle could tell from the way Richard spoke that

he had no objections to Darcy forming an attachment to their governess, she found the idea mortifying.

What would our family and friends think if he were to marry our governess, not to mention the embarrassment poor Marianne would suffer!

Oblivious to her thoughts, Richard sat down beside his wife. Leaning in to give her a kiss, he teased, "It is good to know that after so many years you can still be jealous."

Smiling, Isabelle replied, "A woman has the unique ability to tell when another woman has designs on her man—or on any man for that matter—and that makes us wary. If you wish to call it jealousy, so be it."

"Well, I can assure you that no woman can work her designs on me!"

And I pray that Miss Bennet does not work any on Darcy!

Chapter 7

Matlock Manor
William's Bedroom
The next morning

In the faint light of a single candle, William sat on the edge of the bed considering what to say once he stood face-to-face with Elizabeth.

How does one apologise for ruining a person's life... for that matter, ruining her family's lives? What words suffice to confess I was too cowardly to face her after I learned there was no hope for making everything right?

Irrespective of acknowledging his past mistakes, he knew he owed it to Elizabeth to explain that he did not blame her for what Marianne had done the prior night, nor had he any objections to her being the Matlocks' governess.

Footsteps in the adjoining sitting room announced the valet had arrived with a much-needed pot of coffee, so William stood to greet him. Stephens had been a valet for Richard's father before his retirement and still kept his hand in the profession by serving William whenever he was in residence. As the servant entered the room, the candle atop the tray helped to brighten the area.

"Good morning, Mr. Darcy."

"Good morning."

The valet set the tray down on a dresser and went about the room lighting additional candles. As he did, he glanced at William. "I see you have donned your clothes already, sir."

"I could not sleep, so I began dressing." William held up his cravat. "I left this to your expertise and will welcome your help with my boots."

The valet smiled. "I shall be pleased to assist you after you have had a cup of coffee."

"Thank you for remembering I am not myself until after I have had my coffee each morning."

"In that, you are much like Lord Matlock, God rest his soul."

Whilst he spoke, Stephens added sugar and a dollop of cream to the coffee and stirred the contents before handing the cup to William, who took a sip, murmuring, "Excellent, as always."

Stephens, who had awaited his approval, smiled. "I am glad."

The valet began tidying up the room, and William tried to act nonchalant as he asked, "Do you know if the new governess rises early to walk the estate before breaking her fast?"

Stephens looked surprised. "How would you know that?"

"A long time ago, Miss Bennet and I were close acquaintances. I recall that it was her habit back then. I would like to speak with her privately, and I thought I would walk out early in hopes of encountering her if she still sets out at dawn."

Having overheard two maids talking last evening that Lady Parker had someone reporting to her the instant Mr. Darcy left his room, Stephens said, "In that case, might I suggest that you leave by way of the servants' corridor and re-enter the hallway nearer the stairs to the rear, sir. Unfortunately, some servants are entirely too meddlesome, and you may avoid them by doing so."

"That is a good idea," William replied.

"Now, as to your question. Miss Bennet walks out at dawn whenever the weather permits. She especially loves to circle the pond behind the stables, often stopping to rest in the small gazebo on the righthand side."

"You seem to know a lot about her," William teased.

"She reminds me of my youngest sister, and I have taken it upon myself to keep an eye on her whenever I can."

"You are a good man, Stephens."

"I do my best, sir."

All the world appeared draped in a grey shroud when Elizabeth exited the manor house. She did not mind, for the bleakness matched her present mood. Pulling her shawl tighter against the wind, she dropped her head and walked towards the pond in the distance. Every important decision in her life had been settled during one of her walks, and she was confident she could come to the correct conclusion this morning about another matter of importance—whether she would stay at Matlock Manor.

It would not be long before the sun was up, and she hoped to have made several laps around the pond and come to a decision by then. Once the sun's rays burst through the trees in the distance, it would be time to return to her room, but for now, these precious minutes belonged to her.

As she walked, Elizabeth reflected on the previous night. From the childish scrawl, it was obvious that Ellen had written the note slipped under her door, but how could she have known her sister and cousin were not in their rooms considering she was the first to retire? It had been disheartening that neither Marjorie nor Marianne spoke in her defence when Lady Matlock ordered her to stay behind, especially since she thought she had gained their friendship during their language lessons. And as for Lady Parker, that woman seemed particularly eager to blame her for the girls' prank, whilst Lady Isabelle was only slightly less eager to agree.

What have I done to garner Lady Parker's censure? She has not said two words to me since she arrived. Obviously, she craves Mr. Darcy's attention, so perhaps she has learned about our former connection and is jealous. One thing is clear: Had Mr. Darcy not stepped out of the theatre box when he did, I would have been dis-

missed then and there. Which brings to mind another conundrum. Why did he bother to contradict his relations for my sake?

Her ruminations slowed her progress, and Elizabeth had completed only two circuits around the pond by the time the sun began to rise. In sight of the gazebo, she hurried towards it and took a seat on one of the benches inside. Cook had saved her a blueberry scone, and she pulled it from the pocket of her gown, unwrapped the serviette, and began to eat whilst the morning sky exhibited a brilliant display of colour. As she watched, in her head she composed a list for and against leaving.

The pay and days off are excellent, and I dearly love teaching the youngest children. Still, if Marjorie and Marianne would not take responsibility for their actions when I stood accused of encouraging their disobedience, that does not bode well for my future. Mr. Darcy's defence of me last night can only escalate Lady Parker's animosity, and even though he defended me, from the look on his face when our eyes met in the music room, it is obvious my presence here unsettles him. If I stay, would it be fair to him?

Suddenly, out of the corner of her eye Elizabeth saw something move near the stables. Her heart began beating faster when she realised it was a man and that he was coming in her direction, though he was still concealed amongst the shadows of the building. Straining to identify who it could be, she was able to ascertain it was not one of the grooms, since he wore a gentleman's hat. What's more, whenever he took a step, he relied heavily on a cane. Trying to recall if any of the guests currently at Matlock Manor had a limp, she could not.

Unable to look away, Elizabeth was staggered when he neared enough to recognise. *Mr. Darcy!*

William told himself there was no reason to be anxious about encountering Elizabeth, though his heart seemed determined to reject that argument. It had not raced this furiously since the day he learned that Lady Cornelia was pregnant with another man's child. Subsequently, as he exited the back of the manor, he reminded himself once more that he was forty years of age and not a schoolboy on his way to meet a childhood infatuation.

Usually he walked only short distances since it exacerbated the pain in his knee, and he was well aware of the price he would pay for walking to the pond and back. Though he despised being dependent on his cane, it was the only way he could complete a walk of that distance, and he could think of no better way to speak with Elizabeth in private. The closer he got to the gazebo, the more effort he put into ignoring the pain and disguising the limp; however, by the time he reached the gazebo, he grimaced with every step.

Pasting on a smile at the bottom of the steps, William climbed them whilst simultaneously removing his hat. Then he bowed.

"I hope I did not frighten you by coming here."

Elizabeth's eyes grew as wide as a trapped animal's, and William wondered if she was about to dash off when she stood. Instead, she curtseyed, saying softly, "No... not at all."

"It has been such a long—" William hesitated, then began anew. "Might I enquire about your family? Are they well?"

"My parents died years ago; however, Jane, Kitty and Mary are married with families of their own, and they are all well, I thank you."

Noticing that she failed to mention Lydia, William said, "I am familiar with the sorrow of having lost both parents. I am, however, pleased to know that your sisters are well."

Glancing at the cane, Elizabeth said, "I see you are injured. I pray it is nothing serious and that your recovery will be swift."

Self-consciously, William hung the cane over the rail surrounding the gazebo. "My injury was years ago, and there is no hope of further improvement. Still, I am grateful for your concern."

An awkward silence fell, leaving them staring at one another. William recovered first.

"I came because I wish to assure you that I do not blame you for Marianne's actions of last night. Even if I had not interrupted her and Marjorie in their scheme, I would never have believed you encouraged either of them to disobey."

Against her will, Elizabeth's eyes filled with tears. She dropped her head, attempting to blink them away. "Thank you for your faith in my character."

"I have faith in you, Miss Elizabeth," William replied, unwittingly using her Christian name.

"Since I am in service, I believe it would be best if you address me as Miss Bennet."

"We have known each other for such a long time that I may forget. If I do, please know that it is unconsciously done." Encouraged by Elizabeth's small smile, William stepped closer. "I also wish to assure you that I have no objections to your being the Matlocks' governess. In fact, I believe Richard could not have found anyone more capable or with a better understanding of children and young people."

"You are too kind."

William's expression immediately turned melancholy. "You give me too much credit. In truth, were I kind, I would have warned all of Meryton about Wickham the moment I learned he was there."

Elizabeth was astonished he brought up the subject and that he was taking the blame for what had happened. For a brief moment she was unable to speak over the lump that had formed in her throat. Finally, she managed to say, "Sir, after reading your letter, I understood completely why you did not."

Her compassion overwhelmed him. "You suffered all these years because of my failure to act, and yet you defend my honour?"

"Surely you have not blamed yourself for my circumstances all this time? I received an offer of marriage, but I declined it and chose to go into service."

"Why would you?"

Elizabeth looked away, unable to meet William's eyes. "The reason no longer exists." Then, offering him a wan smile, she added, "I am content with my lot in life."

"When Richard spoke of your qualifications, I was not surprised. I recall how effortlessly you made my sister feel at ease when the two of you met at Pemberley. At that time, Georgiana was a very awkward and shy girl, but you made her feel special. It meant a great deal to her... and to me."

"Miss Darcy is a sweet person. Anyone would be at ease in her company. How is she?"

"She is doing very well, I thank you. She married Gregory Langston of Sussex about four years after your visit to Pemberley. They are the parents of three children—Gregory, who is seven, Anne, who is five and Margaret, who recently celebrated her second birthday. They reside at one of his family's estates in Edinburgh, where he oversees their international shipping business."

"Edinburgh? That is a long way from Derbyshire. I imagine you miss her terribly."

"I do. If not for Marianne, I might have gone mad after Georgiana married and moved to Scotland. As it is, Marianne and I are fortunate if we see her and her family twice a year."

"Speaking of Marianne, seldom have I seen a more accomplished young lady."

"What a nice compliment. Thank you."

Elizabeth noticed that William had begun twisting the brim of his hat mercilessly, a trait she associated with lesser men, not with someone of the Master of Pemberley's stature. Puzzled as to why a man who had never been reluctant to speak his mind appeared anxious, she understood when at length he continued.

"I also came here this morning to ask your forgiveness. I should have returned to Meryton after... well, after the calamity regarding your sister and Wickham, and explained why I did not—"

"You owed me no explanation then, nor do you now," Elizabeth interrupted, reaching to clasp his hand and give it a sympathetic squeeze. "I held no expectations that you would ever renew our acquaintance after Lydia—" Her voice broke, and, pulling a handkerchief from her pocket, she began dabbing at her eyes as she turned away.

That mere touch sent frissons through William and completely disintegrated the wall he had erected to protect his heart.

Stepping close behind her, he gently clasped her arms. "Elizabeth, you must allow me to—"

Suddenly, Stephens was rushing towards the gazebo. "Mr. Darcy. Forgive me for interrupting, sir, but Lady Marianne is looking for you," he declared breathlessly. "She vowed to find you, and when she mentioned checking the stables to see if you had ridden out, I volunteered to look there."

William's spirits had fallen the moment the valet spoke, and reluctantly he let go of Elizabeth to address him. "Thank you for your thoughtfulness, Stephens. I will meet you at the stable shortly, and we will return to the house together."

As the valet took his leave, William turned back to Elizabeth. Stepping around so he faced her, he could not help but notice the initials on the handkerchief she held. Upon realising they were his, he was instantly transported to the day he had given it to her. She was preparing to leave Lambton after receiving the news about Lydia, and her eyes had filled with tears when the Gardiners' coach pulled in front of the inn, so he offered her the handkerchief. Once Mr. Gardiner called for her to board the coach, she had tried to give it back, but William had refused, saying, "Keep it until I see you again."

That Elizabeth had kept it all these years was so significant that William lifted her chin and locked eyes with the one woman who still haunted his dreams. Then a feeling he had not experienced since that summer day in Lambton washed over him. No longer able to deny he still loved Elizabeth, he smoothed a lock of silky hair behind one ear and lightly ran his fingers along her jawline. Hope took root when, beginning to tremble, she reached out to him to steady herself.

"Please, Mr. Darcy—" she whispered.

"William," he insisted.

"William, we should not—"

"Should not what, Elizabeth? Admit to honest feelings, or act upon them?"

"What of your family? They will not be—"

"I am forty years old, Elizabeth. At what age am I allowed to consider what I want... what I hope you want?" When she did not answer, he added, "It is imperative I return to the house now, but we have to speak again tomorrow." Grasping both her hands, he brought them to his lips for a kiss. "Promise you will meet me here in the morning."

"I… I promise."

Immediately seizing the cane propped beside the entrance, he smiled at her before slowly disappearing into the distance.

Even after he was completely out of sight, Elizabeth was still trembling as she reached for the shawl she had left lying on the bench and swung it over her shoulders. Pulling it tighter against the shivers coursing through her, she reflected on what just happened. Striving to make sense of it, she took several deep breaths and let them go. *Am I dreaming, or could it be possible that Mr. Darcy still cares for me?*

Not wishing to suffer the agony of dashed hopes again, she told herself that by tomorrow he might regret his behaviour. Still, knowing that locked in the deepest recesses of her heart was a love that proved too strong to die, she could not help hoping his feelings ran as deeply as her own.

It was past time to return to the manor, so Elizabeth forced herself to begin the walk back. Unbeknownst to her, or William, the maid who had been spying for Lady Parker was already on her way to tattle.

As William limped alongside Mr. Stephens, he considered Elizabeth's fears about his family. He knew Isabelle would neither understand nor condone his wish to marry Elizabeth instead of Lady Parker. Richard would take his side, he felt certain, as would Georgiana, but he had no idea how Marianne would react to the news. Still, he could not remove the smile that overtook his face whenever he pictured Elizabeth as his wife—an expression so out of character that the valet could not help but notice.

"Forgive me, sir, if I overstep my bounds, but may I say it appears that your conversation with Miss Bennet was pleasant."

"It was, Stephens, though we still have much to discuss. That is why I plan to meet her again tomorrow morning."

The valet smiled broadly. "Do you think it might be helpful to let Lady Marianne think you are riding of a morning? In that way, she would be less likely to stumble upon you and Miss Bennet."

"It would. And, since I abhor deceit of any kind, I shall make certain to ride tomorrow after Miss Bennet and I have our talk."

"An excellent solution," the old servant replied.

Suddenly, Marianne walked out of the back door of the manor. Seeing William, she rushed towards him. "Papa, I have been everywhere looking for you! I hoped we could break our fast together, since everyone else plans to eat later. You have not changed your habit of waiting to eat until after your ride, have you?"

"I have not," William replied honestly. Sliding an arm around his daughter's shoulder as they walked on to the house, he added, "I should be delighted to breakfast with you. It has been far too long since you and I shared a meal alone in the morning."

"Precisely why I have been looking for you!"

Lady Parker's bedroom

After quickly dismissing her lady's maid, Lady Parker addressed Jenny, the servant she had bribed to keep an eye on William. A little too crossly, she demanded of the plain little woman, "Where have you been? I paid you to keep an eye on Mr. Darcy, and you disappeared! I hope you have a good excuse."

"I *have* been doing as you asked, my lady," the maid responded. "When he did not leave his room this morning as I expected, I entered one of the empty guest rooms with a balcony to watch the stables. That was how I caught sight of a man heading towards them. From the limp, I knew it was him, so I dashed out the back door and rushed to catch up."

"Go on!"

"He entered the stable, and shortly thereafter, came out accompanied by a groom leading a horse. Instead of Mr. Darcy mounting the animal, however, the groom mounted and rode away. Then, Mr. Darcy walked around the stables to the path that circles the pond. I stayed in the shadows, watching, which was fortunate, for I caught sight of Miss Bennet—"

"Stop!" Lady Parker exclaimed. "Do you mean to say that Mr. Darcy was secretly meeting the governess?"

"Whether it was a secret, I could not say. But I watched her enter the gazebo beside the pond, and once Mr. Darcy reached it, he disappeared inside it."

"That whore!" Lady Parker declared. "I may need you to back my story should I divulge their secret."

"That was not our agreement. I was hired to spy, not to be a witness, and especially not against Mr. Darcy! He could ruin me. Besides, from where I hid, the lattice made it difficult to see what happened after they entered the gazebo, and I am not one to make up lies!"

"A fine ally you make! Just keep in mind that if you do as I ask, I will see that you are employed for the rest of your life. Now leave whilst I decide what to do about this."

As the maid began to leave, Lady Parker called after her. "I still expect you to keep our agreement and tell me what Mr. Darcy does, especially of a morning. Do you understand?"

The maid nodded and hurried from the room.

Chapter 8

Matlock Manor
Lady Parker's bedroom
Later that day

Though she spent the better part of the day trying to devise a way to thwart Elizabeth Bennet's plans to seduce Mr. Darcy, as tea time approached Lady Parker had still not settled upon a course of action. She dared not breathe a word to Isabelle of what her spy had seen since her sister was still quite put out with her after Mr. Darcy absolved the governess of all blame during the altercation with Marianne and Marjorie at the ball. In fact, Isabelle had declared she wanted to hear nothing more from her about the governess; however, Amy felt certain that if *she* caught Mr. Darcy and Miss Bennet in a compromising situation, Isabelle would have to listen.

Nevertheless, she knew the idea of spying near the gazebo, on the chance she might interrupt a tète-a-tète, could do more harm than good. Mr. Darcy would not look kindly on anyone inserting themselves into his business, and he might keep up the *liaisons* with Miss Bennet just to prove the point.

The solution came to her out of the blue! It would take Marianne's involvement to make Mr. Darcy reconsider his *friendship* with that woman. She wielded a great deal of influence over her father and could impress upon him how detrimental his behaviour would be, not only to him but to her.

That is the key! Amy concluded. *I shall offer to escort Marianne and Marjorie to Locklear Manor for Clarissa's party, and whilst I am doing that, I shall causally mention that the governess has set her sights on Darcy.*

Very pleased with herself, there was a renewed vigour in Lady Parker's step as she breezed into the hallway and made her way towards the terrace.

In another bedroom

Since admitting his feelings for Elizabeth, it was as though blinders had been ripped from William's eyes, and he saw clearly for the first time in years. Consequently, he had spent the day in the sitting room of his suite writing instructions for his solicitor to use in preparing a marriage settlement. After Elizabeth's response that morning, he was convinced she would accept his offer, so once he was done with the settlement, he planned to begin making notes regarding his will. That he would change to include Elizabeth and any children born of their union.

Their children! The mere thought produced a smile he could not expunge.

Every so often, a niggling voice whispered it was too late for another chance at happiness, but he ignored it. To believe there was no hope of marrying Elizabeth would only plunge him deeper into the melancholy that had dogged his steps since 1812. *No! After gaining her consent, I will send off this letter and she and I will begin planning our wedding.*

There was, however, still the matter of Marianne. His daughter was pampered; he would concede that. The misery caused by Lady Cornelia's subterfuge, and the loneliness after Georgiana's marriage, had made his life almost unbearable, and it had taken all the fortitude he possessed to keep from succumbing to the grief. Fighting it had left little time to curb Lady Isabelle's influence on Marianne, and she had drilled the *ton's* rules regarding rank and class into his daughter's head at every opportunity.

William could not predict how Marianne would react to the news that he was going to marry Elizabeth, but he prayed she would be welcoming. *Besides, if anyone can win Marianne over, it is Elizabeth.*

Just as this thought came to mind, the door opened, and Richard walked in. "Darcy! I was hoping to best you at a game of billiards, but here you sit writing letters! And not personal letters, I would wager, but business letters. Even with stewards for Pemberley, Darcy House and Rosings, you never truly escape your responsibilities, do you?"

"I hope one day you will take on at least part of the responsibility for Rosings."

Richard shook his head. "I have not yet got the hang of managing Matlock Manor, so I cannot say I look forward to helping you manage Rosings."

"Never fear, Cousin. In time, you will look back and realise it was not terribly difficult," William replied. Folding and sealing the letter to his solicitor, he stood. "I am finished."

Though William's greatest desire at that moment was to speak to Elizabeth, rather than wait until morning, he knew doing so would draw the suspicions of Isabelle, Lady Parker and Lady Gordon, which would distress the woman he loved. Therefore, he added, "Now, I should be delighted to follow you to the billiards room and relieve you of another pound."

Richard's easy smile was replaced by a look of suspicion. "Wait! Your attitude is too cheerful for my taste. I have better luck fleecing you when you are morose, so tell me: What do you know that I do not?"

"Your luck will not be sufficient no matter my mood," William teased. "But I cannot deny I am more hopeful today than I have been in years."

"May I assume Miss Bennet is the reason?"

"You may, but please do not breathe a word of this to anyone, especially not Isabelle. I want to be certain Elizabeth feels the same way I do before anyone discovers our relationship and tries to interfere."

"I will not insult you by denying Isabelle would interfere. God bless her. Interfering is embedded in her lineage, but may I ask when you expect to be certain of Miss Bennet's feelings?"

"I am meeting Elizabeth again in the morning."

"I see," Richard said sombrely.

"Do you foresee a problem?"

Richard shook his head. "None whatsoever; however, I have to admit I am surprised at how quickly your opinion regarding that lady has changed. Only days ago, you argued that a reconciliation with Miss Bennet was quite impossible."

"I believed then that it was," William said, turning to stare out the window. "When I left the house this morning, it was with the intention to reassure her I did not hold her accountable for Marianne's actions last night and to tell her I was not upset that you hired her to be your children's governess. Then, if the time seemed appropriate, I meant to apologise for not explaining my actions after the accident."

William paused. "All I know is that at some point, she touched my hand and I felt like I had been struck by lightning. She began to cry, and before I could offer her my handkerchief, she pulled one from the pocket of her gown—though not an ordinary handkerchief."

"What do you mean, not ordinary?"

"The handkerchief was mine, Richard! My initials were embroidered in the corner. Do you know what that signifies?"

"Suppose *you* tell me."

"It meant Elizabeth did not despise me. If she had, she would never have kept it all these years." Incredulously, William shook his head. "The instant I saw it, I was caught up in a vision. It was as though I was watching myself pass the handkerchief to Elizabeth on the day she left Lambton with her uncle."

William went on to explain how he had insisted Elizabeth keep the handkerchief until they met again.

"You should have listened to me earlier, Darcy. I tried to tell you that when we discussed the governess position, Miss Bennet did not act as though she hated you. On the contrary, your wellbeing was her paramount concern."

"My culpability in regard to her circumstances scarcely allowed me to hope." Then William appeared to brighten. "In any case, the vision made me realise I still loved Elizabeth with every fibre of my being, and I could not bear to lose her a second time."

"Did you tell her that?"

"We were interrupted, so I did not have the chance. I plan to tell her tomorrow, and then ask her to marry me."

"Forgive me. I have no wish to play the cynic, but have you considered how Marianne will respond?"

"I have, but I am resolute that I will follow my heart, regardless of my daughter's sentiments."

"If my good opinion means anything, I am proud you have come to that conclusion. You were an exemplary brother to Georgiana and are an excellent father to Marianne. It is high time you seized a bit of happiness for yourself."

"In all these years, I learned one lesson well: Happiness is fleeting. Now that I am blessed with another chance with Elizabeth, I intend to make the most of it."

"Bravo! To that end, I would offer one more word of advice. Miss Bennet may not relish being subjected to our family's prejudices a second time. Address the matter straightaway. Convince her that you are not a slave to what our family thinks before Lady Amy has time to strike."

"I had already thought of that."

"My friend, I am hopeful your discussion with Miss Bennet comes to a happy resolution for your sake and hers. Both of you have been alone far too long."

"I could not agree more, Cousin," William said, giving Richard one of his rare smiles. "Now, let us see if you are capable of cancelling the pound you owe me!"

The classroom

After Mr. Darcy's actions that morning, Elizabeth was having great difficulty concentrating on the lesson she had prepared for the children. This had not escaped Ellen's attention. Holding up her hand, the precocious child waited silently to be called upon. Seeing that the two youngest children were engrossed in drawing, Elizabeth crossed the room to squat beside Ellen's desk.

"Yes, Ellen?" she said quietly.

"I would like to know if it is possible for us to finish our lessons in the garden like Marianne and Marjorie do?"

"It is almost time for their lesson to begin, so we cannot today. We may do it tomorrow if the weather is fine."

"Oh, but Marjorie and Marianne are not having lessons today."

"How do you know that?"

"This morning I overheard my sister complain to Mother that she had no time for lessons. She said she had to supervise the packing of her clothes for Locklear Manor, or she would have to wear her maid's horrible choices. Mother agreed that she and Marianne could both forego the lessons until after they return from the birthday party."

"Oh?" was all Elizabeth managed to say before a knock on the classroom door demanded her attention. As she stood and turned, the door opened to reveal Lady Isabelle.

"Miss Bennet, I have decided to cancel the language lessons for my daughter and her cousin until after they return from Locklear Manor. There is much preparation still to be done if they are to leave the day after tomorrow."

"As you wish," Elizabeth replied, bobbing a curtsey.

"Now, children," Lady Isabelle said. "Pay attention to your lessons. Miss Bennet assures me that you are progressing well, and we all know what that will mean at the end of this month."

"Presents!" Emily and Evelyn cried simultaneously.

"But only if you keep to your studies," their mother added. After smiling at Elizabeth, she exited the room.

"Please finish writing your numbers through ten before you leave," Elizabeth told her students.

Evelyn and Emily began following her instructions, but Ellen did not. Instead, she gave Elizabeth a knowing smile whilst saying in such a low voice her sisters could not hear, "See, I told you so."

It was all Elizabeth could do to keep from laughing. "Sometimes I think you are much older than your years, Lady Ellen."

"That is what Cousin Darcy said."

"Oh, he did, did he? What else did your cousin say?"

Ellen smiled mischievously. "That if a girl swears to keep a secret, she must do everything in her power to keep it."

"Mr. Darcy is a very wise man."

"He has always been my favourite cousin because he takes the time to talk to me. He and I are great friends and have been for as long as I can remember."

Elizabeth pursed her lips so as not to smile. "I understand why you like him so much."

Suddenly, the door leading into the nursery opened, and the nanny poked her head in. "Is Lady Emily ready for her nap, Miss Bennet?"

"Naps are for babies!" Emily cried, suppressing a yawn.

"Be that as it may, your mother wishes you to take a nap before dinner," Elizabeth said.

By then the older girls' maids had come for their charges, so Elizabeth added, "Since Lady Ellen requested it, tomorrow we shall have classes in the garden, if weather permits. At least you have that to look forward to."

Her pronouncement seemed to cheer them, and as her pupils left the classroom, Elizabeth returned to her own rooms.

The Billiards room

After dinner, the ladies decided to retire early, so Richard asked William if he wanted to play one more game of billiards. It was well past midnight when there was a knock at the billiards room door. Just as it opened, Richard turned to see Mr. Goings holding a silver salver with a letter atop it.

"An express rider just delivered this, my lord," the butler

said, stepping forward to present the tray. "I thought I should bring it to you directly."

Richard took the letter. "Thank you, Goings." As the butler exited the room, he read the name on the missive and held it out to William. "It is for you, Cousin."

Instantly alarmed, William stiffened. Taking it from Richard, he broke the seal and began to read. After a second or two, he said, "I must leave immediately. There has been another fire at Pemberley."

"Good Heavens!" Richard cried. "Surely, they have not burned the house?"

"No. The oldest stable, the one that houses dairy cows and goats," William answered, whilst he finished reading the rest of the missive. "Four grooms were hurt removing animals from the structure, but, thankfully, their injuries are not life-threatening. Only two animals were lost."

"This proves the first fire was arson, does it not?"

"Mr. Sturgis writes that is the opinion of Lambton's constable. In any case, I must return to Pemberley immediately. If Stephens is available to help pack my trunks, I shall try to leave in the early hours of the morning."

"What about your appointment with Elizabeth?"

William glanced at a clock on the mantel, noting how late it was. "She is likely asleep already, and since I plan to leave before she wakes, I shall have to write her a note explaining what precipitated my departure and express my desire to return as soon as possible."

"Whilst you write the note, I shall locate a footman to fetch Stephens."

Unbeknownst to William or Richard, the maid spying for Lady Parker had followed them to the billiards room. Aware that the large closet in that room had another door that opened into the hallway, she slipped inside from the hall and cracked the door to the billiards room enough to listen to their conversation. As soon as Richard went to find a footman and William headed to his bedroom, she rushed to inform her benefactor of what she had heard. Certain that Lady Parker would not be angry at being awakened after she revealed the news, Jenny was relieved to learn she was not mistaken.

"I am glad you thought to wake me. Something must be done about the letter Mr. Darcy plans to leave Miss Bennet." Lady Parker paced across the room several times before suddenly stopping. "You must think of a way to steal the letter. Do you understand?"

The woman's eyes widened with fright, and her nod was unenthusiastic.

Seeing her fear, Lady Parker said, "Think, girl! Is there no way you can slip into Miss Bennet's room and remove it before she wakes?"

"Her maid never uses the servants' corridor—everyone says it is because she is too broad to go through it. I suppose I could slip in and out of her suite that way."

"Of course! That is an excellent solution!" Lady Parker reached into a drawer of her dresser. Bringing out a shilling, she gave it to the maid. "What was your name again?"

"Jenny, ma'am."

"Well, Jenny, if you bring me the letter in the morning, another shilling will be yours in addition to what I have paid you already."

"I will do my best, my lady," Jenny said. Bobbing a curtsey, she rushed from the room.

William's bedroom

Dreading not being able to meet Elizabeth in the morning, William's hand shook as he poured out his heart in the note. When he had finished, it contained nearly as many ink stains as those Charles Bingley used to send him. The remembrance produced a smile. Then, recalling Bingley's current circumstances, the smile vanished.

You cannot dwell on the past! That is what almost destroyed you!

That thought alone forced him to forge ahead, and he began to read what he had written.

My dearest Elizabeth,

By the time you read this, I will likely be halfway to Pemberley. Regrettably, you had been asleep for hours when I received an express informing me of another fire at my estate, else I would have told you this in person.

A stable was burned, two animals killed, and several grooms injured. Thankfully none of their injuries are life-threatening. Since this is the second fire at my estate, I fear it is only a matter of time until another attempt is made and someone is killed. We must find the perpetrators before that can happen. Consequently, the constable in Lambton requested that I return to Pemberley immediately.

Obviously, we cannot meet as planned, and for that I apologise profusely. Please believe me when I say it pains me greatly to postpone our conversation. To that end, I shall handle my duties at Pemberley and return to Matlock Manor as soon as possible. I pray that you understand and, dare I say, that you are anticipating our next meeting as eagerly as I.

Your devoted servant,
William

William had just finished reading the letter and was sealing it when Richard walked through the door, followed by the valet.

"Lord Matlock tells me you wish to leave before dawn, sir," Stephens said.

"Yes," William replied. "Moreover, my hope is to return in a sen'night; therefore, I plan to leave my formal attire here. I see no reason to carry it back and forth, as I will have no need of it whilst I am away."

Stephens smiled. "I understand."

"I will leave you and Stephens to sort out what goes and

what stays," Richard declared. "Meanwhile, if you like, I shall take your letter and slip it under Miss Bennet's door before you lose it."

William handed the missive to his cousin. "I have always been able to count on you."

"That is what cousins are for!"

Jenny watched as Richard slipped the note from William under Miss Bennet's bedroom door before she rushed to the servants' quarters. Wishing to wake ahead of Elizabeth's maid, she hoped she would fall straight to sleep, so that when Hardwick knocked on her door in the morning, she would be rested enough to hear and respond.

Hardwick, a footman, was one of the first servants up, since it was his duty to add wood to the fire in the kitchen before the cook started her day. Knowing he was infatuated with her, Jenny had taken advantage of the situation by having him knock on her door before heading to the kitchen each morning so that she could keep an eye on Mr. Darcy for Lady Parker.

If Hardwick does not fail me, I should have plenty of time to steal that letter.

Chapter 9

Matlock Manor
The next morning

There was more hope in her heart than Elizabeth knew she should have as she walked towards the gazebo. Though she tried to tell herself she was attaching more significance to Mr. Darcy's interest than she ought, her heart raced just as wildly as it had when she had first caught sight of him the previous day. Even then, watching him struggle to walk with the cane, she realised his injury had taken nothing away from his masculinity—a quality that had appealed to Elizabeth from the very start of their acquaintance, though she would not admit it at the time.

Nor did it detract from his handsome face! Elizabeth could not hold back a smile at her heart's gentle reminder.

Deciding to forgo her usual practice of circling the pond to make certain they had plenty of time to talk, Elizabeth went straight to the gazebo. Unwittingly holding her breath as she sank down on the bench inside, she soon realised what she was doing and, letting go the breath, smiled at her foolishness. So many thoughts kept racing through her mind, that it came as a shock when the sun's rays broke through the trees in the distance, blinding her. That was the moment Elizabeth realised that had William intended to come, he would already have been there.

Not anticipating the level of pain that washed over her with that realization, Elizabeth struggled to maintain control as tears began silently rolling down her face. Attempting to compose herself before anyone saw her, she wiped them away with the backs of her hands as she scurried towards the back of the house, all the while thinking of excuses why William had not kept his promise. Then, realising she had made these same excuses when he failed to return after Lydia's ruin, her spirits fell even further. Disappointed at leaving herself open for heartache again, Elizabeth vowed not to dwell on Mr. Darcy a second longer.

Once she reached the rear door of the house, she ran straight into Mr. Stephens, who was going into the garden.

"Miss Bennet, you do not look well. May I be of service?"

"I am well, I thank you," Elizabeth murmured, rushing past him into the manor.

Watching her leave, one thought plagued Stephens. *Could her state have anything to do with Mr. Darcy's departure?*

In a bedroom

Lady Parker's maid, Lucy, had already helped her dress and was finishing her hair when there came a knock at the door.

"Do not bother answering that. Just finish with my hair and return to your room. And this time go out through the servants' corridor"

Lucy put a few more pins in her mistress' hair before curtseying and exiting through the corridor as instructed.

Lady Amy stood and crossed to the door. Opening it, she found Jenny standing without. Grasping the informant's arm, she pulled her inside. Then, sticking her head out the door, Amy looked up and down the hall. Relieved that no one appeared to have noticed anything, she quickly closed the door.

"Come here via the servants' corridor in the future and make certain my maid is in her apartment before you do. Is that understood?" At Jenny's nod, she continued. "Good, for should anyone discover you eavesdropping, I do not want them to associate you with me. Do you understand?"

The maid nodded again, so she continued, "Did you get it?"

Jenny pulled a letter from her pocket, and Amy's shoulders sagged with relief.

"Thank heavens!" she said, grasping the note William had written to Elizabeth, instantly breaking the seal. The more she read, the angrier her expression became.

"Why that stupid, stupid—" Realising she needed to watch what she said in the maid's presence, Amy composed herself. "You may go now."

"What about the shilling you promised me?"

Irritated at the maid's gall, Lady Parker marched to the dresser, retrieved a shilling and tossed it to Jenny.

"What am I to do now that Mr. Darcy is not here?" the maid asked.

Vexed that she had not thought that far ahead, Amy was silent for a moment. Then she said, "For now you will eavesdrop on Lord Matlock and my sister. Try to overhear whatever they say regarding Mr. Darcy or Miss Bennet and be certain to write down everything. I must accompany Lady Marjorie and Lady Marianne to Locklear Manor and will not be available to hear what you have learned until I return."

"Since I am not assigned to the family floor, I do not see how I can possibly—"

Exasperated, Lady Parker interrupted. "Surely you have a friend or two amongst the servants who work on this floor and would be willing to exchange positions occasionally for a small portion of that shilling. Just be certain the housekeeper does not learn of it."

"I... I suppose I can arrange it."

"Good, for I do not wish to hear any more excuses."

Pemberley
That same day

Just as William's coach was approaching the circular drive in front of Pemberley, Mr. Claridge, the constable in Lambton, descended the front steps. The butler, Mr. Walker, was still at the front door, and upon catching sight of the coach, he hurried back inside. Knowing the master well, he felt certain William would insist on meeting with Mr. Sturgis and Mr. Claridge as soon as he alighted from the vehicle. To that end, he wished to stop Mr. Sturgis before he disappeared downstairs.

As a footman opened the coach door and William stepped out, the constable cried, "Mr. Darcy! I just spoke with Mr. Sturgis. I wished to know if he had heard from you."

"When I got Sturgis' letter, I decided to return straightaway. I saw no need to send a reply."

By then, footmen had retrieved William's trunk and were carrying it up the steps, so he waved a hand in that direction. "I pray you will not mind returning to the house. I would like to go over the details of all that is known thus far."

"I am at your disposal."

The constable and the steward informed William of what had been done to catch the perpetrator, which included interviewing all the outside servants and the tenants, most especially those living nearest the pasture where the first fire started.

"What is the point of questioning the tenants again? They denied seeing anything after the first fire, did they not?" William asked.

"Yes. Though, in my opinion, some seemed reluctant to answer my questions. I toyed with the idea that the first fire might have been accidentally sparked by children, which would explain a reluctance on the parents' part to own to the truth," Mr. Claridge stated. "In any case, having no witnesses, I hoped the damage done by the first fire would be enough to discourage it from happening again." He shook his head. "Apparently, I was wrong."

"I thought it an anomaly, so we were both wrong," William said sombrely.

"After the second fire, Mr. Claridge and I felt we should impress upon the tenants that this time the damage was too serious to be ignored," Sturgis said. "Two animals were lost, and four people injured, any one of whom might have died. If this keeps up, someone likely will."

"Moreover, after inspecting the site of the latest fire, I thought they could have been set by different people," Mr. Claridge added.

"Pray tell me how you arrived at that?" William asked.

"The first fire started in the pasture and burned in the direction the wind was blowing—towards the hay shed. It was almost as though the building was caught in the fire accidentally. Upon examining the second fire, however, it quickly became clear it started in the paddock just outside the stable. According to your servants, bales of hay purchased to replace those lost in the first fire were being stacked there until the construction of another shed."

William shook his head. "I do not know what to think. I have always treated my tenants and servants fairly. Why would anyone want to do harm to Pemberley?"

"Might I suggest you offer a reward for information leading to the conviction of the perpetrator to find out?" Mr. Claridge ventured. "Money often loosens tongues."

William threw the pen he had been absently rolling between his fingers onto the desk. "I feel I have no choice but to take your advice." To Mr. Sturgis he said, "Have placards posted about Lambton offering fifty pounds for information that leads to a conviction."

Mr. Claridge stood. "I should leave, but before I go, I would advise you to increase the number of guards watching the estate, especially at night."

"Normally there are a dozen men who do nothing but ride the perimeter, some during the day and some at night," William said, "but I will consider adding more to watch the buildings after dark."

"Pray try not to worry, Mr. Darcy," the constable added. "I have read that people who repeatedly set fires are caught in the end."

William's brows furrowed. "Somehow that does not ease my mind."

The constable smiled wanly. "No. I suppose it would not." He paused at the door. "No need for a servant to see me out."

After Claridge left, William turned to Sturgis. "I am going upstairs to wash off the dust and change clothes before we go over other estate matters. I will send for you when I am ready."

"I shall be in my office when you need me."

As soon as the steward left, a feeling of loneliness, such as William had not experienced in years, overwhelmed him. He attributed it to leaving Elizabeth when they had come so close to a reconciliation. Crossing to a large cabinet built into the back wall, he unlocked it and opened the doors. As it had done numerous times over the past fourteen years, a portrait of a young woman with dark curly hair and ebony eyes greeted him from where it was safely stored. Lifting the portrait from its perch, he brought it out of the cabinet to study.

It had taken a portraitist, originally summoned to Pemberley to paint a portrait of Georgiana, several attempts to capture this likeness of Elizabeth. William had thought it a good resemblance until he saw her at Matlock Manor. It was then he realised the portrait had not come close to capturing either her beauty or her spirit.

Not wanting to explain his possession of the likeness should Elizabeth think him foolish, and unable to bear the thought of having it destroyed, he meant to move it to another place before they married. He concluded the attic was just the spot. There, it could reside forever amongst scores of portraits too numerous to put on display. He could trust Mr. Walker to keep his secret and reminded himself to instruct the butler to wrap the portrait in brown paper before summoning footmen to carry it upstairs. Suddenly, he recalled that Walker planned to retire at the end of the year, and another thought came to mind.

With Mrs. Reynolds gone, how will I ever manage when you leave? I will never trust any of my servants as I trusted the both of you.

Sighing, William picked up the portrait to return it to the cabinet; however, just before doing so, he placed a gentle kiss on the lady's lips as he always had. Then, with one last look, he set it in the cabinet and locked the doors.

On the road to Locklear Manor

By the time the coach carrying Lady Parker and her charges to Locklear Manor was nearly to their destination, it had begun to rain. It was not a gentle rain, but a heavy downpour accompanied by occasional peals of thunder. Though sorely needed, a rain of this magnitude following months of dry weather rarely promised welcome news for the residents of Derbyshire. Once the rain began, it usually continued for days, leaving roads impassable and bridges close to being washed away.

It put Amy's nerves on edge, since she did not wish to be away from Matlock Manor any longer than necessary, lest Mr. Darcy return and be free to resume his courtship with Miss Bennet.

Unable to think about anything since the journey began save Elizabeth Bennet's hold on Mr. Darcy, Amy was well-prepared to make her case against the governess the first chance she got. Noticing that Lady Marjorie and Lady Marianne had grown quiet because of the storm, she decided the present might be her best opportunity.

"Since you young ladies are preparing for your debuts, I feel certain that my sister has warned you about men whose only goal is to catch your eyes and turn your heads from the sound advice of your parents."

Both girls nodded.

"I thought as much. Still, I feel I must ask: Has Isabelle warned you about calculating women who think nothing of ruining your chances for an advantageous marriage by furthering their own circumstances?"

"She has not mentioned any such thing to me," Marjorie declared.

She looked to Marianne who quickly volunteered, "Nor to me."

"The best way to impress upon you the danger would be to tell you the heart-breaking story of a dear friend I shall call Lord A," Lady Amy continued. "That poor man's wife died many years ago, and since her death, he has focused all his attention on rearing his children. Last season his oldest daughter—I shall call her Sarah—was at the age to make her debut. Sarah was an obedient young woman and careful not to fall under the influence of unsavoury men, yet she had never been warned about unsavoury women."

Both girls were now listening attentively, so Amy continued. "One year ago, Lord A's governess retired due to illness, and she recommended her niece take her place. The niece, a pretty woman of one and thirty, was an excellent teacher who got on well with the children, and soon she had ingratiated herself to the entire family with her gaiety as well as her abilities. To make a long story short, she quickly had Lord A under her spell, and barely a month before Sarah was to be presented at court, he dismissed all propriety and swept her off to Gretna Green where they married."

"How horrible that must have been for Sarah," Marianne whispered.

Dramatically bringing her hand to her heart, Lady Parker pretended to feel the imaginary Sarah's pain. "It was. Sarah's debut ball was a disaster. Though I was not in attendance, I was told that they were shunned by the *ton*, save for a few trusted friends of her father's. Even then, they did not allow their eligible sons to attend—not that they would have wished to! What mortification it would have been to marry Sarah and be forced to introduce the governess to your acquaintances as your new mother."

"What happened to Sarah afterwards?" Marjorie asked.

"Receiving no creditable offers of marriage, Sarah had no choice but to accept an offer from a merchant from Liverpool. He is rich, I will give you that, but he is not welcome in polite circles."

"How could her father do something so foolish, knowing full well how it would affect his daughter?" Marianne asked.

"In poor Lord A's defence, I must point out that he was never handsome and is no longer a young man," Lady Parker said. "I believe he saw a chance to regain his youth."

"Are you saying that is a good excuse?" Marjorie asked.

"Not at all! But you will learn that most men can be played the fool by a pretty woman," she replied.

"Frankly, I do not have to worry about this," Marjorie said. "Father loves Mother very much, and he would never be so—"

Immediately, it dawned upon Marjorie to whom the warning applied. Silently, she looked to Marianne, whose eyes widened in horror. Then, she addressed Lady Parker, "Please tell me you are not speaking of my father."

Amy dropped her head. "Would that I could."

"Name the woman!"

"Unfortunately, it is Miss Bennet."

"Surely, you jest," Marianne replied with a laugh. "Miss Bennet does not seem the type to—"

"The women who appear to be the most innocent are often the most dangerous," Lady Parker stated.

"I have never even seen them speak," Marjorie added.

"Oh, believe me, they do. In fact, I have it on good authority they met at the gazebo by the pond every morning he was at Matlock Manor."

"That is preposterous! I... I do not believe it!" Marianne declared. "My father is not the kind of gentleman to associate with those beneath him. Furthermore, he particularly keeps his distance from females who try too hard to gain his attention — whether tenants, servants or women of the *ton*."

"Be that as it may, given the right incentive, any man can be seduced— even married ones. I know, for I have been a witness to such things since I debuted in society."

By then Marianne's eyes were full of angry tears. "Who told you this?"

"A trusted maid who, at my request, was keeping an eye on Miss Bennet."

"And you just happened to spy on my father, too?"

"Accidentally, yes. After witnessing her reaction to your father that night in the music room, I felt something was not quite right. I was sceptical of my sister's complete faith in Miss Bennet; thus, I took it upon myself to make certain Isabelle was correct to trust her."

By now Lady Marianne was livid. "I must stop this, but how? If I try to ask Papa about it, he will just get angry. He tells me constantly not to interfere with his business."

"May I suggest your best course of action is to allow Miss Bennet to overhear a conversation between you and Marjorie— one in which you discuss her liaisons with your father. Let her know her plans to seduce him are no longer secret. You must also state in no uncertain terms how much you despise the thought of having her as a mother and how humiliating it would be to introduce her to your friends. If she has an ounce of pride or decency left, Miss Bennet will leave Matlock Manor, never to pursue your father again."

Marianne heaved a sigh. "I cannot think of another way." Addressing her cousin, she said, "Will you help me, Marjorie?"

"You know I will."

"Thank you. Before I retire tonight, I will write down what I will say and what you should reply. We need to practice until it sounds natural. Then the next time we are under the same roof as Miss Bennet, we shall execute our plan."

"I apologise, for I know this is upsetting, Marianne," Lady Parker said. "Still, I felt you would want to know rather than risk be taken unawares should something happen."

"You owe me no apology," Marianne said. "I appreciate your

warning. I would just die if Papa married that woman, and I am thankful that there may still be time to thwart her scheme."

Just then the coach came to a stop in front of Locklear Manor. Several footmen rushed down the front steps with umbrellas in hand to assist the occupants out of the vehicle. Before they could, however, Lady Parker said, "Girls, I do not think I need to caution you not to tell Isabelle, Richard, or Mr. Darcy how you found out about Miss Bennet. If you do, I will hear about it endlessly."

"You may rely on me," each said before exiting the coach.

Chapter 10

Matlock Manor
Lady Matlock's study
Three days later

It had rained every day since Lady Parker and her charges had set out for Locklear Manor. Since there was nothing to do but stay inside, the occupants of Matlock Manor were doing just that. This included Lord Matlock, who had called his steward into his office very early to work on estate matters, something he usually put off until he had taken his morning ride.

Normally Elizabeth met with Lady Matlock the first thing every Monday to discuss what the children were studying and how well they were doing; consequently, she was in her employer's study that morning when the door suddenly flew open and Richard rushed in. He was followed closely by Isabelle's mother, Lady Gordon.

"You are interrupting our conference," Lady Matlock said. Though she said it teasingly, there was a hint of annoyance in her tone. "I will be free to speak with you shortly. I suggest you wait for me in the blue parlour until then."

Instantly recognising the concern written on the interlopers' faces, Elizabeth braced herself as Richard began to speak.

"Forgive me, Isabelle, but this cannot wait," Richard replied.

Then, holding up a letter, he added, "This express arrived just now from Locklear Manor. After reading it, I asked your mother to join me here to—" He stopped as though trying to think.

Meanwhile Lady Gordon had gone to her daughter's side, and as she placed a comforting hand on Isabelle's shoulder, Richard continued.

"Please remember your condition and try to remain calm."

Immediately, Isabelle's face grew white and one hand came up to clasp her throat. "Is it the children... or my sister? Has any harm come to them?" she asked fearfully. "Are they dead?"

"Now, my dear, please do not be alarmed," Lady Gordon said. "No one is dead; they are merely ill."

"Who is ill?" Lady Matlock demanded of Richard. "Tell me this instant!"

"It seems one of the young ladies who attended Clarissa's party, a Lady Sophie, became ill the very next evening. According to the physician who was summoned, she presented the same symptoms as those suffering with the stomach ailment that prompted our early departure from Brighton. An article in the last London newspaper stated that the malady had spread east to Ramsgate and north to London, though it appears new cases are dwindling in the worst hit areas. Apparently, this young woman had been staying with cousins in Ramsgate before travelling here and must have contracted the ailment then."

"Why would anyone with good sense expose others to this dread disease?" Isabelle asked.

"As the paper pointed out, symptoms often do not appear for days, so Lady Sophie probably had no idea that she would become ill."

"Does Lady Blakely say our family has been stricken?"

"The letter is not from Lady Blakely. It is from a physician, Dr. Connelly. He writes that he had been summoned to Locklear Manor to examine Lady Sophie, but by the day after his arrival all the young women there for the party, as well as Lady Blakely, your sister, and Lord and Lady Martindale had fallen ill. Thus, it fell to him to notify the families of those stricken. He asked me to notify Darcy. He writes that he has quarantined the house and separated those who are ill from those who are not by moving them downstairs. Moreover, he insists we stay away from Locklear Manor until he has determined the danger of the disease has passed. Of course, I do not intend to obey him."

"My poor Marjorie," Isabelle said as she stood. "I shall accompany you. I can stay with those who are not ill and be close in case—" Her voice broke as she came around the desk.

Richard grasped her shoulders. "My dear, Marjorie is going to be fine. Trust me and stay here with your mother. I shall see to our family."

"They will likely require frequent changes of clothes, not to mention bedsheets. And who will bathe them? A woman would be of more use than a man."

"I should be the one to go," Lady Gordon declared.

"You are not in good health, Mother," Isabelle countered. "And they warned us in Brighton that this disease is most perilous to the very young, the elderly and those who have been ill."

"At least you did not call me elderly," Lady Gordon replied wryly. "Still, Richard is correct. You must think of the child you are carrying."

Isabelle sank into a chair. "I thought I could stay clear of the sickness if I stayed downstairs."

"Let me go," Elizabeth declared. As all eyes turned to her, she continued, "I am strong and healthy. Moreover, whilst I was employed as a companion in Wales, I assisted the local physician in our village during the influenza epidemic that swept that country in 1816. My employer, Lady Edith, turned her home into a temporary hospital, and Mr. Garrick taught me how to attend the patients without becoming sick. In addition, he taught me how to recreate his remedies. In fact, I still maintain a bag of herbs and medicines. I always keep it close at hand."

"Your constitution and background certainly qualify you as more useful than either of us," Lady Gordon replied. "But it is not your responsibility."

"I am grateful for your offer," Lady Isabelle said, "but Mother is right."

"Do not be grateful!" Elizabeth cried. "Be sensible! I care

about your family, and I am willing to be of service. Please let me."

Hesitant at first, Richard knew that this was the only sensible solution. "Since you put it that way, we humbly accept."

"Will you notify Darcy before you leave?" Lady Isabelle asked.

"No. We will be hard-pressed to get to Locklear Manor in this weather, and the roads we travel are better than those between here and Pemberley. I shall see how everyone at Locklear Manor is faring before risking a courier's life to notify my cousin."

"I understand. We know once Darcy hears his daughter has taken ill, he will go straight to Locklear Manor without any concern for his own safety," Isabelle added.

Richard sighed, then addressed Elizabeth. "I wish to get started soon. I will ask your maid to go along for propriety's sake, though she will lodge with those who are not sick once we get there. Can you be ready to leave later this morning?"

"I can be ready as soon as my clothes and medicine bag have been packed," Elizabeth replied, picking up her ledgers and heading towards the door.

Just as she reached it, Isabelle said, "I shall pray God's protection over you and all my loved ones, Miss Bennet."

"I appreciate that," Elizabeth replied. "I discovered during the epidemic in Wales that prayers helped when nothing else would."

Having said that, she disappeared down the hall.

Pemberley
William's study
That same day

William was disappointed the storms had begun before he was able to return to Matlock Manor and Elizabeth. Though his coach might navigate the muddy roads between Pemberley and his cousin's estate intact, the bridges between the two were often underwater in deluges such as these, presenting an entirely different hazard. All he could do now was pray for the rain to end, the mud to dry, and the creeks and rivers to return to the confines of their banks.

As he saw it, the only good thing to come from the rain was the absence of more fires. As he went over the list of supplies the steward had given him that morning—materials Mr. Sturgis felt were necessary to begin rebuilding the stable—he was distracted by the sound of voices in the hall outside his study. Waiting for the expected knock on his door, William was not surprised when it came.

"Come!"

The door opened, and Mr. Walker stepped just inside. "Sir, one of the tenants asked if he might speak to you right away. I tried to tell him it might be best if he made an appointment, but—"

"Never mind, Walker," William said. "I have finished reading Sturgis' report. I would like to hear what the man has to say."

"As you wish," the butler replied. Turning to someone outside the door, he said, "The master will see you now, Mr. Wainwright."

As the butler left, a white-haired man of about five and fifty came into the office, looking as though he had the weight of the world on his shoulders. William recognised him as a faithful tenant who had been with Pemberley for the better part of twenty years and the previous year had buried his wife.

Mr. Wainwright motioned for someone in the hall to join him. Two dark-haired boys, approximately ten and twelve years of age, entered the room.

"Mr. Darcy, sir, these are my cousin's children, Toby and Luke." He tapped the one nearest him on the shoulder, and the boy performed an awkward bow, which was quickly repeated by his younger brother.

"Their mother died eight years ago, and their father passed recently. As their only relation, it fell to me to take them in."

"That is admirable of you, especially given your recent circumstances."

"It has not been easy," Mr. Wainwright agreed as he nervously rolled a well-worn hat in his hands.

"I imagine not; however, I do not think you came here today to introduce your cousins."

Wainwright's eyes fell to the floor. "I came about them fires."

William's brow furrowed. "You wish to collect the reward for information about the fires?"

"No, sir. I came to tell you that it was these boys what set the fire that burned the shed. I suspected they might have, but they always denied it; however, after you posted the reward, they confessed."

"Tell me what happened."

"I had cut down a tree to enlarge my garden. The fellow I finally found who was willing to buy the wood lived clear across the river. As I left to deliver the wood, I told the boys to haul what limbs and brush remained to a low spot near the river using the cart and donkey. After a couple of trips, they decided it would be less work if they burned it."

"In the middle of the driest summer we have had in years?" William asked incredulously.

"I blame myself for their foolishness. You see, they had watched me burn small piles of brush in the freshly turned soil of my garden. They did not realise I burned it there because a fire could not spread. Their mistake was in carting the brush over the hill to a place where they thought I would never see the ash. In their impatience, they tried to burn it all in one pile. You know what happened after they set the fire and the wind picked up."

William addressed the boys. "So, you disobeyed your cousin who graciously took you in and, as a result, burned Pemberley's pastures and one of our sheds?"

"We did not mean to, sir!" the oldest boy cried. "When Luke and I saw the fire was spreading, we tried to put it out, but it was too late!"

"Why not alert your neighbours?" William asked. "The other tenants might have kept it from reaching the shed had they known about it sooner."

Toby's head dropped. "We were afraid that if our cousin found out what we done, he would send us to an orphanage."

"Ridiculous!" Mr. Wainwright said. Then he urged the boy, "What else do you have to tell the master?"

"Me and Luke did not start the fire that burned the daily barn."

"Why should I believe you?" William asked.

The boys looked at one another anxiously. Then Toby replied, "We told because we were afraid whoever set the other fire would set more fires."

"And we did not want the blame for them, too," Luke added.

Assuming a scowl, William stood in order to appear more fearsome. "You were right to confess. Moreover, you should thank God that your cousin is such a valued tenant that I do not plan to bring charges against you. Nonetheless, your misdeeds shall not go unpunished."

Both boys' eyes grew wider as they awaited his judgement.

"In addition to your chores at home, you will work in Pemberley's stables each afternoon. I will have my stablemaster meet with your cousin to determine what chores you will handle. Any wages you would have earned will be used to pay off the lumber for the new shed. Is that understood?"

Relieved, the boys nodded fervently.

William then addressed Mr. Wainwright. "I shall let the constable know, and I imagine he will want to question the boys."

"I understand. And, sir, I thank you for showing mercy."

"Let us hope this will serve as a valuable lesson."

"Aye. I pray it will."

Locklear Manor

Just as the housekeeper set the tray of tea on a table at the top of the stairs, Dr. Connelly walked out of Lady Clarissa's bedroom. Shaking his head, he said, "That young lady is too stubborn for her own good. She has refused to drink much of anything. I pray the maid has more success with her than I."

Locklear Manor's long-time housekeeper sighed. "Perhaps I should not say this, but Lady Clarissa has always been too obstinate, which is why I had Cook brew her favourite tea in addition to boiling more water to drink. I hoped the tea might induce those who are sick to drink something."

"Just do not let them have cream in the tea."

"No, sir. Please do not worry. If anyone can convince her to drink, it will be Gladys or Martha," she said, mentioning the two upstairs maids who were helping care for the sick. "They have always coddled her." Then, noting the physician's weary appearance, she asked, "Did you get any rest?"

"I recall sleeping for short periods of time in between being summoned to one patient or another."

"Will you not stop and have a cup of tea?" Mrs. Duncan asked. She pointed to a chair beside the table. "Sit here, and I will serve you."

"I have more patients to see," the physician protested, though he sank down in the chair. "Still, perhaps half a cup with sugar may be just the thing to revive me."

Instantly, Mrs. Duncan poured a cup, added two lumps of sugar, and handed it to the physician. As he wearily brought it to his lips, she said, "I wish I could be of more help. You have your hands full with only Gladys and Martha assisting you."

"They are performing admirably, and I wish to keep as many people away from the sick as possible. It would never do for you to come down with this horrible disease, for you are vital to keep the house running efficiently whilst Lady Blakely is ill. That is why I asked you to leave the trays here instead of going any farther."

"I shall do what you think is best."

Recalling those he had banished to the lower floors, Connelly asked, "Is Lord Blakely still unaffected? According to his wife, he has a heart condition, and it would not do for him to catch the disease."

"Lord Blakely is doing well. So well, in fact, that he pesters me constantly to ask you how he might help."

"I shall not change my decision to keep him isolated."

Mrs. Duncan peered down the long, empty hall. "How are the rest faring?"

"Lady Sophie is much better, most likely because she was the first one to come down with the illness. Her mother and father are still too sick to leave their beds, as are Lady Clarissa, Lady Marjorie and Lady Marianne. It appears Lady Parker and the other young ladies—Lady Charlotte and Miss Katherine—were not as affected. Nevertheless, they require care."

Once the physician finished his tea, he set the cup on the table and picked up the tray. "I must see about the others. Perhaps between the maids and myself we can convince everyone to drink some tea."

Suddenly a door about half-way down the hall opened and Gladys walked out. She was holding an armload of sheets as she made her way towards them.

"More laundry," Dr. Connelly sighed. "That has become a never-ending task, has it not?"

"It has, but I have learned to keep the wash pots full of boiling water. Sheets and gowns alike are washed as soon as they are changed."

"There! That is what I meant by running the house efficiently," the physician said. "It would be impossible to keep illness from spreading without handling such things properly."

"When you put it that way, it makes my contribution seem noble," the housekeeper replied.

"Never doubt that your part is important," Dr. Connelly said. "Now, I am off to see about Lady Blakely."

"Tell my mistress all the servants are praying for a swift recovery for her and all those who are ill."

"I shall. Thank you, Mrs. Duncan."

Locklear Manor
That evening

Darkness came early because of the steady downpour, and it was pitch black by the time the Matlock coach reached the

Blakelys' estate. Richard was not surprised when no one rushed out to greet them, since the house had a large yellow flag hanging from the tall columns on either side of the portico, as well as across the front door. Each had *quarantine* painted across it.

As soon as one of his footmen jumped down to open the door, Richard climbed from the vehicle and reached back in to hand out Elizabeth and her maid. An umbrella was quickly opened, and he took it from the footman to escort the ladies to the front door. After rapping on it longer than it would normally have taken to rouse someone inside, the door finally creaked open enough for a man to shout, "Go away! We are under quarantine!"

Richard pushed the door open, startling the footman who had shouted the warning. As he led Elizabeth and her maid inside, a very agitated woman came rushing towards them across the foyer. From her appearance, Richard assumed she was the housekeeper.

"What in the world!" she exclaimed. "Are you daft? No one is supposed to cross a threshold with quarantine warnings on the door."

Resisting a smile, Richard said, "I have not often been called daft, and I assure you that I am perfectly sane. I am Lord Matlock, of Matlock Manor, and this is my children's governess, Miss Bennet. She and I are here to care for my daughter, my niece and my sister. Now, I suggest that you show us to our rooms so that we may change clothes and then familiarise ourselves with what is being done."

"Lord Matlock!" the woman exclaimed. "I apologise if I offended you, sir, but I am afraid that even *you* are not welcome here, according to Dr. Connelly."

"Ah, yes, the good physician," Richard said. "And who might you be?"

"Forgive me. Your presence upset me so, I completely forgot my manners. I am Mrs. Duncan, the housekeeper. Lady Blakely left me in charge since she was taken ill."

"Well, Mrs. Duncan, I suggest you find Connelly and tell him I wish to speak with him."

Though flustered, the servant demonstrated she was not about to be accommodating. "Wait in the drawing room," she said, motioning to a nearby doorway. "I shall fetch him."

As Richard watched the tall, white-haired woman ascend the stairs, he was reminded of Mrs. Reynolds, his cousin's late housekeeper. He had always admired that woman and was almost as bereft as Darcy when she died.

You would never have let me get past the front door, Mrs. Reynolds. They just do not make housekeepers like you anymore.

He offered Elizabeth an arm. "Shall we, Miss Bennet?"

To her maid he said, "Follow us please. Hopefully, we shall shortly learn where we are to reside."

Chapter 11

Locklear Manor
The next day

If Dr. Connelly had been less than welcoming to those who had trespassed the quarantine the day before, he could not have been more pleased when he awakened naturally, instead of being roused to attend the sick. When he had first talked with Elizabeth, she surprised him by recounting her previous experience caring for those who were ill and, consequently, he had allowed her to be in charge whilst he rested. As a result, he had slept soundly for the first time in days.

When he rose to enter the dressing room and begin his day, it occurred to him that he had been fortunate Miss Bennet had defied his orders; however, thoughts of the gentleman who escorted her to Locklear Manor were of a different nature. Though Connelly found Lord Matlock's keenness to help his family admirable, he had much rather that gentleman had stayed at Matlock Manor until summoned. He supposed his defiance was likely due to the fact that Lord Matlock was used to giving orders and had been hard to appease until convinced everything possible was being done for his family. After that, upon being informed that he would not be allowed contact with them, he had graciously offered to take charge of any duty. In the end,

Dr. Connelly had assigned him the task of fetching countless buckets of hot water to keep him occupied.

There was a knock on the door, and he reached for a towel to dry his face. Crossing the bedroom, Connelly opened the door to the hall to find Gladys waiting without.

"Sir, Mrs. Duncan informed me that Cook has food prepared, and the trays will be up shortly. Shall I leave yours in the sitting room?"

"Yes, thank you," he replied. Then he added, "I pray the tray includes a pot of hot coffee. I am weary of tea."

"I will make certain it does."

As she went to leave, the physician called out, "Wait!" and Gladys turned to face him. "You were privy to my conversation yesterday with Miss Bennet, and you have witnessed how she conducted herself last night. In your opinion, is she as skilled a nurse as she implied?"

"I have never seen anyone more fastidious. Just as you instructed, she insisted that Martha and I wash our hands between nursing patients. Moreover, she gave us strips of muslin and asked each of us to cover our nose and mouth when we go into their rooms."

"Some physicians ascribe to this, and I cannot argue with the logic," Connelly replied. "Where is Miss Bennet now?"

"She has been at Lady Martindale's side the better part of the night. That poor woman has not recovered as quickly as her daughter and husband."

"I feared her poor health might be against her. I shall see her as soon as I finish dressing. Just leave my tray in the sitting room if I have not returned by the time Mrs. Duncan brings it up."

"As you wish."

Lambton

Weary of being indoors and eager to learn the condition of the roads, as soon as the rain ended, William ordered his carriage readied. He then instructed the driver to make for Lambton, using the excuse that he needed to check on the progress of the lumber orders he had made to rebuild the shed and the stable. As he feared, the road proved to be a thick layer of mud, and it took more time than usual to reach the village. Nonetheless, the horses managed to keep their footing, and ere long the carriage pulled to a stop in front of the sawmill located at the far end of the main street. William got out of the vehicle to confer with the owner.

After concluding his business, he re-entered the carriage and ordered the driver to take him back to Pemberley. At the same time, Mr. Claridge, who had stopped to speak to the local grocer, noticed Darcy's carriage. Excusing himself, he rushed towards the vehicle shouting for the driver to stop.

Just as the driver reined in the horses, William opened a window. Seeing the constable, he opened the door and waited for him to reach the carriage.

"Thank goodness I saw you," Mr. Claridge declared breathlessly as he reached the vehicle. "You have saved me braving the mud all the way to Pemberley."

"Come inside and sit down."

The constable entered and sat opposite William. "A witness has come forward to offer information regarding the fires. He is supposed to meet me at my office in a few minutes to explain more fully. Do you have time to accompany me and listen to what he has to say?"

Surprised to hear they had a witness so soon, William replied, "Certainly."

Not long afterwards, they were seated in Mr. Claridge's office when the back door opened and a man who had a cap pulled low over his forehead and the lapels of his coat turned up came in. He swept the well-worn cap from his head and bowed.

"Mr. Darcy, this is Mr. Johnson, the man I spoke to you about," the constable said.

After each acknowledged the other, William said, "Please, take a seat. I am eager to hear what you have to say."

Nervously, the man sat down, and began talking animatedly. "Like I told Mr. Claridge, I saw something happen at work that made me think one of your servants might be stealing liquor from Pemberley and selling it to my employer."

"Where do you work?" William asked.

"At a pub between here and Sheffield—The Grey Goose."

"I certainly want to find out who has been stealing my liquor, but what does that have to do with the fire?"

"Please hear me out, sir. Several days ago, I went in early to replenish the wood in the kitchen before the pub opened. Hearing voices, I opened the back door and found the owner, Mr. Gregson, and a man dressed in your livery. They were busy unloading wooden crates from a wagon. The owner got very angry and ordered me back inside. I went, but I waited near the door to hear what I could. That is when I heard Gregson say, 'When can I expect another shipment?' The other bloke said, 'I will have to think of another way to distract them. I cannot risk setting another fire.' Later, I opened one of those crates and found it full of brandy in fancy bottles."

"Do you know the man's name?"

"No, sir," Mr. Johnson replied, "but I can tell you he is extraordinarily tall—well over six feet—and he has reddish, brown hair and a large scar on the left side of his face."

Recognising the culprit, William let go a heavy sigh. "That description fits one of my footmen. I should like to investigate more thoroughly before confronting him, though if he has been selling my imported brandy, he most likely has hidden a good deal of money somewhere. And there is always the possibility he had help stealing the liquor and setting the fire."

"You make a good point," Mr. Claridge said.

Then William addressed Mr. Johnson. "If what you have said leads to a conviction for the fires, I shall gladly pay you the reward. Moreover, if we can prove he was selling Pemberley's liquor to your employer, I will reward you for that as well."

Mr. Johnson looked pleased. "I am a Godfearing man and

working for a thief does not sit well with me. If the fellow with the wagon is an arsonist, I will be proud to have helped catch him." Standing, he added, "I have to be at my job shortly, and I do not want anyone to see me talking to either of you, so I will go out the way I came."

After Mr. Johnson departed, Mr. Claridge said, "I shall await word from you before I bring the pub owner in for questioning."

"It should not take long to search the servants' quarters. Expect to hear from me by the day after tomorrow at the latest."

Locklear Manor
Three days later

Dr. Connelly was pleased with how well his patients were progressing, including Lady Martindale, who had been the one most ill. Barring unforeseen circumstances, he had decided to lift the quarantine in two days' time, which was also when he planned to return to his office in Sheffield, roads permitting.

As it happened, the next morning Lady Marjorie and Lady Marianne were well enough to break their fast together in the sitting room that adjoined their bedrooms. Whilst they ate, Marjorie brought up the unfortunate circumstances in which Marianne found herself.

"After all that Miss Bennet has done for you—for both of us, really—how can you go through with letting her know you do not want her to marry your father?" Marjorie lamented. "It seems too cruel to even consider telling her now."

"One thing does not preclude the other," Marianne replied matter-of-factly. "I am grateful for her care, but even if I were not here, she would have come to help you. And, although I appreciate her kindness, it does not negate the humiliation I would experience if Papa were to marry her. That is just too horrible a thought to contemplate! Can you imagine having to introduce her to my friends as my mother?"

Marjorie sighed heavily. "I do not know how you will get through it."

"I will, for I must. My father is blind to the disaster that marrying Elizabeth Bennet would create for both of us. I have no choice but to make my feelings known and pray she will do the right thing."

"I suppose you are right."

"I am."

Unbeknownst to either woman, Elizabeth had entered Marianne's bedroom with a tray containing the last draught that Dr. Connelly had ordered for her. Hearing her name mentioned, she was curious. She set the tray on the bedside table and crossed to the open door to eavesdrop. After hearing what was said, she forgot the tray and rushed back into the hall and straight to her bedroom.

Once there, all the heartache Elizabeth had suffered since William left Matlock Manor without saying goodbye overwhelmed her and she began to weep. Lying down across the bed, she allowed herself to cry until there were no tears left. Then, she forced herself to consider what Marianne had said.

Someone must have seen Fitzwilliam with me at the gazebo and went straight to Lady Marianne with the news. But who? And who else knows? Most likely Lady Parker does since she takes such great interest in Fitzwilliam; however, if Lady Matlock knew, would she not have riddled me with questions before now?

Sitting up, she turned so that her legs hung off the bed. *In any case, I cannot possibly return to Matlock Manor, so I will ask Lord and Lady Martindale if they will allow me to travel to London with them. After all, she has been very appreciative of my care and offered to assist me if ever I needed another position. If they are kind enough to agree, I must be ready to leave when they do.*

Sliding off the bed, she walked to the closet where she found her small trunk and pulled it into the middle of the room. Quickly, she began placing all the things she had brought with her into it, including the clothes Mrs. Duncan had washed and brought upstairs that morning.

I must inform Lord Matlock. I shall leave him a letter. That way he will not have the chance to question my reason for leaving.

Elizabeth looked in the drawers of the furniture in her room but found no writing materials. Making a mental note to ask that her dinner be served in the parlour on this floor where she knew there was a writing desk, she walked to her dressing room. Splashing water on her face, she pinched her cheeks in a bid to conceal the fact she had been crying. Satisfied that she looked unaffected, Elizabeth headed to her sitting room where her breakfast tray would be waiting. She expected Dr. Connelly would join her there shortly to discuss each patient's condition before she lay down to rest whilst Dr. Connelly attended them.

Pemberley

A quick inventory of the cellar revealed six cases of expensive, French brandy in addition to several cases of port were missing. Moreover, a surreptitious search of all the footmen's apartments revealed that only the suspected footman's room contained evidence. There they found three bottles of brandy hidden under blankets in the bottom of a trunk and several hundred pounds stuffed inside the lining. When confronted with the evidence, the footman confessed to stealing and selling the brandy, though not to setting the fire.

After the constable brought in Mr. Gregson for questioning, the proprietor turned against Darcy's footman, as Mr. Claridge suspected he might. He claimed he had no idea the brandy was stolen, even though a footman would never have had such expensive liquor in his possession unless it was. It had taken bringing in Mr. Johnson to testify to compel both perpetrators to confess to everything.

As the footman told it, when the majority of Pemberley's

servants rushed to the balconies at the back of the house the day the shed caught fire, he realised he could slip into the cellar and pinch a bottle or two of wine without being seen. It had been so easy that he had taken two crates of brandy before the house returned to normal. After selling those, he decided to set the stables on fire, believing a fire of that magnitude would give him even more time and he had been correct.

After the footman's confession, he and the inn owner were gaoled until they could be transported to the county seat for trial. William had returned to Pemberley exhausted, where he was forced to wait for the roads to dry in order to return to Elizabeth.

Locklear Manor
A parlour

When dinner was mentioned that evening, Elizabeth asked for her tray to be taken to the parlour near her room, explaining that she needed to write a letter to her sister and would make use of the writing desk there. Having spoken with Lady Martindale about travelling to London with their party, she was assured she was not only welcome, but she could stay with them once they reached town. Declaring that it would not be necessary, Elizabeth requested discretion about her plans, saying she would inform Lord Matlock of her intentions before they departed Locklear Manor.

Her ladyship was curious about her reasons for leaving his employ, so Elizabeth said she felt the position was never ideal since she had been friends with members of Lord Matlock's family long before she went into service. Her explanation seemed to pacify Lady Martindale, who said nothing more about it.

Relieved to find the parlour empty, Elizabeth closed the door and hurried to the writing desk. Once she sat down, she tried to compose her thoughts before putting pen to paper. When at last she knew what she wished to say, she pulled paper from a drawer and pen and ink from a stand.

Lord Matlock,

You will recall when I took the position as governess, I stated that if my presence made any of your family uncomfortable, I would leave. To my regret, I believe that is precisely what has happened. Therefore, please accept this letter as my resignation, effective immediately.

Forgive me for not telling you this in person, but I thought it best not to discuss how I arrived at my decision. By the time you receive this letter, I will be on my way to London with Lord and Lady Martindale. They have graciously offered to let me travel with them.

I humbly ask that you send my belongings still at Matlock Manor to my sister's address in London, which I have written at the bottom of this letter.

Let me close by saying I truly enjoyed working with your children. They are not only intelligent, but kind-hearted, which is a true reflection of you and Lady Matlock. Tell them I will miss them and to Ellen say that I have faith in her ability to teach the little ones until another governess is hired.

I would like to make one last request. I know this is improper, but will you please put the enclosed letter into Mr. Darcy's hands? I would not have him believe I left without saying goodbye.

Sincerely,
Elizabeth Bennet

Elizabeth had originally planned to write a message to William at the bottom of Lord Matlock's letter; however, after further consideration, she worried that he might follow her and demand an explanation.

It would hurt Fitzwilliam if he knew what Marianne thinks of me, and it could drive a wedge between them. Instead of telling him the truth, I must make him despise me by saying things to wound his spirit. Tears blurred her vision. *How can I do that whilst saying goodbye to the only man I ever loved?*

Pulling a handkerchief from her pocket, she dabbed at her eyes as she began to write.

Mr. Darcy,

It is fortunate that Providence called you away from Matlock Manor when it did, for it afforded me time to think more clearly. Otherwise, I might have been swept up by emotion and come to a decision we both would regret.

Just as we recognised years ago, our circumstances are so dissimilar as to make any union between us unthinkable. To those in your sphere, I would never be found acceptable as the Mistress of Pemberley, and frankly, it would be too great a burden to struggle against their prejudices now.

I am an excellent governess and pride myself in that ability, so do not think me disheartened. I have learned how to make the most of the opportunities I have been given, and I am quite satisfied with my lot.

I will always remember our acquaintance fondly and pray that you will do the same.

Sincerely,
Elizabeth Bennet

By the time Elizabeth finished writing the letter, it was stained with tears. Quickly dabbing the paper with her handkerchief, she blew on the paper until it dried. Satisfied that William would never notice the stains, she sealed the letter and then placed it inside the one meant for Lord Matlock. Then she sealed that one as well.

Soon after she finished, Gladys appeared, carrying her dinner tray.

Setting it down on a circular table in the middle of the room, she declared, "Mrs. Duncan said Cook was making beef with potatoes and carrots today. It smells good!"

Forcing a smile, Elizabeth said, "I am certain I will like whatever it is."

"Just leave the tray here when you are finished, Miss Bennet."

With the maid's departure, Elizabeth's smile vanished.

Chapter 12

Locklear Manor
Two days later

Though Lord Matlock wished to be among the first to leave the manor, Lady Parker had created a scene over a missing shoe, which necessitated a search of the entire floor until it was discovered to have been in her trunk all along. Meanwhile, the families of the other young women affected had arrived to take them home, which meant their coaches were already ahead of his in the queue of departing vehicles.

With nothing to do but wait patiently in the foyer for his family to come downstairs, Richard encountered Lady Blakely, who had just come inside from seeing off other guests.

"Please allow me to apologise again, Lord Matlock," she said. "I still cannot believe a simple birthday celebration could go so horribly wrong."

"You had no way of knowing one of your guests would arrive ill," Richard replied. "Isabelle and I certainly do not hold you responsible."

"You are both very kind."

Just then Lady Parker, Lady Marjorie and Lady Marianne began to descend the stairs, followed closely by Elizabeth's maid Essie.

When Richard realised Elizabeth was not among them, he asked, "Where is Miss Bennet?"

"I have no idea," Lady Parker replied sharply.

"I have not seen Miss Bennet since the day before yesterday," Marianne volunteered.

"Nor have I," Marjorie added.

Lady Blakely interrupted their conversation. "I thought you were aware that she left earlier with Lord and Lady Martindale. As I understand it, they are escorting her back to London."

Richard quickly thought of a lie to hide the fact that he had not known. "Ah, yes. She did say that she was going to visit her sister for a short while. I cannot blame her; she was exhausted."

Suddenly Essie rushed forward, holding out a letter. "Miss Bennet asked me to give this to you before we left for Matlock Manor."

Taking the missive, Richard broke the seal. Noticing a note enclosed for Darcy, he stealthily slipped his cousin's letter behind the one addressed to him and began to read.

After Richard had finished reading, he folded both letters and put them in his coat without any explanation. Then, he announced, "We must be on our way."

"Are you not going to tell us what she said?" Lady Parker asked.

"I do not think it any business of yours," Richard replied tersely. Then waving a hand towards the door, he added, "We will not reach home today if you keep dawdling."

Marjorie and Marianne exchanged knowing glances. They had found the tray with the draught that Elizabeth had left in Marianne's bedroom and suspected she had overheard their remarks about her unsuitability as Marianne's mother—a theory re-enforced by the fact that Elizabeth had avoided them ever since.

Matlock Manor
That same day

As Lady Gordon joined her daughter in the music room whilst her granddaughters practiced the piano, she accepted a cup of tea from a maid, picked up a biscuit and sat down.

She leaned close to Isabelle. "I do hope Richard returns before Mr. Darcy arrives. I would hate for you to have to explain Marianne's whereabouts."

"Believe me, Mother, I could not agree more," Lady Matlock replied. "I have been uneasy since I received Darcy's letter saying he was returning today. How unfortunate that Richard should have to face his cousin before he has had adequate time to rest from this whole ordeal."

"Do you know for certain Richard has not sent Mr. Darcy word of what happened?"

"He said not. And you know how Darcy feels about being kept in the dark about anything that concerns him."

"Well I, for one, will not blame him if he gets angry," Lady Gordon said. "Think how you would feel knowing your child was near death and no one informed you."

"Richard said the only person that ill was Lady Martindale, and she recovered."

"Still, you know how Mr. Darcy dotes on that child."

Isabelle sighed. "I do. Yet I have to agree with Richard that it would have put two lives at risk to notify him when we first received word. Not only would the messenger have been in peril, but Darcy would have risked his life to get to Locklear Manor. And by the time the rains subsided, everyone was doing so well it seemed pointless to send an express."

"I agree, my dear. Still, you can rely on Mr. Darcy having his say when Richard arrives. That is how men act when they have no control over a situation. Moreover, I suspect his concern will extend beyond Marianne. Whilst it may not be obvious to you, I believe he is in love with Miss Bennet."

Isabelle's head whipped around. "On what do you base your opinion?"

"The way he looked at her the first time he saw her in the

music room led me to suspect there was something more than friendship between them."

Isabelle sighed. "I fear you may be correct. And if Darcy sets his mind to marry her, there is nothing anyone can do. He has always done as he pleases."

"Not always! I remember how his horrible relations forced him to marry that worthless creature!"

"It is unfortunate Lady Cornelia had no scruples. He would have made her an excellent husband had she only given him half the chance."

Glancing to her youngest granddaughters, who were too busy watching Ellen play to listen, Lady Gordon said quietly, "She could not control her wantonness that long." Then, she stood and crossed to the tray of refreshments. Selecting another biscuit, she took a bite before adding, "Frankly, I think Mr. Darcy would do well to wed Miss Bennet. Not only is she lovely, I found her very intelligent, and she has a good sense of humour—qualities my Amy has never possessed."

"Mother!"

"Simply the truth, my dear. Your sister never cared about anything but the latest fashions, and she is too self-centred to make any man a good partner."

"Unfortunately, I cannot disagree about her selfishness, but I was hoping that marrying Darcy would force her to act like an adult."

Suddenly a maid appeared in the doorway. "Lord Matlock has arrived, my lady."

Both women set down their cups and promptly walked towards the foyer.

One hour later

When Isabelle entered her husband's bedroom, she found him relaxing in the large upholstered chair next to the windows. His head lay back against the cushioned surface and his eyes were closed. Crossing the bedroom, she went behind the chair and leaned down to kiss the top of his head before beginning to massage his shoulders.

"Did the girls tire you, my dear? You look even more exhausted than when you first arrived."

Without opening his eyes, Richard replied. "They did, but I was so pleased to see them that I hated to tell them I needed to rest."

"They kept asking when you would return, and when I told them that you were on your way home, they became so excited."

"They were very happy to see me until they asked about Miss Bennet. It was distressing to watch them go from laughter to tears so quickly."

"They are heartbroken, to be sure. Will you not share with me the true reason she left? Did my sister do or say something untoward?"

"I know only what Miss Bennet wrote in her letter, but I suspect there is more to the story. God help Darcy when he finds out she is not here."

"Do you think her absence will be that great a disappointment?"

"You have no idea, sweetheart."

Isabelle sighed. "I am sorry that it falls to you to tell him. Darcy will be angry enough that you did not inform him of the illness at Locklear Manor. Then to hear about Miss Bennet—"

"I expect he will be livid at first, but eventually he will concede I did what was best under the circumstances. As for Miss Bennet, I pray the letter she left for him is kind."

Suddenly there was a knock on the door. "Come!" Richard called.

The door opened, and a footman stepped inside. "Pardon the interruption, sir, but you wished to know when Mr. Darcy arrived. He went directly to his room."

"Thank you, Mansfield."

As the footman left, Richard stood. "Off to the Colosseum to face the lion."

"Good luck, dearest," Isabelle said, rising on tiptoes to give him a quick kiss. "I shall pray Darcy remembers that you risked your own health by going to Locklear Manor to care for Marianne."

Richard stopped before exiting the room. "Unfortunately, it was Miss Bennet who cared for Marianne and the others. All I did was carry water," he added as he walked through the door.

William's bedroom

When Richard entered the room, he found Mr. Stephens hanging his cousin's clothes in the closet and William in the dressing room splashing water on his face. As William reached for a towel, he saw Richard standing in the doorway.

"Stephens tells me there is no need to dress for dinner. He said everyone has decided to eat in their room tonight. A bit odd with so many people in residence, is it not?"

"To tell the truth, Cousin, I arrived just ahead of you. I escorted Marjorie, Marianne and Lady Parker home from Locklear Manor, and we are all weary. We thought it best to eat in our rooms and retire early."

"Good heavens! That was a long time to celebrate a birthday."

"In truth, the party was not why they were there so long."

"Oh?" William said, the first tinge of concern entering his voice.

"Sit down, and I shall tell you about it."

"That bad, eh?" William said, forcing a smile.

"Please. Just sit down and listen."

He sounded strangely agitated, so William did as he asked.

Richard turned to his servant. "Leave us, please, Stephens."

With a nod of his head, Stephens left the room. By then William was becoming nervous. Still, he said nothing as his cousin began to relate all that had happened whilst he was at Pemberley. After Richard finished, he waited for William's reaction. He did not have long to wait before his cousin leapt to his feet.

"I shall never completely trust you again! What if Marianne had died and I was not there?"

"I would have sent for you had the physician thought Marianne was in any danger. As it was, from the beginning he expected her to make a complete recovery."

"What makes him an authority? I imagine he has lost many a patient he thought would live."

Richard tried not to smile. "Listen to yourself, Darcy. You sound like a madman."

"When it comes to my family's wellbeing, I am proud to be labelled as such."

"Regardless, Marianne is completely well, and there was no real need to worry. However, there is something else I must tell you."

"For heaven's sake!" William said, throwing up his arms. "I am not a child! Just tell me!"

"Miss Bennet accompanied me to Locklear Manor to care for the girls and Lady Parker. Isabelle could not go in her condition, and Lady Gordon is not strong enough. Miss Bennet insisted she was the most qualified to care for them, and as it turned out, she was right."

Richard went on to tell William about her work during the influenza epidemic in Wales and how competently she had stepped in to help Dr. Connelly tend the patients at Locklear Manor.

During Richard's long-winded explanation, his cousin's apprehension grew and when at length William spoke, he had to brace himself to keep his voice from breaking. "Richard, are you trying to tell me that Elizabeth did not survive the disease?"

"Of course not! I apologise if I gave you that impression. It is just—she decided not to return to Matlock Manor as our governess. Instead, she left me this letter of resignation and returned to London with Lord and Lady Martindale."

Richard held out the letter and was surprised by the tremble in his cousin's hand as he took it. By the time he was done reading, William's face was so full of grief that Richard prayed Elizabeth's letter to him might offer some comfort.

Quickly pulling it from his coat, he said, "Miss Bennet asked me to put this into your hands."

After reading his letter, William shook his head numbly. "I cannot believe she would change her mind after—" He stopped, running his fingers through his hair as he began to pace the floor. "When last we spoke, she acted as though she still cared for me. Something must have happened to make her decide that leaving was preferable to seeing me again! Is there something you are not telling me?"

His voice carried more despair than Richard had heard in years. Wishing he did have an explanation, he reached out to grasp his cousin's shoulder and give it a squeeze. "I swear I know of nothing."

Mindlessly William nodded, refolded Elizabeth's letter and put it in his pocket. "If you do not mind, I wish to be alone."

"Are you not going to greet Marianne before you retire?"

"Her maid said she had eaten and retired already, which is probably for the best. I need time to digest all that I have learned. I will see her in the morning."

"As you wish."

After the door clicked shut behind Richard, William sank down in a chair, closed his eyes and tried to imagine a future without Elizabeth.

Two days later

Since learning that Elizabeth had fled to London, William had become more sombre than ever. Moreover, he spent more time in his bedroom than with the family, a situation that was beginning to grate on Marianne's nerves. Seeking to draw her father out of his isolation, she bade him to come to the music room to listen whilst she and Marjorie performed a duet. All the family had gathered, as much to reassure themselves of Darcy's wellbeing as to hear the music, for he had not finished eating an entire meal since his return to Matlock Manor and was beginning to look gaunt.

As Marianne and Marjorie performed, Lady Parker kept up an embarrassing display of ill manners by talking throughout their performance. Hoping to impress William with her knowledge of the composer of that particular song, she spoke so loudly that Lady Gordon finally hushed her, causing her colour to rise in anger. She scowled throughout the rest of their song, and it was only after Ellen and Evelyn played a duet that she deigned to speak again.

"I swear that your youngest children play almost as well as many of my acquaintances, Isabelle! I cannot bear to hear most of the ladies in our circle perform."

"If the girls play well, we have Miss Bennet to thank," Lady Matlock answered. "Her tutelage contributed greatly to their proficiency."

Vexed by the mention of the woman she so resented, Lady Parker went silent. Ellen, however, was not of the same mind. Halting before beginning another song, her eyes filled with tears as she said, "Miss Bennet was the best teacher I have ever had. I cannot believe she is gone."

Her two younger sisters readily joined in, with Evelyn adding, "We miss her so much, Papa! Can you not go and get her?"

"I am sorry, Poppet, but I cannot force Miss Bennet to return."

"Do not worry," Marianne declared confidently. "Your father will soon hire another governess, and you may like her even more than Miss Bennet."

"I will not!" Emily cried, stamping her foot. "Miss Bennet was kind, and we had such fun at our lessons."

"And she cared about us!" Evelyn added.

"Nonsense!" Lady Parker declared. "You will have many governesses before you leave the schoolroom. My advice is not to get too attached to any of them, and you will not be disappointed."

Unable to bear any more, William stood. "If you will excuse me."

"Must you go, Papa?" Marianne cried from her position in the chair next to his. She reached for his hand. "Stay and listen to Aunt Amy play."

"I must leave for Pemberley in the morning, and I wish to be well rested."

Surprised, Richard said, "You just arrived. Can you not stay a few more days?"

"I have buildings under construction, so I am needed there." He looked to Marianne. "If you wish to remain here, of course, you may."

Worried about his increasingly despondent attitude, Marianne needed to make certain her father did not slip further into melancholy. "I shall return with you."

"Then I suggest you retire soon, as well."

William leaned over to place a kiss on her forehead. Then he quit the room, leaving everyone staring after him.

London
The Cowans' residence

Jane opened the door to the bedroom where her sister had been staying since her unexpected return. She walked in and placed a tray with food and tea on a table next to the window, pulled back the curtains and raised the sash with no attempt to be quiet.

"Lizzy, it is time you ate something and then explained to me why you have returned to London."

"Please go away!" Elizabeth groaned, pulling the counterpane over her head. "I am not hungry."

Jane sat down on the edge of the bed and pulled the covers down. "I had hoped that once you had rested from that terrible ordeal at Locklear Manor, you would confide in me. I am through waiting, so sit up and eat whilst we discuss why you decided to leave Lord Matlock's employment."

Elizabeth had no choice but to comply. Sitting up, she brushed the hair from her eyes, murmuring, "I... I no longer felt comfortable being around them."

Jane's eyes grew large. "Did Lord Matlock do anything untoward?"

"Oh, no! He has always acted like a gentleman."

"Then what changed? In your last letter you said you were delighted with your position and—" Seeing tears fill Elizabeth's eyes, Jane declared, "Oh, Lizzy! Is it Mr. Darcy? Tell me he did not dash your hopes again!"

"If he has any part in my decision, it is because I have neither seen nor heard from him since he returned to Pemberley after the fire."

"Then, what else upset you?"

"Whilst I was at Locklear Manor, I overheard Lady Marianne tell her cousin that she would be embarrassed to introduce me as her mother. I do not know how she learned of Fitzwilliam's attention, and only God knows if he actually planned to offer for me again, but she made it clear she would not be happy if he did. His daughter has every right to her view, but it was disheartening to hear her opinion of me, especially since I thought we were becoming friends."

Jane pulled Elizabeth into her arms. "Oh, Lizzy! What a horrid thing for her to say—especially about someone who risked her life to care for her."

"My life was never in any great danger."

"Many people have died from the disease, Lizzy! Why do you think my children are in Birmingham with Jonathan's brother? And Aunt Gardiner, her children and grandchildren are all at their seaside cottage at Southend." [3]

"I was beginning to wonder why the house was so quiet."

"I told you about the children the night you arrived, but you probably do not remember because you were so exhausted that you went straight to bed. I also sent our housekeeper to look after them."

"Then why are you not in Birmingham with them?"

"Jonathan wanted me to go, but I know he would never tell me if he fell ill. I just wanted to make certain the children were

---

3   *Southend-on-Sea* *commonly referred to simply as* *Southend*, *is a town in southeastern Essex, England. It lies on the north side of the Thames Estuary, 40 miles (64 km) east of central London.*

away from this dread disease and being well-cared for. Besides, I am strong and in good health."

"As am I."

"Have it your way. You always do."

Throwing back the covers, Elizabeth rose from the bed and crossed to the window. Admiring the clear blue sky, she murmured, "Fourteen years have passed since I foolishly refused his offer, and nothing has changed. Old prejudices still carry the day."

"Anyone who would not rejoice to have you in their family is too foolish for you to spend one minute of your time dwelling on their disapproval."

Elizabeth smiled. "Spoken like a prejudiced sister!"

"I may be prejudiced, but I have every right to be!" Jane said. "You are the most intelligent, giving, tender-hearted, thoughtful—"

"What? No mention of my beauty?"

"Oh Lizzy, I long for you to marry and be settled, preferably near me so that we may see each other whenever we wish."

"I think it is time I visited Southend!" Elizabeth replied wryly.

"You are so stubborn."

"A Bennet trait, I fear."

"Be that as it may, surely you do not hold Mr. Darcy responsible for what his daughter said?"

"I cannot pretend it does not matter," Elizabeth replied. "They have a close bond, and I would not do anything to ruin it."

"But Mr. Darcy has a right to his opinion, too, and you need to know what that is."

"Oh, Jane, it is all so confusing! The last time we were together I was so overcome." Elizabeth tried to swallow against the large lump now forming in her throat. "I would have fallen into his arms had he reached out to me." She shook her head emphatically. "No. I can never see him again and most likely will not have to. A fire at Pemberley was the reason he returned, yet he felt no obligation to inform me before he left. I believe that was because he realised that he should not renew his offer. It is just unfortunate that his daughter does not know that as yet."

"And if you are wrong and Mr. Darcy intends to return?"

"The letter I left for Fitzwilliam will dissuade him from following me."

"Oh, Lizzy. What did you do? What did you say?"

"I merely stated the truth: Our circumstances are still so dissimilar as to make any union between us unthinkable."

"I hope you know what you are about, for I do not."

"I am resolved that I made the right choice," Elizabeth replied. "Now, please promise never to speak of it again."

Without waiting for a reply, she strode to the tray on the table, lifted the lid and took a deep breath.

"These rolls smell heavenly!"

Chapter 13

Matlock Manor
Days later

Richard was in his study working on matters of business, when he heard the knob turn and the door creak open. Instead of a servant entering, however, Ellen stuck her head inside.

"Papa, may I speak with you, please?"

Unable to keep from smiling at the daughter he thought most like himself, Richard tried to appear firm. "Are you not supposed to be helping your sisters with their lessons?"

"I left Evelyn and Emily practicing their numbers, and what I have to say will not take long. It is very important, though."

"Then, I suppose you had better tell me." Richard laid down his pen and turned in his chair. As he held out his arms, Ellen raced towards him. Once she was settled in his lap, he asked, "Now, what is so important?"

"I think I know why Miss Bennet left us."

With a mix of dread and anticipation, Richard replied, "Go on."

"I was outside of Marjorie's bedroom this morning when I heard—"

"What did your mother and I tell you about eavesdropping?"

"I was not eavesdropping, I promise! Mama asked me to tell

Marjorie to return the easel she had borrowed from the class-room. All of us must have an easel if we are to paint."

"Of course you must. So, what did you hear?"

"I heard Aunt Amy say, 'Do not tell anyone that you suspect Miss Bennet overheard you and Marianne discussing her. You had no way of knowing she was listening. Besides, her nosiness merely hastened what Marianne had already planned—to let that little whore know she would never be accepted as her mother.' I do not know what a whore is, Papa, but it sounds evil."

Knowing his innocent daughter would never use such a word unless she had overheard it, Richard's ire rose instantly. "It *is* evil, and to refer to Miss Bennet in such a manner is not only untrue but despicable. I am pleased you thought to tell me, so I may speak to your aunt. Now, go back to your classroom and paint a lovely picture for me. I shall look in on you this afternoon to see how you are faring."

Slipping to her feet as her father stood, Ellen stammered, "But... but, are you not going to take me with you to confront her?"

"I do not want anyone to know that it was you who informed me," Richard stated. "If anyone asks, just pretend you know nothing." Smiling, he leaned down to place a kiss on her forehead. "Now run along, Poppet, and try not to worry. I will set things to right."

"Thank you, Papa!"

With a quick hug around his waist, Ellen exited her father's study much happier than when she had entered. As for Richard, the fake smile on his face swiftly changed to a scowl. Placing the papers he was reading in the top drawer of his desk, he locked it and stood.

Time to inform Isabelle of her sister's part in Miss Bennet's departure.

Lady Matlock's study

"I cannot believe my sister's gall!" Isabelle declared, coming around her desk to stand in front of Richard. "It is bad enough that Amy is involved, but instructing the girls to keep quiet—"

"When we speak to her and Marjorie, I want to leave Ellen's disclosure out of the discussion. We shall infer it was a servant who informed us."

"I agree."

Suddenly there was a knock on the door. "Come!" Isabelle called.

"You sent for me, Mother?"

"I did. Pray sit down."

Seeing the expressions on her parents faces, Marjorie's anxiety grew as she sank into a wooden chair in front of her mother's desk. "What is the matter?"

"It is regarding Miss Bennet, and we think you know exactly what the matter is," Richard replied.

Marjorie's eyes closed. "How did you find out?"

"That is not important," Richard stated. "What *is* important is for you to tell us why you began to plot against Miss Bennet and what happened at Locklear Manor to make her leave."

Swallowing hard, Marjorie said, "It began in the coach on the way to the party. Aunt Amy ..."

After Marjorie had been apprised of her punishment and sent to her room, Isabelle sent a maid to fetch her mother and sister.

"Why involve your mother?" Richard asked.

"I want Mother to hear everything, so Amy cannot twist the truth. I am certain my sister will pout and keep her distance—at least until she thinks of a way to get back into our good graces—but there is no way to know what she would tell Mother."

Soon both ladies entered the room.

"Mother... Amy. Pray be seated."

"Why do I feel as though I am a child about to be upbraided?" Lady Gordon teased.

"It is not you who should be scolded, Mother," Lady Matlock

said, turning to Amy. "It is my sister. I wanted you here so you would know exactly why we are angry."

Whilst Lady Gordon's expression changed to one of anxiety, Lady Parker's expression reflected defiance. "I have no idea to what you are referring. I have done nothing wrong!"

"Your conversation with Marjorie this morning was reported to me," Richard stated. "When Isabelle and I questioned her, she confessed everything you said to her and Marianne about Miss Bennet as you travelled to Locklear Manor."

Amy smirked and declared unapologetically, "I was only stating a truth we all hold dear! Servants and the gentry do not mix, much less marry. Surely you agree with me, Isabelle! I have heard you say the same thing often enough."

"I admit that I have been critical of certain people in the past, but the circumstances regarding Darcy and Miss Bennet are entirely different. After all, when their relationship started, she was a gentleman's daughter from Hertfordshire. It was well before she went into service."

"Still, she has been a servant for over a decade!" Amy argued. "She is no longer worthy of acceptance into our circle."

"I have heard enough of that nonsense!" Richard declared. "Marjorie also said you encouraged them not to tell us that Miss Bennet most likely overheard a conversation where Marianne declared she would never accept Miss Bennet as her mother."

"I do not deny it! I knew you would act just as you are now, so I think I was justified in having done so!"

Richard crossed the room to stand towering over Lady Parker. Eyes ablaze, he said, "You had better pray you have not done permanent damage to Miss Bennet's relationship with my cousin, for if you have I will never receive you in any of my homes again. After all, it would be cruel to force Darcy to endure the company of the woman who is the source of his misery."

"Misery? Good heavens! I was merely trying to save him from being lured into marriage by a woman totally beneath his station!" Amy crowed. "Besides, I am your wife's sister, and Isabelle will never allow you to banish me!"

"Richard is the head of this family," Isabelle replied. "I not only agree with him regarding your treachery, but should he decide to ban you, I will abide by his wishes."

"Mother, are you going to say nothing?" Amy shrieked.

"I am afraid that I agree with Richard in this matter," Lady Gordon replied. "If you have ruined Mr. Darcy's chances for happiness, he should not have to suffer your company again."

Hearing this, Lady Parker quit the room in a flurry of swishing silks, murmuring profanities as she went.

Richard sighed heavily. "That went about as well as I expected."

Lady Gordon stood. "I apologise for my daughter's misdeeds, Richard. Would that I could do something to make amends. Perhaps I should write a note of apology to Mr. Darcy."

"I am afraid that would make little difference," Richard answered.

Lady Gordon nodded. "I shall go to my room and instruct my maid to begin packing. My daughter needs to vacate your home, and I intend to see that she does."

"You will always be welcome here," Richard said.

"I appreciate your kindness. Still, it is time that Amy retrieved my granddaughter and we all visited Bath. The latest news from London is that the sickness has not reached there. Now, if you will excuse me, I shall be in my rooms."

As she exited the study, Richard addressed his wife. "I plan to leave for Pemberley before dawn. Marianne owes her father the truth and an apology."

"How do you propose to challenge Marianne when Darcy is so protective of her?"

"I will surprise her by bringing up the subject during dinner. My cousin has a right to know that his own daughter has deliberately damaged his relationship with the woman he loves."

Isabelle's face crumpled as though she might cry. "I must confess that I am guilty, too, for I also feared having Miss Bennet as a relation. It was only after seeing how hurt Darcy was upon hearing she had fled to London that I began to regret my position. After all, who am I to tell Darcy he cannot have the woman he loves, when I was blessed to marry the man I love?"

Richard pulled his wife into his arms, placing a kiss on her forehead. "I love you, too, sweetheart."

"I still vividly recall those who advised me against marrying you because you were not an heir when we met."

"Thank God you did not listen to those old biddies," he said, coaxing a smile from her. "And I am very relieved to hear that your attitude has changed. For far too long I have felt uncomfortable with your ideas about rank and status, though I kept my thoughts to myself."

"Why did you keep silent?"

"I suppose because I thought I had no right to object. After all, I was aware you ascribed to the *ton's* nonsense before our marriage, though I believed you acted more from habit than malice." Suddenly he became sombre. "I hope Marianne will tell Darcy the truth and that he will listen when I advise him to find Miss Bennet and tell her that he loves her still. Otherwise, I fear she may be lost to him forever."

"I shall pray that Miss Bennet will not hold our prejudices against Darcy," Isabelle said, her eyes filling with tears. "If she does, he may never forgive me or my family."

"Only God can make things right between them now, but I believe He knows they were formed for one another, just as you and I were, and that is why He brought them back together."

"What a lovely thought," Isabelle replied, her voice more hopeful. "I shall think on that when worry threatens to overwhelm me." Then she added glumly, "Oh, darling, though I know you must, I cannot bear to see you leave again. We have been apart far too much of late."

"I know, dearest," Richard replied. "What say you and I spend the rest of the day in our suite and let the children survive without us?"

A long, passionate kiss was to be his answer, and afterwards they walked arm in arm back to their rooms.

Pemberley
That same day

It had been days since she and her father had returned from Matlock Manor, and Marianne was beginning to worry about his state of mind. Normally, she could coax him from one of his foul moods by asking him to ride with her of a morning, or play a game of chess after tea, or Vingt-et-un after dinner. Nothing seemed to interest him since he learned Miss Bennet had left Lord Matlock's employ.

In fact, her father had routinely begun to leave the house at dawn and not return until well after dark. He excused the practice by saying that he had to supervise the rebuilding of the shed and stable. In addition, he complained of not being able to sleep, so he retired directly after dinner. It was the only meal they shared of late, and it was always spent with Marianne carrying the conversation whilst he occasionally murmured a terse response.

Determined to rise early enough to confront him before he left the house, Marianne was dressed for riding when she entered the breakfast room only to find it empty.

Mrs. Brown walked in behind her and Marianne turned to address the housekeeper. "I see my father has already left to supervise the construction."

"Oh no, my lady," the housekeeper answered. "The master left for London about an hour ago. He asked me to give you this note when you came downstairs to break your fast."

She held out a letter, and Marianne took it, replying wanly, "Thank you."

Sinking down into one of the chairs at the table, she broke the seal and began to read.

Dearest Marianne,

My solicitor requested I attend him regarding some legal papers I had asked him to create. I decided last night that it would be best if I left for London this morning. Since you have just recovered from the dread disease that is still plaguing London, I did not think it wise to take you with me.

Rather than argue the point, I felt it better that I leave before you woke. I should not be away long if all goes as planned. I have asked Mrs. Brown to supervise you whilst I am away, and I expect you to obey her.

Papa

Since she had been old enough to understand, her father had never gone anywhere without discussing it with her first if he could not take her with him. His departure today was so unlike him that Marianne's first inclination was to cry; however, she did not wish the housekeeper to think her a spoiled child.

Pasting a serene look on her face, she stated, "Since father is away, I will need a footman to accompany me whilst I ride. Will you ask Mr. Walker to send one to the stables?"

"Are you not going to eat something first?"

"At present, I have no appetite. Perhaps I will after I have had my ride." Having said that, Marianne exited the room.

Mrs. Brown was not fooled in the least.

I do not know what happened at Matlock Manor, but I have not seen Mr. Darcy in such a state in the six years I have been his housekeeper. If I did not know better, I would think someone had died.

Knowing that eventually she would learn what had occurred, she headed downstairs to speak to the butler about securing a footman.

That evening

Without anything to hinder its progress, Richard's coach made the journey to Pemberley in a timely manner, arriving just as the sun was setting. When he stepped out of his conveyance, he was a bit surprised to find only two footmen came down the steps to greet him. Even as he approached the front door, it was a footman who opened it, acknowledging him with a bow.

Nonetheless, by the time he stood in the centre of the foyer, Mr. Walker made his appearance as he rushed around a corner.

"Lord Matlock! We were not expecting you."

Richard handed his hat to the butler. "I decided to come quite suddenly." Before he had time to say more, Marianne came flying down the grand staircase, only to stop halfway when she recognised him.

"Oh, it is you, Cousin Richard."

"That is a fine greeting," Richard replied with a wry smile.

"I apologise," Marianne said, as she descended the rest of the stairs more sedately. "I heard a maid say there was a coach coming down the drive, and I hoped Father had returned."

"Darcy is not here?"

"He left for London very early this morning, sir," Mr. Walker stated.

Richard stared at the floor as though trying to decide what to do. "It may be best that I talk to you and Darcy separately in any case."

"You… you wish to speak to me?" Marianne repeated uneasily.

"I do." To the butler, he said, "Lady Marianne and I shall be in Darcy's study should anyone need us."

Mr. Walker knew the master had given his cousin a key to the study, so there was no question that he could use the room whenever he wished. "Yes, Your Lordship."

"But… but, do you not wish to change clothes first?" Marianne ventured. "Or perhaps have some refreshments?"

"I think the sooner we have our discussion, the better," Richard replied, waving an arm in the direction of the hall leading to the study. "Shall we?"

The study

If Richard thought Marianne would regret her actions as quickly as Marjorie had, he was mistaken. Not only was she unrepentant, she seemed as happy as Lady Parker had been to expound on the differences between Miss Bennet's rank and her own.

"I cannot see why you think that expressing my true feelings was wrong. Better for Miss Bennet to learn now that I would be embarrassed to introduce her as my mother than after some hastily-arranged marriage—and I have no doubt that was her goal."

"Indeed? Then explain to me why she left my employ rather than stay and fight for Darcy."

"I have had time to consider that, and I have come to the conclusion that she wanted Papa to chase after her. That is why I am so upset that he went to London alone." Angrily she tossed a nearby pillow onto the settee across the room. "All these years Papa has stayed true to my mother's memory, and if he succumbs to this woman's treachery, his devotion will be for naught."

"True to your mother's memory? Where did you get that idea?"

"It makes perfect sense. That is why he never married again. He was so in love with Mother that after she and their child died, he never trusted his heart to anyone else."

"Perhaps I should not correct your ill-conceived notion, but God knows Darcy never will. Unlike you, he cares more for your feelings than his own."

"What an unkind thing to say, Cousin! I did not think to ever hear you speak to me in this manner."

"I apologise if the truth wounds you, but you need to hear it."

Beginning with the summer he and Darcy met Elizabeth, Richard told Marianne everything that had happened between her father and the woman he loved. This included how he was injured trying to rescue Lydia and that by the time he had recovered, he feared Elizabeth hated him for not being able to save her sister.

"That was why Darcy never tried to contact her."

"Is that not evidence enough that Miss Bennet was never worthy to be a part of our family? After all, her sister was a fallen woman who ran off with a man who was not her husband."

"Before you disparage Miss Bennet's family, perhaps you should hear more about your own. Your mother was a widow when she met Darcy, and she was already with child when they married."

"That does not surprise me! I have heard that couples often anticipate their vows."

"Would it surprise you if I told you the babe was not Darcy's child? Lady Cornelia was known for her—shall we say *liaisons*—with the second son of Lord Haggard. He was studying the law and was willing to marry her, but she wanted to be a rich man's wife. So, she set her sights on my cousin."

"That is a lie!" Marianne interjected with eyes ablaze.

Undeterred, Richard continued. "If Darcy had not been so melancholy over the loss of Miss Bennet, my mother could never have talked him into marrying your mother. You see, at the time your grandmother and my mother were close friends, and I believe they planned the marriage to solve Lady Cornelia's predicament."

"I do not believe you!" Marianne cried, coming to her feet. "Why would you darken Mother's memory with these lies when she is not here to defend herself?"

"Do you really think I would invent lies when Darcy may never forgive me for telling you the truth? Whether you believe it or not, I swear what I have said is true. Isabelle knows it, as does her mother, and they will confirm what I have said if you ask."

Marianne had begun to pace. Suddenly she stopped, picked up a vase, and sent it crashing into the brick hearth. "They would lie, too, if you asked it of them."

"So now *everyone* is a liar. You are nearly old enough to make your debut, yet you act like a spoiled child denied something you want. Ask yourself this. Why are there no portraits of your mother at Pemberley or at Darcy House in London?"

She looked pensive for a moment before answering. "I assume Papa had them removed to lessen his pain."

"There is something you need to see. Apart from Mr. Walker, no one knows about this but Darcy and I."

Retrieving the set of keys he had used to open the study, he searched through them for a particular one, stood and turned to open the cabinet in the wall behind the desk. After looking through it, he seemed puzzled. "What could Darcy have done with it?"

"With what?"

Without replying, Richard walked over to the intricately embroidered bell pull, gave it a tug, and waited for the butler. Not long afterward, Mr. Walker entered the room.

"You called, sir?"

"I did, Walker." As soon as the butler came forward, Richard asked, "Where has Darcy put the portrait?"

"The portrait?"

"Come now, you know as well as I that Darcy has kept a portrait locked in this cabinet for the last fourteen years. Where is it?"

Sheepishly, the butler answered, "Just before he left for Matlock Manor on the last occasion, he asked me to cover it with brown paper and have a footman carry it to the attic. He said something about not wanting someone to see it."

"Show us where it is."

Walker glanced worriedly at Marianne. "But... but Mr. Darcy did not wish for—"

"I am well aware of my cousin's wishes concerning his secret, but Miss Marianne needs to understand her father's attachment to the portrait."

Suddenly, Walker understood.

"Follow me."

Finding the painting was not difficult, as it was the only object in the room not covered by layers of dust. Walker brought it forward and propped it on a table against a wall. Richard dismissed him, promising to rewrap the portrait once Marianne had viewed it. After the butler left, he pulled a knife from his boot and cut the cord holding the paper in place.

As he began to unwrap the portrait, Marianne's eyes grew wider, and once it was fully visible, she stammered, "Why would Papa possess a portrait of Miss Bennet? Granted she is much younger, but it is definitely she!"

"This is not Miss Bennet. It is merely a close resemblance created by an artist from Darcy's memory. He had Georgiana's portrait painted not long after your mother died and paid the man to stay and complete this one afterwards. I have always believed that having Georgiana's portrait painted was only an excuse to have this one created, for Georgiana had sat for one only two years previously. I remember when I first discovered Darcy with this portrait in his study. He said he had the artist sketch ten or twelve likenesses before he was sufficiently satisfied to let him proceed with the portrait."

Marianne's voice broke when next she spoke. "I... I do not understand. He never acted as though he regretted her."

"Can you truthfully say you never noticed his melancholy? After Isabelle and I married, I was not in his company as much, but whenever I was, I could tell he carried a deep-rooted sorrow."

"I suppose I thought being grave was just part of his nature."

"Then you were wrong, just as you were wrong about his attachment to your mother."

Marianne found it difficult to swallow against the large lump forming in her throat. "If it was as you say—"

"If you still doubt his regard for Miss Bennet," Richard interrupted, "suppose you take a better look at the wedding ring the woman in the portrait is wearing."

Stepping closer, Marianne leaned in for a better look. Then she gasped. "It is Lady Anne's wedding ring! She is wearing it in her portrait in the gallery." Quietly she added, "It *is* as you say. Papa must have loved her very much."

"He loves her still."

Tears began to run down her face. "I never knew myself until this moment. I have always known Papa loved me, despite the fact I was not his child, for he treated me as though I were. And when Lady Parker said he was meeting Miss Bennet in the gazebo, I was overcome by jealousy. I never wanted him to marry again, for I feared a new wife, and possibly children, would take my place in his heart."

"Do you think I love Marjorie any less because I love her sisters or her mother?"

"I never considered that."

"The love that Darcy has for you will always exist, just as his love for Miss Bennet will."

"All this time ..." She stopped, unable to continue.

"Now that you know what heartache you have caused two, good people, what will you do to rectify your mistake?"

"First, I must apologise to Papa and ask his forgiveness. Then, I must face Miss Bennet and explain how wrong I was to say such horrible things about her. I will ask her to forgive me for my jealousy and not to hold my hatefulness against Papa because he loves her still."

"I intend to follow Darcy to London tomorrow. I cannot take you with me, but I will deliver any apologies you wish to send him or Miss Bennet, should I find her."

"Do you think there is still a chance for them to find happiness?"

"Whilst in His Majesty's forces, I learned that as long as there is breath, there is hope."

Chapter 14

London
Darcy House
Five days later

At the floor-to-ceiling windows of a small parlour on the up-permost floor of the house, Mrs. Barnes stood looking towards Hyde Park through a telescope she had taken from another room with every intention of returning it before the master noticed it was missing. Unbeknownst to her, Mr. Barnes had stopped at the door upon seeing such an odd sight and approached her to learn what was so fascinating that his wife had employed a telescope to view it. Though startled when he suddenly appeared beside her, the housekeeper did not speak but kept to her surveillance.

Once he had assessed the scene below, Mr. Barnes teased his wife. "If your interest is in that fellow standing at the gate, my dear, I fear he is a bit too young for you."

"Oh, pish!" Mrs. Barnes said, smiling and slapping at his arm. "I was not looking at him. I was trying to decide if the gentleman seated on the bench nearest the fountain is the master."

"Whether it is or not, you know he will be upset if he catches you spying."

"I am *not* spying!" she protested. "I am merely *concerned*. When I asked him this morning why he had not touched his food, Mr. Darcy became annoyed, and not a minute later he left the house without bothering to call for his horse to be saddled. I watched him strike out and cross the street with that detestable cane more than an hour ago. We both know he cannot walk that long. He should have returned by now."

"I warned you not to mention how little he eats. He does not like it when you coddle him."

"I do not coddle him! It just worries me to see him so thin. I know he is not eating enough to keep a bird alive. That is all!"

The butler put an arm around his wife's shoulders. "I know it worries you, my love. It worries me, too. After all, we have watched him grow from a gangly child to an adult, and we love him as though he were our own. Of course, we coddle him."

"And worry about him."

"And worry about him," Mr. Barnes repeated.

"The trip from Pemberley always aggravates that old injury, and though it has been two days already, he still grimaces whenever he takes the stairs. He should never have gone for a walk in the park today," Mrs. Barnes declared. "I fear he may be sitting on a bench somewhere, in pain and unable to return to the house."

"If it will make you feel better, I shall send a footman to locate him, even though it may make his disposition even worse should he be found."

"I do not think it can get any worse. Besides, knowing he is well will ease my mind," she replied, turning to place a kiss on her husband's cheek. Just as she refocused on the park, a carriage pulled to a stop in front of the house. "We have company!" she announced. "I thought the knocker was off the door."

"It is," Mr. Barnes said, stepping forward to look down and see who was exiting the vehicle. "Did Mr. Darcy say that he was expecting Mr. Allen today?"

"He did mention something about a meeting, but I assumed he meant to go to the solicitor's office."

"We must hurry," he said, taking her hand. "Show him to the library and placate him with tea and refreshments whilst I send a footman to locate Mr. Darcy."

William's study

Grimacing as he took his place behind the huge mahogany desk, William apologised. "I am sorry you had to wait, Allen. I had not forgotten our meeting, but I lost track of time."

Observing the young man he had served since long before George Darcy's death, Mr. Allen said, "Fitzwilliam, you are thinner than I have ever seen you. If I did not know better, I would think you were ill. Have you suffered from that awful stomach ailment that has wreaked havoc on so much of England?"

"Thankfully, no. I assure you that other than the pain of walking a bit too much this morning, I am fine."

"Ah, yes, the injury to your leg. Forgive me, but you manage so well I sometimes forget about that. How long has it been?"

"Fourteen years."

"Should it not be less painful by now?"

"Because a bone was crushed, my physician said I will never be entirely free of pain. Still, if I take care and do not stand or walk for too long, I can minimise it."

"I suppose that is better than losing a leg. If I recall correctly, at the time of the accident, they wanted to amputate and would have done so if Colonel Fitzwilliam—excuse me, if *Lord Matlock* had not been there to object. A fine man, your cousin, though I cannot get used to calling him anything other than colonel."

William flashed a rare smile. "I agree. Richard is a fine man and I have not grown accustomed to his title, either."

Opening the satchel in his lap, the elderly gentleman pulled out a file and laid it atop William's desk. "Since you are in Town so infrequently, I know you must have much to do. Therefore, I will address the reason for my call without delay. As per your letter, these are the settlement papers you asked me to draw up."

Instantly, an expression of sadness crossed William's face. Wishing he had not impulsively sent the letter regarding a settlement before gaining Elizabeth's consent, he was unable to meet the solicitor's eyes.

"They will not be necessary now," he murmured quietly

Mr. Allen leaned forward. "Excuse me?"

"I acted too hastily in having you prepare them. The lady refused my offer, so the settlement papers are no longer needed."

Unable to believe any woman in her right mind would turn down an offer from Fitzwilliam Darcy, Allen stammered, "Might... might I suggest you retain them? Surely she will reconsider."

"I can assure you that will not be the case." To change the subject, William reached into a desk drawer to bring out a blank bank cheque. "If you will tell me the amount, I shall pay you now for preparing them. That will save you the trouble of sending a bill."

"I thought to wait until you had decided on the changes to your will and include everything then."

"Naturally, there will not be any changes to my will, either."

Mr. Allen was beginning to understand why his client seemed so dispirited. "I will send it tomorrow, if that is acceptable."

"It is," William replied. Standing, he held out his hand, and Mr. Allen grasped it.

"I wish our meeting could have concluded on a happier note," the solicitor said.

He was almost to the door when he was overwhelmed with the feeling that he should say what was in his heart.

Turning to William, he said, "Fitzwilliam, I know I am not your father, though I am old enough to have been. However, I wish to say what I think George would say if he were here."

When William raised no objection, he continued, "I watched you do a fine job of raising your sister and seeing her successfully married. Moreover, you assumed responsibility for a child who was not your flesh and blood and have raised her as your daughter. Soon, Lady Marianne will take her rightful place in society, and before you know it, she, too, will marry. You are still young enough to choose a new path for your future. My prayer is that you will not let what just transpired discourage you. Do not stop until you find a woman you cannot live without—one who, God willing, will give you children. You have done your duty, and now it is time to raise sons and daughters of your own."

"I am grateful to have had your counsel all these years," William replied, "and I appreciate that your concern is heartfelt. I promise to keep what you have said in mind."

Mr. Allen smiled. "I hope you do. Nothing would make me happier than to prepare new settlement papers and revise your will to include a wife and more children."

For a long time after Mr. Allen's departure, William sat on the balcony outside his study, sipping brandy, and contemplating his solicitor's advice. Regrettably, each time the man's words played again in his mind, William stumbled over the one thing that made following his counsel impossible.

Unfortunately, the one woman I cannot live without is you, Elizabeth.

The next day

By the time he had arrived in London the prior evening, Richard was very tired and it was fast growing dark. He decided to get a good night's rest at his townhouse before calling on his cousin early in the morning. Now that the sun had risen and he was well rested, he was on his way to Darcy House.

As the carriage halted in front of his cousin's residence, Richard noted the knocker was not on the door. Unlike Pemberley, several footmen rushed down the steps to open the carriage door and steady the horses. As he stepped out of the vehicle and began up the steps, the front door opened, and the butler stepped onto the portico.

Mr. Barnes looked relieved to see him. "Welcome back to Darcy House, Lord Matlock. I am so pleased you have come."

"I take it my cousin *is* in, though there is no knocker on the door."

"Yes, my lord," Walker replied. Then, looking about and seeing no one close by, he added, "Mr. Darcy has not been very sociable since his arrival."

"When has my cousin ever been sociable?"

"At times he is less so than at others."

"It cannot be easy for you and Mrs. Barnes."

The long-time servant lowered his voice even more. "Frankly, we have been worried that he seems to have fallen back into old habits. He scarcely eats, and he keeps to himself. He has spent more hours locked away in his study than riding, and you know how he used to love riding of a morning or late in the evening. I hope your arrival will cheer him."

"I fear what I have to say will definitely not cheer him, at least at first. Still, my hope is that it will eventually bring him happiness of a lasting nature."

"Mrs. Barnes and I shall pray that it does." By then both men were standing in the foyer. As Walker took Richard's hat, he tilted his head towards the grand staircase. "At present, Mr. Darcy is in his rooms. Do you wish me to announce you?"

"I had rather you did not," Richard said with a wry smile. "I have always found it best not to give my cousin any warning."

The Cowan Residence
Cheapside

Jane stood at the rear door of the house watching as her sister rested on one of the wooden chaises Jonathan had ordered for the terrace. Having spent too much time in her room since her arrival, Jane had insisted Elizabeth take the air with her whilst a maid changed the bedding. As she was preparing to join her sister, however, she was suddenly struck with the realisation of how much Elizabeth had changed since she left Cheapside to become the Fitzwilliam's governess.

Though her sister had faced setbacks after going into service, Jane had watched as time and again Elizabeth drew upon a spirit of optimism from somewhere deep within; a spirit that always left her with renewed hope for the future. It appeared to Jane, however, that this time was different. That realisation left her stunned until Lizzy noticed her and cried, "You promised to sit with me and enjoy the sun!"

Recalled from her distressing thoughts, Jane went through the door. Once she reached the chair next to her sister, she sat down and lay back, closing her eyes. Soon, a big smile split her face. "I fear that Jonathan should not have had these constructed. I forget all about running the household the moment I lie back in the sun."

"This is heavenly," Elizabeth agreed. "After I leave, I think I shall miss sitting here with you most of all."

Jane's eyes popped open. "Leave? You just arrived!"

"Of all people, you should know that I am not a woman of leisure, dear sister. I must begin searching for another position."

Jane sat up and turned to place her feet on the bricks of the terrace. "Elizabeth Bennet! You are incurring no expenses whilst you are here! So I will not have you talking about going back into service so soon. Rest and enjoy being with me, just as I am enjoying being with you."

"I cannot impose indefinitely on you and Jonathan."

"Jonathan is thrilled you came. Many of his men were either sick or caring for sick family members. With you here, he felt less guilty about leaving me alone whilst he worked such long hours."

"Your husband is generous to a fault, but I do not feel comfortable about not contributing to my keep. Besides, the papers contend that the disease has run its course in Town, so his men should return to work soon."

Jane sighed. "I was not going to mention it, but he asked Markus to bring the children home. They should be here tomorrow."

"I shall be glad for the opportunity to see them before I accept another position."

"My prayer was that you would stay long enough to get to know—"

"Jane, I feel as though I have lost the only man I will ever love for a second time. You cannot possibly expect me to consider other men when my heart is still broken."

"You are correct. I apologise."

Elizabeth moved to sit on the chaise with Jane. Giving her a hug, she said, "I knew you would understand."

William's rooms

Richard found the door to the sitting room open, so he slipped in. Not seeing anyone, he opened the door to William's bedroom to find he was not there either. Just as he turned to leave, he caught sight of his cousin through the French doors that opened onto the balcony.

He stopped to observe William before going any farther. His cousin was sitting in an upholstered chair with one leg propped upon a footstool layered with pillows. Dressed in only a shirt and breeches, the knee that gave him so much misery was fully displayed, wrapped in layers of muslin strips that had been soaked in salve, just as Richard had so often seen it in the past.

"May I tell the master that you are here, Lord Matlock?"

Richard turned around to find William's long-time valet behind him. Tall and completely grey-haired, the distinguished-looking Mr. Martin carried a tray with a pot of tea.

"I wanted to observe him first, Martin. You and I both know that Darcy will never admit to being in pain—at least not to me. Tell me honestly. How is he faring?"

"His knee is very painful today. I just finished applying the concoction that Dr. Graham prescribed for when it is particularly painful. That should give him some relief for several hours."

"Does he still require laudanum?"

"Not regularly, no," the valet answered. "He will not take that unless he has gone for days at a time without sleep and then only a scant spoonful."

"I am glad to hear it. I saw too many men ruined by laudanum when I was in His Majesty's service. Other than the pain in his leg, does he have any other complaint?"

The valet sighed. "He seems very despondent, sir. I thought perhaps Lady Marianne's absence might be the reason."

"I fear you are mistaken," Richard replied. "Normally, I would not share this, but I want you to be aware of the depth of my cousin's misery so that you may keep a careful watch over him. Darcy is downcast because he believes the woman he loves does not return his affection."

"I cannot fathom any woman being so foolish."

"Nor can I, but misunderstandings happen. That is why I am in London—to correct that mistake. Knowing Darcy as I do, he could refuse to listen and may even order me to leave. If that is the case, I will need your assistance. I know that you care for my cousin and would not want anything to happen to him."

"Oh, no, sir!"

"I am requesting that if he orders me to leave, you do not let him out of your sight. You must inform me immediately if he begins to drink heavily, asks for too much medication, or decides to leave London. I will be at my townhouse and will respond immediately."

"I will be pleased to assist however I can," Mr. Martin said. "Now, I had better take this tea out, or he will wonder what has kept me."

"Go ahead! I shall be right behind you."

William was thumbing through the post and did not notice as Richard walked out behind the valet. After Mr. Martin set the tray down and poured a cup of tea, William took one sip before declaring, "Drat!"

"Is it cold?" the valet asked.

"No. The tea is fine," William answered, holding up a letter. "I completely forgot that my godson is to be married the end of this week!"

"You have a lot on your mind, sir," the valet stated. "If you do not need anything else, I shall be in the dressing room seeing to the necessary garments for your journey."

"Thank you, Martin."

With the valet's departure, Richard came into view. "Lord Beauford's son is getting married again? I thought Viscount Righton's wife died only a few months ago."

"Where the devil did you come from?" William asked.

"Why from Derbyshire, as if you did not know," Richard replied, trying to lighten the mood.

"You know what I meant," William snapped. "And why is it my servants never announce you anymore?"

"Oh, come now, Cousin! You never cared about such things in the past. Barnes told me you were upstairs, and I followed Mr. Martin onto the balcony. There is no conspiracy."

"From now on I wish to know when you arrive."

"Why? To keep me from hearing your secrets?"

"I have not been able to hide anything from you since I started wearing breeches."

"This is true," Richard said, suppressing a smile. "So, as I was saying, if memory serves, Righton's wife died recently. Is he not in a bit of a rush to marry again?"

"Actually, it will be a year next month, and she left him with four small children to rear. I am surprised he has not married before now."

"That long? Time certainly flies." Richard watched William read the letter again. "Given your current condition, surely you will not attend." At William's look of incredulity, he added, "It does not take a genius to see you are in pain."

"If I stayed home every time my leg pained me, I would never go anywhere. Having said that, I *would* prefer to miss the wedding and send a gift but, alas, as his godfather, I cannot."

"Where is the wedding being held?"

"That is where the issue lies. They are having it at their cottage in Southend."

"That is no cottage! It has at least fifteen rooms and is a good fifty miles down a barely passable road. If you are in pain now, how will you cope after making such a trip?"

"I shall just have to take Mr. Martin. He can wrap my leg again once we arrive," William answered. "Now, it is time you explain what brings you here."

"I went to Pemberley, and they told me you were in London, so here I am."

"That does not answer my question."

"In your present frame of mind, I fear you may not appreciate why I came."

"Which is?"

"I came in hope of repairing your relationship with Miss Bennet."

William dropped his head. "Then you have wasted your time. Elizabeth made it clear in her letter that she had rather continue in service than be married to half a man."

"I do not believe she said that," Richard retorted.

Reaching under a stack of papers, William pulled out Elizabeth's letter and began to read parts of it.

"*It is fortunate that Providence called you away from Matlock Manor when it did, for it afforded me time to think more clearly. Otherwise, I might have been swept up by emotion and come to a decision we both would regret later.*

And then this! *I am an excellent governess and pride myself in that ability, so do not think me disheartened. I have learned how to make the most of the opportunities I have been given, and I am quite satisfied with my lot.*

"Is that not clear enough?" William demanded. "She had rather continue as a governess than become my wife."

"Only you would interpret her words in that manner," Richard replied. "And for heaven's sake, stop calling yourself half a man!"

"What do you call someone who cannot walk more than a hundred yards without crippling pain, who rides with the greatest of difficulty and is useless on a ballroom floor?"

Richard did not answer, for by then he had noticed something peculiar about the letter. "Let me see that."

William handed him the missive and watched, puzzled, as his cousin held it up to the sun. "What are you looking for? Something to prove Elizabeth wrote it?" William said sarcastically.

"A fine, vellum paper such as this does not have blemishes. Therefore, I can only conclude that these dark smudges are teardrops. Miss Bennet must have been crying when she penned this."

Since that was contrary to the explanation William had invented for himself, he snatched the letter from his cousin's hand. "You assume too much."

"Do I? Or is it you who has assumed too much?"

William shifted uneasily in his chair. "I refuse to discuss Elizabeth's motives any longer."

"If you refuse to discuss her, I shall not be able to tell you why she left my employ in such a hurry."

William released a heavy sigh but did not reply.

"Do you wish to know?"

Reluctantly, he nodded. Richard began to explain what Ellen had overheard and to relate his subsequent discussions with Marjorie and Lady Parker.

"She may be your sister, but I loathe that woman's condescending attitude. That she would plot against Elizabeth does not surprise me in the least," William continued, his voice rising in proportion to his anger. "She has relentlessly pursued me since her husband's death, even though I have made it abundantly clear I am not interested."

"I apologise. I should have put my foot down sooner, for apparently Amy also suggested that your daughter and mine let Miss Bennet overhear them talking about why she would never be accepted by our family and, in particular, by Marianne as her mother."

William's brows furrowed. "I find it hard to believe my daughter would be involved in something so cruel and deceitful."

"Marianne is young and impressionable. It was easy to convince her that she was protecting you from a conniving woman out to trap you in a marriage that would elevate Miss Bennet's status whilst ruining your own. Add to that the suggestion that such a marriage would ruin Marianne's chances to make an advantageous match, and you have the perfect argument for following my sister's advice."

"You speak as though you have already talked to Marianne."

"I have."

William's expression darkened. "Did it ever occur to you to ask my permission? She is *my* child?"

"First of all, if she is old enough to interfere in your relationship with Miss Bennet, she is no child. And, secondly, my Marjorie is only a year older, and I was no harder on Marianne than I was on my own daughter."

"Still, to confront her whilst I was not—"

"Darcy, I thought both of you would be at Pemberley. When I discovered you were in London, I felt I had no choice but to ask her about Marjorie's confession. If there is a chance you might be able to turn this disaster around, you have to act now."

William came to his feet, hissing with the pain. "What did Marianne tell you?"

Richard pulled Marianne's letter from his pocket and held it out. "This letter speaks for itself."

William took it and began reading.

Papa,

If you are reading this, then Cousin Richard has told you how horrible I was to Miss Bennet. I beg you to forgive me for being so unkind and disapproving. You see, it was only after Richard told me of your prior acquaintance that I truly understood how foolish I had been to think she was playing you for a fool.

I am genuinely repentant and have written a letter of apology to Miss Bennet, which Richard promised to deliver should he find her. If possible, I would willingly apologise to her in person as well.

Oh, Papa! Please forgive me. I am heartbroken to think

how much I have hurt you and her.
Love,
Marianne

After he read the missive, William stood staring at it for a long time.

At length, Richard said, "Darcy, I apologise if my actions upset you, but I felt you deserved to know the truth."

William nodded.

"I shall leave and let you ponder the matter. Just send word when you are ready to look for Miss Bennet. I have the address of her sister in Cheapside and of her uncle's warehouse.

As Richard turned to leave, William spoke. "Forgive me. I... I am angry at myself, not you. I should have taught Marianne more concern for those who are not as wealthy as we are and who do not have our connections. If she is too proud, it is my fault."

Richard closed his eyes and let go a deep sigh. "You are like a brother, Darcy. No! I am closer to you than I was to my brother. I would never purposefully hurt you."

"I know. Just as I would never purposefully hurt you."

With that William went silent again, and Richard left to return to his own townhouse.

Chapter 15

London

Thinking William would want to begin looking for Elizabeth the next day, Richard rose early and dressed to await his cousin's summons. When a summons came, however, it was not from William, but from his valet. Mr. Martin's missive was short and to the point.

Mr. Darcy is planning to leave London today.

When Richard arrived at Darcy House, he asked Mr. Barnes to announce him and followed the butler up the stairs. Mr. Martin was helping his master dress as they entered the bedroom.

Richard barely waited to be announced before saying, "Since you are leaving London, does that mean you have discovered where Miss Bennet has gone?"

"I have not. And how do you know I am leaving? It was only this morning that I decided to go."

As Mr. Martin straightened his master's cravat, he shot an anxious glance in Richard's direction.

Skimming the room, Richard quickly found a plausible answer. "Your trunk has been pulled from the closet. What else could it mean?"

William seemed satisfied. "Lord Beauford asked me to come

early, so I am travelling to Southend. That will allow me more time to rest before the ceremony."

"Surely you want to make things right with Miss Bennet before you leave."

William dismissed his valet, and as soon as Mr. Martin departed, he addressed Richard's question.

"I have had plenty of time to reflect on all that you told me, and I am of the opinion that Elizabeth did not leave because of something she overheard. As appalling as that would be, I believe she fled because she did not want to tell me that she would not welcome another offer of marriage from me."

"Darcy, you cannot possibly believe that."

"The Elizabeth Bennet I knew would never let other people's opinions govern her choices. She once told me that she was resolved to act in a manner which would constitute her own happiness. Even if she had overheard Marianne and Marjorie, had she still had feelings for me, I believe she would have stood her ground. On reflection, it seems clear she had no idea I suffered from... from *limitations* until the day I joined her at the gazebo. After that, it was merely a matter of time until she fled to avoid an offer she could not accept."

"I never took you for a coward, Cousin."

William whirled on him angrily. "I could easily have facilitated a compromise to make Elizabeth my wife, but I did not. It took all the willpower I possess to let her walk away."

"I think you are mistaking surrender for strength."

"Strength? You have no idea the torment I went through after the accident, for I kept the worst of it to myself. But the pain in my body was nothing compared to the chasm in my heart—knowing I failed Elizabeth, and in doing so, had lost her forever. And now to lose her a second time—"

"You did your level best. That is all anyone could ask."

"But it was not enough! Then, after my marriage, I realised Aunt Eleanor had conspired with Cornelia's mother to play me for a fool! I felt as though it would have been better if I had died in the accident. The only thing that kept me from utter despair after Cornelia died was knowing Marianne had no one else to care for her."

"What Mother did was horrendous, and I told her so."

"I am grateful for your support."

"I know there is much I do not understand about your relationship with Miss Bennet," Richard continued. "Still, I stand by my opinion that you are a coward when it comes to one thing: risking your heart again."

William closed his eyes. "For years I was uncertain if I was going to survive losing Elizabeth. Now, I had rather we part like this than hear her say that she does not want me."

Richard crossed the room to clasp his cousin's shoulder. "Love is never easy, Darcy. Go after her! Hear the truth from her!"

William slowly shook his head. "My mind is made up, and I hope you will accept my decision."

Richard crossed his fingers. "I will try."

"Would you like to accompany me to Southend-on-Sea? I am sure Lord Beauford would not mind. He remembers you from visits to Pemberley when we were boys. He asks about you often."

"No. I think I shall stay here and finish some work I have neglected for far too long."

"I should return in a sennight. If you are still here, perhaps we can dine together."

"I shall look forward to it."

After leaving Darcy House, Richard instructed his driver to head towards Cheapside. He intended to call on Elizabeth's uncle at his warehouse to ask his help in locating the address she had provided in her letter. Moreover, he wished to do it all before the day was over.

The Cowan residence

The coach bringing the children home arrived just before tea. Jonathan, who had come home early from work to welcome them, stood beside Jane and Elizabeth on the portico, waiting for the vehicle to come to a stop. Once it had, they rushed forward to greet the children and their housekeeper.

Elizabeth was as eager to see her nephews and nieces as their parents were and as she welcomed them it was not lost on her that if she had accepted Mr. Darcy's proposal in Kent, she would likely have children of similar ages by now. After accepting gentlemanly kisses on the cheek from Thomas and David, she stooped to receive hugs and kisses from the youngest two, Betsy and Susanna.

"I am so glad you are here, Aunt Lizzy," Susanna, said. "When we got the letter from Mama saying you had come, I prayed you would still be here."

Before Elizabeth could answer, six-year-old Betsy added, "I did, too, Aunt Lizzy. Will you stay with us a long time?"

"I have no idea," Elizabeth said with a wistful smile. "But I plan to make the most of our time together before I leave again."

"Children!" Jane declared, "I know you must be famished. Go inside and change clothes. Then, meet us in the dining room where cakes, sandwiches and tea are waiting to be served."

Squeals of delight rang out as the children sprinted towards the house with their parents on their heels, ineffectually warning them not to run.

Jane and Jonathan's departure left Markus and Elizabeth alone. He was standing with his hat in his hands, watching her, which made Elizabeth nervous. As she struck out towards the house, Markus hastened to catch up with her, and they walked alongside each other silently until they reached the steps to the portico.

"Miss Elizabeth. I am so pleased you are here, for I have long wanted to know you better."

Elizabeth, who had kept her eyes averted, was surprised, for in the past Markus had been too shy to speak first. Immediately, the thought occurred to her that Jonathan might have encouraged him to be bolder.

"I feel we already know each other well, Mr. Cowan."

"Markus," he corrected her.

"Markus," she repeated. "After all, my sister and your brother have been married more than a decade, and we have been in each other's company many times."

"But we have never had opportunity to talk privately. I hope to remedy that whilst we are here."

Elizabeth swallowed with great difficulty. "As I am an unmarried woman, it is only proper that we are not left alone."

Having reached the front door, she forced a smile at the footman posted there before hurrying across the foyer to the stairs. Halfway up, she met Jonathan coming down. He was treated to an equally contrived smile as they passed without speaking.

In the foyer below, Markus was left staring after her. When his brother joined him, he said, "Elizabeth does not seem eager to know me better."

"Jane always said Lizzy is headstrong, and I have to agree. Still, my sister needs to marry and settle down, and who better to do that with than you?"

"You make it sound so simple, but when I mentioned talking privately, she resisted."

"Something happened at her last position which left Lizzy more despondent than I have ever seen her. She asked Jane to keep secret what occurred, so I do not know the particulars. Still, if ever there was a time to persuade her to give up a life of service, it is now."

Unconvinced, Markus only nodded.

"Try not to let Lizzy's attitude dissuade you," Jonathan said, slipping an arm around his brother's shoulder. "Jane believes Lizzy is close to agreeing that marriage would be in her best interest. Now, let me show you to your room."

Cheapside
Gardiner's Warehouse

After getting lost in Cheapside, Richard finally located Mr. Gardiner's warehouse. To be truthful, he might have found it sooner had he not been concentrating his attention on the smaller establishments. As it turned out, Elizabeth's uncle had one of the largest warehouses in that part of town. From the outside, it was plain that the establishment encompassed two neighbouring warehouses that had been combined. One could go in either building entrance and use the connecting passage-way to reach the other warehouse whilst browsing the goods for sale. Richard found the design most inventive and spent a bit of time admiring the selection of merchandise. Then, spotting an older gentleman behind a counter, he walked in that direction.

"Excuse me. Would you be the proprietor?"

"Oh, no, sir!" the man answered. "That would be Mr. Gardiner."

"Would you please tell him that Lord Matlock would like to speak with him?"

"Certainly. Please wait here. I believe he is still in his office." The man went towards the back of the facility and disappeared through a doorway.

Not long afterwards, a portly, grey-haired man came out and headed straight towards him. Upon reaching Richard, he held out a hand, though his expression was full of uncertainty.

"Edward Gardiner, at your service. I assume you are Lord Matlock."

Richard shook the hand. "I am. It is a pleasure to meet you."

Mr. Gardiner looked Richard over guardedly. "Have you come about my niece, or are you here to purchase something?"

"I have come about Miss Bennet."

"Then please follow me to my office so we may talk in private."

Richard followed the man to the back of the building, through a door, and down a panelled corridor, which ended at an ornately carved door that led into a well-appointed office.

Once inside Mr. Gardiner's office, that gentleman motioned for Richard to have a seat in a large leather chair in front of a magnificent, mahogany desk. Then he went to a cabinet upon which sat a pot of tea and some china cups. Taking one of the cups, he held it up, asking, "Would you care for some tea?"

"I would."

"Sugar?"

"Two lumps would be perfect."

After setting Richard's tea in front of him, Mr. Gardiner fixed his own cup and moved to sit in the chair behind the desk. The minute Elizabeth's uncle was seated, Richard seized the opportunity to get straight to the point.

"I am here because I would like to speak to Miss Bennet and hoped you would know where I might find her."

"I do know, but from what I have heard, she left your employment in a state of upheaval. Her sister, Jane, has been very worried about Lizzy because she has become a virtual recluse since her return to London."

"That is why I have come, to try to set things to rights."

"I do not understand."

Richard took a sip of his tea, then said, "I have reason to believe she is in love with my cousin and fled my employment to avoid facing him when he returned to my home. I wish to assure her that my cousin is deeply in love with her, as well."

"Your cousin?"

"Fitzwilliam Darcy of Pemberley in Derbyshire."

Mr. Gardiner looked down at his desk as though considering Richard's declaration. At length he said, "If Mr. Darcy is in love with Lizzy, why is he not looking for her instead of you?"

"Simply because my cousin is too much of a gentleman to force a meeting."

"Excuse me? I do not have the pleasure of understanding you."

Richard leaned forward, his expression growing solemn.

"May I ask for your discretion regarding what I am about to say? My cousin is a very private man and would not appreciate my discussing this with you."

"You have my word."

"Years ago, Darcy suffered a grave injury to his leg that left him with a limp. The injury, which prevents him doing many things other men take for granted, happened after you and your party left Lambton when word reached Miss Bennet that her sister had fled with Mr. Wickham."

"So you know of Lydia's ruin?"

"Only because Darcy almost died in a coach accident trying to retrieve her. He talked a good bit in his delirium."

"I had no idea he was injured trying to save Lydia."

"Neither does Miss Bennet. He is too proud to tell her. Moreover, he thinks his infirmity repulses her and that she left my employment to avoid telling him she does not wish to marry him."

"My Lizzy is not a shallow person. If she loved him, any incapacity would not matter."

"I believe that. And, I would be negligent if I did not mention my wife's sister, Lady Parker, made the situation worse by suggesting to Darcy's daughter and mine that they let Miss Bennet overhear them say marrying her would ruin my cousin's reputation. You have to understand that Lady Parker has relentlessly pursued Darcy since her husband died, and she recognises Miss Bennet for the threat she is to her plans."

"I see," Mr. Gardiner said. Clutching his chin with one hand, he rubbed a thumb slowly across it whilst pondering what to do. Finally, he came to a decision.

"As Lizzy's protector, I request you not contact her until I grant you permission. She is so fragile at present that she told Jane she wishes to hide from the world. Should we force a meeting with you, she could flee London without any of us knowing where she has gone."

Though disappointed, Richard understood. "I only wish to resolve any misunderstandings and give my cousin and Miss Bennet the chance to be happy."

"I appreciate your purpose in coming here. I will speak to Lizzy without divulging you are in Town and see how she reacts when I suggest she needs to face her fears instead of running from them."

Richard nodded, then reached into his pocket and brought out one of his cards. "Please contact me after you have spoken with her."

Mr. Gardiner took the card and read it. "I shall."

Southend-on-Sea
That evening

By the time William's coach arrived at Lord Beauford's house, he was bone weary and ready to retire. That was not to be, however, for his host insisted he eat dinner with him and his family and the guests who had already arrived for the wedding. With no convenient excuse to decline, William had Mr. Martin help him change clothes and rewrap his knee in new muslin strips, howbeit without applying the foul-smelling salve, and went downstairs to join the others.

Just as he entered the parlour where everyone had gathered to await the bell announcing dinner, he was accosted by one of the most irritating matrons of his acquaintance—Lady Allcorn.

"Oh, Mr. Darcy!" the elderly lady exclaimed as she came towards him clutching the hands of two young women who looked to be in their early twenties.

From their red hair, round, plain faces and portly figures, it was obvious that they were relations of Lady Allcorn. William braced himself for the confrontation.

"I was delighted to hear that you were attending Viscount Righton's wedding. We see so little of you in London these days that I told my daughter I simply must bring the twins with me, since you have never met either of them."

Busily trying to think of what to say, William had not replied when Lady Allcorn began the introductions. "Mr. Darcy, this is Lady Peregrina, my Margaret's oldest, and this," she pushed the other one forward, "is Lady Florinda, the second born. Peregrina, Florinda, this is Mr. Fitzwilliam Darcy of Pemberley in Derbyshire."

William performed a curt bow whilst the young ladies curtseyed, saying in unison, "Pleased to meet you, Mr. Darcy."

"Likewise," William managed to murmur.

The ladies' eyes sparkled as they awaited William's next words, but the introduction was followed by an awkward silence. Suddenly, someone slipped an arm through his. "There you are, Mr. Darcy! I was wondering what was taking you so long."

William turned to see a beauty with light brown hair and blue eyes, of approximately three and thirty years, wearing a gown the colour of her eyes. She was smiling at him as though they shared a secret. William was so shaken by her gall he could not speak.

That seemed to suit the woman, who addressed Lady Allcorn and her granddaughters. "I am sure that you ladies will excuse us. Mr. Darcy and I have much to catch up on."

As she guided him away from Lady Allcorn's trap, she whispered, "Just follow my lead."

She guided him out of the parlour and into the hallway where she stopped to explain. "I saw that look of desperation on your face and felt I simply must rescue you from that woman and her ugly ducklings."

William could not hold back a smile. "Thank you, but tell me: Why should you help me when we have never met? Which begs the question, how do you know my name?"

"I am not surprised you do not remember me, but I certainly remember you," she replied, smiling beguilingly at the man she had never forgotten. Even though his hair was interspersed with silver, she thought William more handsome now than before. "I had not reached my majority when my brother began attending university with you."

"Your brother?"

"Lord Tolbert."

"Then you must be Gwennie."

She laughed. "No one has called me that in years, and my mother would be quite put out if she heard you." She looked around. "She is somewhere in the crowd."

"And your brother? Is he here?"

"Barrett lives in Ireland with his wife and three children. We do not see him as often as we would like."

William nodded. "I do not recall reading about your marriage. Is your husband here, too?"

"I have never married," she said, smiling conspiratorially. "When I was younger, I did not believe in that storied institution, and at my age, decent men are hard to find. Barrett inherited our father's estate in Ireland, and I am to inherit my grandmother's small estate in Sussex after mother passes. You cannot imagine how many offers I get from men who only want me for what I will have eventually."

"I believe I can."

Lady Gwendolyn instantly flushed crimson. "How foolish of me! Of course, you would be very familiar with that problem."

Just then the butler stepped into the hall and rang the dinner bell. Gwendolyn looked to William.

"Will you escort me to dinner and sit beside me? That will make mother very happy, and it will keep me from being forced to carry on a conversation with some old bore." She added with a wink, "Besides, it will save you from having to entertain the twins—one on either side."

William held out an arm. "Shall we?"

Chapter 16

Lord Beauford's cottage
Two days later

Lady Gwendolyn Tolbert had been smitten with Fitzwilliam Darcy since the age of fifteen, when her breath had been stolen by one smile from her brother's handsome new classmate. She had accompanied her mother to Cambridge to visit Barrett at the house he, Mr. Darcy and Lord Applegate had rented whilst attending university. From that day forward, she had made it her quest to learn everything possible about the man from her unsuspecting brother in the letters they exchanged and during his visits home. The first and most important thing she discovered had been reassuring, for Barrett revealed that Mr. Darcy had resolved not to marry until after he finished university, which would allow her time to grow up.

After that, whenever she brought up the subject of his friend, Barrett had extolled Darcy's kindness, intelligence and sense of honour. Having no doubt that Mr. Darcy would never leave his wife in the country whilst he cavorted all over London with courtesans as she had heard men of the *ton* often did, Gwendolyn set her cap to marry him. Subsequently, whilst Barrett attended Cambridge, she visited frequently in order to make an impression on the man of her dreams; however, although Mr.

Darcy was always kind, his attentiveness had never gone beyond a greeting and a few polite questions regarding her trip.

As a result, by the time he and her brother graduated, Gwendolyn had been out in society for a year and had given up on Mr. Darcy. Having witnessed many of her friends' marriages turn to imprisonments once the vows were spoken, she was in no hurry to pick a suitor from the admirers relentlessly dogging her steps and was easily convinced to accompany her mother to visit relations in Spain.

Upon her return to England, she learned not only had Mr. Darcy almost been killed in a coach accident, but he was newly engaged. The announcement reporting his engagement to Lady Cornelia was particularly galling because Gwendolyn knew the woman. Deeply disappointed that Mr. Darcy had chosen someone so dreadful for a wife, she had sailed to Ireland to live with her brother and his new wife, hoping to purge him from her heart. It was only after her mother's declining health had forced her return to England years later that Mr. Darcy crossed her mind again.

At the moment, Gwendolyn considered herself most fortunate to have stumbled upon her brother's other housemate whilst in London. Lord Applegate had informed her that Mr. Darcy had been a widower for the better part of fourteen years. Moreover, he enquired if she planned to attend the wedding of Viscount Righton in Southend because it was rumoured Darcy would be in attendance since he was Righton's godfather.

"You may not realise this, but meeting Darcy by happenstance these days is nearly impossible," Lord Applegate had said with a laugh. "He lives like a hermit at Pemberley. I cannot boast of having seen him more than once in the last year."

Gwendolyn had laughed along with Lord Applegate, but as soon as they parted, she had used her connections to gain an invitation to the wedding. Determined to make the most of the opportunity to be reacquainted with the one man who still made her heart flutter when he came to mind, she had rushed to Lord Beauford's cottage a few days early, hoping Mr. Darcy would do the same.

Gwendolyn had not been disappointed, for shortly after she arrived, Fitzwilliam Darcy had too. Rescuing him from the clutches of Lady Allcorn that day had been particularly fortuitous, for Barrett had often mentioned how much Darcy detested being confronted by conniving women. However, by the next day, Gwendolyn worried that Mr. Darcy might have thought her too brazen, as well. When she had no luck finding him amongst the guests, she had her maid enquire among Lord Beauford's servants and learned Mr. Darcy had kept to his room that day.

It was not until the following morning that she caught sight of him again. Walking onto the balcony of her bedroom, she spied William standing on the terrace below. He was watching workmen erect a white tent in the lower portion of the yard, so she rushed down the stairs and out of the house as quickly as possible.

Approaching him, she said, "It is a beautiful day." Seeing William flinch, she quickly added, "Forgive me. I did not mean to startle you."

"No need for apologies," William said, turning to observe her. "I fear I was lost in thought and did not hear you coming."

"Might I offer a penny for those thoughts?"

William smiled wryly. "They are not worth nearly that much."

"Still, I would love to hear them."

At length, William murmured, "I was just thinking that when life seems to be going well, something always comes along to spoil it. Happiness never seems to last very long."

"Spoken like a true cynic."

William dropped his head. "I should not have answered so candidly. You now know why I am rarely invited to these events. One wishes to invite pleasant company, not curmudgeons."

"Yet, you are here!" she said with a laugh.

William had to laugh as well. "Only because I am the groom's godfather."

"I find your honesty refreshing. Pretence is boring. Besides, what good is conversation if it is all a lie?"

"Then you are certainly *not* like most of the women of my acquaintance."

"I am pleased that you have finally noticed."

"What do you mean?"

"I tried to gain your notice the entire time you were at Cambridge with my brother. And all the while, you had no idea I existed."

"You were merely a child then."

"I was fifteen when we met and nineteen by the time you graduated."

"In my mind, you will always be Barrett's baby sister."

Smiling beguilingly, she answered, "Do I look like someone's baby sister now?"

"No," William replied, his eyes taking in every inch of her. "Definitely not."

Her laughter rang out. "Thank heaven!" Gwendolyn quickly changed the subject. "Why is the tent being set up there? It needs to be along the beach where guests can have a better view of the ceremony inside the gazebo."

"Lord Beauford thinks storms may set in before the wedding, and a tent on the beach is more vulnerable to the wind. Where it is presently, it is anchored to posts in the ground."

"I suppose he is right," Gwendolyn said with a shrug. Then, stealing a sideways glance at William, she added, "I was just about to take a walk along the beach. Would you care to join me?"

"I am afraid that my valet is expecting me. The trip here aggravated an old injury, and if I am to attend the wedding without having to rely on my cane, I must return to my room and let him work his magic on my knee. Given enough rest, the pain will diminish."

Gwendolyn's brows knit. "I had no idea you were still suffering. You do not act as though you are in pain."

"After fourteen years, one learns to live with it."

She smiled compassionately. "How much rest is required?"

"Another day off my feet should be sufficient."

"Perhaps the day of the wedding, after the bride and groom have left on their honeymoon, you and I could walk down to the gazebo.

"I plan to leave directly after the ceremony."

"You cannot be serious!" she exclaimed. "Lord Beauford will be hurt if you do not stay. He planned dinner and dancing for all his guests so they would not have to travel until the next day. Besides, how far would you get before darkness would make it necessary to stop at an inn? Surely, you would be more comfortable here."

"My plans are open to change. Were the rain to—"

"Exactly!" Lady Gwendolyn interrupted. "Now, I shall leave you to your valet. Perhaps with a little luck, he will work wonders, and you will consider asking me to dance."

"I think not."

Lady Gwendolyn smiled brilliantly. "Ah, I recall your dislike of the activity. I will not mention dancing again if you will at least accompany me to dinner."

William forced a smile. "I had much rather dine than dance."

"Excellent!" she said. "Now, I shall leave you to your valet's care and try to find someone else to walk with me today."

Hurrying towards the house, she turned to catch his eye and gave him one last smile before disappearing inside.

London
The Cowan residence
That same day

Elizabeth had been disconcerted since her uncle's visit the day before. Edward Gardiner had never been one to pry; instead, he would wait patiently until she was ready to discuss her concerns. To have him enquire as to why she left Lord Matlock's employment and suggest she face her fears rather than run from them had caught her entirely off-guard.

She had politely answered that she was not running from

her fears—though she was no longer certain that was true—but she simply wanted to work outside the sphere of Lord Matlock's influence. Her uncle had not appeared satisfied by her explanation. Instead, he challenged her to get in touch with her former employer and be more specific about why she left, so there would be no misunderstandings when she applied for another position.

In addition, Elizabeth had grown increasingly tired of trying to avoid Markus' attempts to engage her in conversations about marriage. All of these burdens propelled Elizabeth to make a spur-of-the-moment decision, and the moment Jane entered her room she blurted out her request.

"Will you please ask Jonathan to lend me your coach so I may join Aunt Gardiner and our cousins at the sea?"

"What has made you decide to leave us so suddenly? Did Uncle Edward persuade you to join them?"

"No, but I suspect he may have spoken to Lord Matlock. If the earl is in town, he could appear on your doorstep at any second."

"Would that be so terrible?"

Tears filled Elizabeth's eyes, and she turned to cover her face with her hands. Instantly Jane was behind her sister, wrapping loving arms around her. "Oh, Lizzy, please do not cry."

Elizabeth withdrew a handkerchief from her pocket and dabbed at her eyes. "I am not crying," she said. Then, taking a deep breath to calm herself, she shook her head as though to make the tears disappear. "It is—I wanted to keep my reasons for leaving his employ vague. If I speak to Lord Matlock, he could ask questions I do not want to answer. Such as whether or not I am in love with Fitzwilliam. I could not possibly compose myself enough to convince Lord Matlock that I am not. Once he knows, his cousin will know, and I will be exposed as a fool still in love with a man too far above my station."

"As I have said before, suppose you are wrong. What if Mr. Darcy *is* in love with you?"

"I am certain Lady Parker reminded Mr. Darcy that a marriage to someone so far beneath his rank would affect his daughter's chances for a good match, and that is why he departed so suddenly. But even should he love me, I would only become a wedge between him and his daughter, and I could not live with that on my conscience."

"It is impossible to win an argument with you!" Jane declared. Then her voice softened. "At least you are not leaving because of Markus." At the incredulous look that crossed Elizabeth's face, Jane added, "Or are you?"

Elizabeth sighed. "Markus is partially responsible for my wanting to leave. I hinted I am not interested in him, but he refuses to listen. I believe Jonathan has influenced him into pressing me to accept an offer, for Markus has never acted like this in all the years I have known him."

"Jonathan has said nothing to me about such a scheme, but I know he worries about you, just as I do. And, of course, he thinks his brother is a good match for you. He believes Markus will make a good husband and father."

"I am certain he will—for a woman who returns his affection. I appreciate Jonathan's concern, but you must make him stop trying to pair us. This is my life, and I intend to live it my way."

Now tears filled Jane's eyes, making Elizabeth feel guilty. Pulling her sister into an embrace, she added, "I would not hurt you or Jonathan for the world, or Markus for that matter, but I must do what I know to be right."

When Jane did not answer, Elizabeth pulled back to look at her. "Now. May I please borrow the coach to visit our aunt in Southend-on-Sea?"

Jane produced a weak smile. "Of course you may."

Elizabeth kissed her sister's forehead. "Thank you! I believe that being able to walk on the sand, sit by the sea, and listen to the waves may be just what I need to lift my spirits."

"You may be right. When do you want to leave?"

"Tomorrow morning."

"Then you will need all of your clothes readied," Jane replied, blinking back tears. "I shall tell the maid to see to it and to begin packing your trunk."

Jane looked so forlorn that Elizabeth added, "I promise to visit you again before I take another position."

Smiling wanly, Jane said, "I will hold you to that."

Cheapside
Gardiner's Warehouse
The next day

Being anxious to set things to right and not having heard from Mr. Gardiner, Richard decided to seek out Elizabeth's uncle again. After entering Mr. Gardiner's warehouse, he found the man with several of his employees on the dock in the rear of his business. They were cataloguing a new shipment of goods, and Richard waited until they had finished to call above the noise of the alley.

"May I speak to you, Mr. Gardiner?"

Once he recognised Richard, Gardiner appeared perturbed. "Lord Matlock, I was just about to send you a letter, but since you are here, it will save me the trouble. Please follow me to my office."

Once there, Mr. Gardiner sank down in the chair behind his desk and began nervously twirling between his fingers the pencil he had been using to mark his inventory. Richard, growing impatient, was about to ask after Elizabeth when Mr. Gardiner began to speak.

"To be truthful, I was not certain until a few minutes ago that I should allow you to speak to Lizzy."

"What happened to change your mind?"

"I received this note from her sister, Jane." Mr. Gardiner reached for a piece of paper on the corner of his desk and read it again silently. "It seems that after I spoke with Lizzy, she decided to leave London."

"She has left already?" Richard asked incredulously.

"Yes," Mr. Gardiner said, sighing heavily. "I had hoped she would decide it was in her best interest to speak with you, and then I could reveal that you were here. I had no idea she would leave so abruptly."

"You did warn me that she might flee."

"Still, I never expected it to happen so quickly. To be honest, I have never seen my niece afraid to face any problem. That is what bothers me the most—that she does not appear to want to know all the facts. Still, once she does, if she clings to her opinion, I will have to respect her wishes."

"I completely agree. I only want her and Darcy to know exactly how the other feels. If their love for each other cannot overcome what they perceive as obstacles, then perhaps it was not meant to be." He watched Edward Gardiner nod in agreement before asking, "Do you know where Miss Bennet went?"

"To Southend-on-Sea. With the sickness in London, I sent my wife, children and grandchild to a cottage I own there."

Richard could not suppress the smile that crossed his face. "Southend is only six and thirty miles from London. One can make that trip in a day's time."

"If the weather is clear, they certainly can," Mr. Gardiner replied.

"Where is your cottage located in Southend?"

"Are you familiar with Lord Beauford's estate?"

"I am."

"My property used to be part of that. One of my ancestors worked as a butler for a previous Lord Beauford. Apparently, he was so well thought of that when he retired, a small cottage and the land it occupied were deeded to him. It has been in my family for over a century."

Richard began to chuckle.

"Do you find it amusing that a tradesman would own a cottage by the sea?"

"Nothing of the kind, sir! I find it amusing that Providence seems to be guiding my cousin and your niece back to each other. You see, Darcy is at Southend this very minute, attending the wedding of—"

"Viscount Righton!" Mr. Gardiner interjected, breaking into a smile. "Mrs. Gardiner has talked of nothing else in her letters. It seems Lord Beauford has constructed an enormous gazebo on the beach below the house for the ceremony."

"Will your wife be attending the wedding?"

"We are not familiar with the current Lord Beauford, and I understand the ceremony is limited to relations and close friends, so she will not attend. Still, it is exciting for Madeline to be close enough to watch all the falderal involved in organising a wedding by the sea. You know how excited women get about such things."

"I certainly do." Richard stood. "Now, if you will excuse me, I must pack and be on my way to Southend."

"You do know that Lizzy may not speak to you, even should you travel that far."

"I am determined to see this through. If Miss Bennet will not listen to me, perhaps your wife will and pass along to your niece what I have to say."

"Pray wait whilst I write my Madeline a note explaining everything." Gardiner pulled paper from a drawer in his desk and a pen from his ink stand. As he began to write, he added, "This will save you the trouble of having to convince her first."

"I am most appreciative."

"I could say the same to you. Not many gentlemen of the *ton* would want his cousin to marry someone in service."

"I want my cousin to be happy—as well as Miss Bennet. I have little patience for most of the *ton's* foolishness. I was an army officer far too long not to have common sense."

"Something I have found sorely lacking amongst the *ton*." Richard chuckled. "More often than not, so have I!"

It was not long before Richard was at his townhouse. ordering his clothes packed and his coach readied to leave early the next morning for Southend. He prayed he would be welcomed at Lord Beauford's cottage, but how would he explain his presence there to William?

He refused to worry about it, deciding he had plenty of time to think of an excuse before he arrived. That being settled, he retired early so as to be well rested for the trip.

Chapter 17

Southend-on-Sea
The Gardiners' cottage

Elizabeth had been showered with attention since her arrival. Her youngest cousins, in particular, had monopolised her company that first evening and were again vying for her attention as the family broke their fast together.

"Children, if you do not let your cousin have a few minutes peace, she may never want to visit us again," Aunt Madeline declared, chuckling. "If you have finished eating, I suggest you return to your projects. Abigail, if memory serves, you have an apron to finish, and Martha, you have not finished trimming that new bonnet. Rebecca, the puppy you found needs to go for a walk whilst the sun is still peeking through the clouds."

As the children rose from the table, Elizabeth said, "Please do not blame them, for I have enjoyed getting to know them better. My only regret is that Randall took his family back to London before I arrived."

"He felt his father needed him at the warehouse, and since the sickness has subsided, it was time to return."

Just then, ten-year-old Rebecca came back into the room with a small dog on a rope. "Do you think rain will spoil the wedding, Mama?"

"I have no idea," Madeline Gardiner replied. "But the clouds gathering in the distance do not bode well for a dry ceremony."

Abigail, a romantic at fifteen, sighed. "I think a wedding beside the sea is absolutely perfect."

Her mother smiled. "Perfect it may be, but it is not very practical."

"What do you mean?" Martha, the eldest of the sisters, asked.

"If I recall correctly, they had to limit the ceremony to close friends and family because the yard and gazebo could not accommodate all who wished to attend."

"Who is getting married?" Elizabeth asked between bites of buttered toast.

"Lord Beauford's son, Viscount Righton," her aunt replied. "The ceremony is scheduled for later this morning. Do you remember him?"

"Barely," Elizabeth replied.

"I am not surprised. He was younger than you. His poor wife died less than a year ago, leaving four small children motherless. Naturally, he needed to marry as soon as possible."

"It seems unfair to me that men are encouraged to remarry straightaway whilst women are looked down upon unless they mourn for ages. Men have all the advantages in our society. Women are only pawns on the chessboard of life."

Hearing the bitterness in her niece's voice, Madeline Gardiner hurried the children from the room and poured herself a fresh cup of tea before sitting down beside Elizabeth.

"Jane said she saw changes in you since you returned from Derbyshire, and I understand now what she meant. You were never a cynic before."

Elizabeth's brows instantly knit. "Of late, it has been hard to pretend happiness I do not feel. If that makes me a cynic, then I suppose I am."

Mrs. Gardiner reached over to pat Elizabeth's hand. "If you need a confidante, I am always available. I promise not to offer any advice unless you ask for it."

Smiling wanly, Elizabeth said, "Jane and I have already discussed everything, and we do not see eye to eye on a solution, so I doubt you and I will, either."

"Then, might I suggest you go up to the crow's nest and contemplate what Lizzy Bennet wants for the future. I believe you need to make certain you know where you want to be and why."

Elizabeth gave her aunt a hug, then pulled back, saying, "I believe I will take your advice."

The Gardiners' and Lord Beauford's cottages were the only two dwellings on a lane that began on a bluff and dwindled steadily as it wound down to the sea. Both cottages sat atop a hill, with the soil on the properties becoming sandier the closer it got to the water. A seawall, constructed of heavy timbers, had been built at the edge of the property decades before to keep the land from washing away. If one wished to access the beach, one simply negotiated a series of walking paths constructed of stones, cement and wood. At the wall, steps led to the beach below. Elizabeth had always thought the path to the beach on her uncle's property was magical, for it included several whimsical bridges with statues of fairies and woodland animals along the way.

Most cottages at Southend-on-Sea had crow's nests atop them to provide views of the sea. Some were enclosed with windows, whilst others sported only a roof. Though the Gardiners' cottage was not very large, it included an enclosed crow's nest offering stunning views which occasionally served as a bedroom.

Even as a child, Elizabeth had loved staying in the crow's nest. It contained only a small bed, a dresser with a mirror, and a washstand. Not only was it the quietest room in the house due to its isolated location, but from there one could see for miles in every direction. Once inside, it was easy to imagine one was all alone on a desert island. Moreover, the solitude it afforded had often given Elizabeth's battered soul a chance to heal in the years after she had gone into service.

Keeping up the façade of being content with her life as a governess was becoming more difficult each year. When she first went into service, she had found it fulfilling, but of late she longed for what her sisters had—children of their own. Still, she could not abide the idea of marrying someone simply to have children. No, nothing had changed since she had vowed as a girl to *marry only for the deepest love.*

Recalling how naive she had once been, Elizabeth placed her pencil inside the pages of the journal she had pulled from her bag, laid both on the bed and headed towards a large spyglass lying on a shelf. Grasping it, she walked to the windows facing the sea and lifted the glass to her eye. The wind had picked up, creating foam-tipped waves, and she found the view breath-taking. She spent the next few minutes in her crow's nest ritual—searching the horizon for boats and ships. Later, focusing the glass on the activity on the beach, her eyes were drawn to men on ladders busily fastening white tulle, vines and flowers along the roof of a large gazebo that had been erected on the shore below Lord Beauford's cottage.

How beautiful! I imagine they were afraid to put them up sooner, lest the wind blow them away.

Normally, Elizabeth would not spy on her neighbours, but she was drawn to the wedding preparations like a moth to a flame. Turning to the yard, she discovered a large white tent had been erected which obstructed her view there, so she focused her glass towards the house. There she spied several people dressed in finery standing on the brick terrace. Suddenly, one of the guests—a man—looked in her direction. Had he seen her?

Just as Elizabeth let the glass drop, a tall gentleman joined the others. His similarity to Mr. Darcy made her take another look regardless of being discovered; however, when Elizabeth raised the glass again, he was no longer in sight.

Must I see Fitzwilliam everywhere?

Disheartened, she turned her attention back to the sea. Noting that rain was now visible on the horizon, which made it impossible to see any ships, she lay the spyglass down, deciding not to chance another look at Lord Beauford's estate until the wedding began. Picking up the journal she had tossed aside, she retrieved the pencil sandwiched between the pages and lay back on the bed. Immediately upon opening it, her eyes were drawn to the lines of a poem she had copied to the first page.

No, the heart that has truly loved never forgets,
but as truly loves on to the close,
As the sunflower turns on her god, when he sets,
the same look which she turned when he rose. [4]

Why did I think it a good idea to write that there?

Elizabeth contemplated ripping that page from the journal, then thought better of it. Instead, flipping pages until she found a blank one, she began to record her feelings.

Aunt Gardiner asked what I want for the future, and I have no idea. I must begin looking for employment soon but am in no humour to start.

In the years since Lydia's ruin, the remote chance that Fitzwilliam Darcy could come back into her life had always resided in the far recesses of Elizabeth's heart, keeping a spark of hope alive.

Now that all hope is dashed, can the future hold any endearing charms?

Deciding she could not face the answer to that question today, Elizabeth closed the book again. Exhausted from the long trip the day before, she closed her eyes, and not long afterwards sleep overtook her.

In a dream, she watched herself, dressed in a white gown trimmed with lace, walking down the path to Lord Beauford's gazebo. Suddenly, a man stepped out to wait for her with outstretched arms. Though his face was hidden in the shadows, upon reaching the gazebo, she could see him clearly: *Fitzwilliam Darcy.*

---

4   *Excerpt from "Believe Me If All Those Endearing Young Charms" written in 1808 by Thomas Moore.*

That realisation combined with shouting voices brought her instantly awake.

"Wake up, Cousin Lizzy!" the sisters said in unison.

"The wedding is beginning!" Rebecca declared.

"Thank goodness the rain held off," her aunt added.

Elizabeth sat up to find her aunt and all her cousins at the windows.

"We are each to take turns looking through the spyglass!" Rebecca declared. "Mama said so!"

Martha had already seized the glass and was looking towards Lord Beauford's garden. "Here comes the bride!" she cried excitedly.

"Let me see!" Abigail said, snatching the glass from her sister.

"Now, girls," Mrs. Gardiner cautioned. "You must share, or I will send you all downstairs."

Abigail handed the spyglass to Elizabeth, who immediately focused on the bride. As the woman proceeded to the gazebo, Elizabeth reluctantly handed the glass to her aunt, who helped her youngest, Rebecca, look through it.

"The bride is so lovely," Rebecca sighed, passing the glass to her mother. "Do you not think so, Mama?"

"All brides are lovely," Mrs. Gardiner replied as she took her turn. "I had forgotten how handsome Viscount Righton is, though. That man never ages."

The wedding was short, and none of them got to see many details of it. Still, they were pleased with what they had seen by the time the bride and groom had been pronounced man and wife and the first drops of rain began pelting the gazebo. As the wedding party rushed back up the walk towards the house, Rebecca asked, "What happens now, Mama?"

"There will be a wedding breakfast with lots of food and toasts to the new couple. Then, after a respectable time, the bride and groom will change into their travelling clothes and bid the guests goodbye before departing on their honeymoon."

"What will the guests do then?" Abigail asked.

"I understand Lord Beauford is hosting a dinner tonight, so the guests do not have to travel home in the dark."

Martha sighed. "I cannot wait to be a bride."

"There is no reason to rush," her mother said.

"Oh, Mama," Martha protested. "You always say that."

"I say it because it is true! Now, you have all seen the wedding, so go back downstairs, and let Lizzy have her privacy," Mrs. Gardiner declared. As the girls headed down the stairs, she said to Elizabeth. "I hope you did not mind the interruption. The girls very much wanted to see the wedding."

"On the contrary, I am glad you woke me. I would not have wanted to miss it, either."

Mrs. Gardiner smiled. "I shall leave you to your thoughts, then."

Alone once more, a deep sense of mourning washed over Elizabeth. *You forfeited your chance to become a bride when you fled Derbyshire,* her conscience reminded her.

Since the awning windows which prevented rain from coming in unless it was particularly windy, were open on the back side of the house, she crossed to them and took deep breaths of the fresh, rain-washed air.

Stop feeling sorry for yourself, Lizzy. You will be of no use to anyone if you give in to despair.

After a few minutes, the rain began to wane, and the sound of music drifted up from the cottage below. Lying down on the bed, visions of marrying the man she loved filled Elizabeth's imagination, and she fell asleep dreaming of what would never be.

After the wedding
Lady Gwendolyn's bedroom

Lady Gwendolyn was beside herself with excitement. Not only had she been in Fitzwilliam's company before the wedding, but she had also sat beside him at the wedding breakfast.

Moreover, she had persuaded him to attend the festivities Lord Beauford had planned for his guests tonight.

Now in her room to rest before dinner, she tried on the gown she intended to wear that evening—a gold damask with matching sequins covering the low-cut bodice and short, puffed sleeves. She had brought along her maid, who was proficient in styling hair, and felt certain she would stand out amongst the fresh group of young women who had arrived for the wedding and would be at the dance. Confident that Mr. Darcy would not be interested in women young enough to be his daughter, she looked forward to the evening with great anticipation.

Surveying her reflection in the mirror one last time, Gwendolyn had her maid help her out of the gown and hang it up again. Then she lay down for a nap.

Darcy's bedroom

If William thought that by going to Southend he would have little time to dwell on losing Elizabeth, he was wrong. Not only did she haunt his dreams, she took every step with him and sat beside him whilst he ate. Even Lady Gwendolyn had commented during the wedding breakfast that he seemed millions of miles away. He blamed the pain in his knee for his preoccupation, when, in reality, the culprit was much higher. The pain was in his heart.

The wedding itself had proved a cruel reminder that only weeks before he had imagined a similar ceremony for himself. As Viscount Righton's godfather, he was seated with the family and could clearly hear the vows he had hoped to declare to the woman he loved. It affected him much more than he wanted those sitting around him to know. Men were not supposed to be sentimental, and he had never thought of himself as such; however, he could not help picturing Elizabeth in the place of the bride, and the scene pierced his heart anew.

Spending as little time as possible at the wedding breakfast, he had rushed back to his room at the first opportunity to brood in silence. Now, as he sat on the balcony with his leg elevated, one prayer ran through his mind when he closed his eyes.

Help me endure tonight, Lord, and I will return to Pemberley where I belong.

The Gardiners' cottage
Late that Afternoon

Having left before daybreak, Richard's coach pulled up to the Gardiners' cottage just before dark. As he stared at the door, doubts assailed him. Was he doing the right thing by interfering? Shaking his head as though to clear it, he climbed out of the coach and braced himself to confront Elizabeth.

You have come this far; you cannot let Darcy down now.

Before he reached the front door, it was opened by a young maid. "May I help you, sir?"

Richard removed his hat. "Lord Matlock to see Mrs. Gardiner."

"Of course. Pray wait here, my lord," the maid said, allowing him in.

After a short time, a woman he assumed to be Mrs. Gardiner greeted him. "Lord Matlock, I am Madeline Gardiner. I understand you wish to speak to me."

"I do."

"Pray, be seated, my lord."

There was no foyer in the cottage, for the door opened into a large parlour. As he looked around for a chair, Madeline Gardiner said. "I assume you are here about my niece."

"I am." Before sitting, Richard pulled the letter from Mr. Gardiner to his wife from his pocket. "Your husband asked me to give you this first."

She took the missive, broke the seal and read it before looking up again. "My husband feels it best that you speak to Elizabeth, but I am not certain I agree with him."

"If you have any questions, I shall be pleased to answer them, but let me say this before we begin. I am not here to further any goal other than to compel two people, whom I believe to be in love, to face one another before they make another life-altering decision."

Mrs. Gardiner considered his words. "You have a point. Elizabeth does not want to face you or Mr. Darcy, which worries me. She has never shrunk from confrontation before. May I ask why you think Mr. Darcy does not want to face her?"

"He said as much."

Suddenly the maid returned with a tray of tea and biscuits.

"If you will excuse me, I shall go upstairs and see if my niece will agree to see you."

Richard sat down and accepted the cup of tea and a small plate of biscuits the maid offered. He watched as Mrs. Gardiner went out a side door and thought he heard the sound of footsteps going upstairs. Before long, two sets of footsteps coming downstairs caught his attention. Then the same door Mrs. Gardiner had exited earlier opened, and she walked in, followed by Elizabeth.

Richard leapt to his feet, bowing. "Miss Bennet."

A solemn-looking Elizabeth curtseyed. "Lord Matlock."

Mrs. Gardiner said, "I shall leave you alone to—"

"Pray stay, Aunt. There is nothing Lord Matlock can say that you cannot hear."

Resigned, Madeline Gardiner sat down in a chair and clasped her hands.

"Will you not be seated?" Richard asked Elizabeth.

"I prefer to stand," she stated sombrely. "Moreover, I wish you to know immediately that I have no intention of returning as your governess."

"I never thought you should."

Elizabeth looked taken aback. "You did not?"

"No. I am not here about your employment, other than to apologise for what I learned happened shortly before you left." He pulled a letter from his pocket. "This will explain what I mean."

Elizabeth broke the seal on the letter and began to read.

Miss Bennet,

Forgive me. When I said those horrible things about you at Locklear Manor, it was because I was convinced you were a fortune hunter out to catch Papa's eye. I had no idea of your shared past with my father until Cousin Richard explained everything. Only then did I realise that my animosity towards you stemmed mainly from jealousy.

You see, it has been only Papa and me for many years, and I thought it would always be that way. The idea of him marrying again and perhaps having more children made me physically ill, for I feared they would replace me in his heart. A very wise man helped me to see that my thinking was flawed and there is room in his heart for everyone Papa loves.

I pray I have not done permanent damage to your relationship with my father, for I have seen the agony he has suffered since you left Derbyshire. If I could, I would take back my unkind actions, but that is impossible. I hope you can find it in your heart to forgive me, and that I am able to call you my mother very soon.

With all sincerity,
Lady Marianne

Without any sign of emotion, Elizabeth refolded the letter and put it in the pocket of her gown.

"When next you see Lady Marianne, will you please tell her that I was touched by her apology?"

"Except—" Richard said.

"Except it makes no difference," Elizabeth said. "After Fitzwilliam learned of Lydia's ruin, he left without a word of explanation. He did the same thing when he left Matlock House. I think he has shown his true feelings when differences with his family occur."

"That is simply not true! Darcy wrote you a letter before he left for Pemberley," Richard stated. "I know, for I was the one who slid it under your door."

"I saw no such letter."

"Blast!" Richard roared. "Isabelle's odious sister evidently had something to do with that! Perhaps she had one of the maids steal it, for it was there the night Darcy left."

"Even if that is true, it does not explain why he never returned after I left Lambton to help retrieve Lydia."

"I thought Darcy explained that to you the morning you met at the gazebo."

Elizabeth thought for a moment. "He was going to explain, but I assured him that no explanation was necessary."

"Then you have no idea how his leg came to be injured?"

Elizabeth shook her head.

"After you left Lambton, Darcy was determined to find Wickham and Lydia and force them to marry. Even though a blinding rainstorm was pummelling Derbyshire, he refused to wait until morning. Instead, he struck out for London that evening and his coach washed off the road and down an embankment near Leicester. All aboard the vehicle were killed except my cousin. Fortunately, another coach came by shortly afterwards and offered assistance, or Darcy might also have died in the wreckage."

"He was injured trying to help me," Elizabeth murmured to herself. Then, meeting Lord Matlock's eyes with tears in her own, she added, "Knowing me has brought him nothing but pain. It is best I leave him alone."

"Darcy does not see it that way. In fact, he blames himself for not saving Lydia, and by extension, saving you from a life of service."

"I tried to tell him the morning we talked that he was not to blame. How can he accept as true something so clearly wrong?"

"For the same reason he believes you left my employment because he was going to make you another offer—an offer you could not accept because of his infirmity."

"That is entirely untrue!" Elizabeth cried. "I believed he left Matlock Manor because his daughter did not want to accept me as her mother. *That* is why I decided not to return as your governess."

Richard smiled. "Now, do you understand why I am here? Misunderstandings have kept you and Darcy apart for fourteen years. Do you not think it time you spoke to one another and quit assuming you know what the other thinks?"

Elizabeth hung her head. "I... I am so confused I do not know what I should do."

"Well, let me add this bit of information for your consideration. My cousin is nothing if not proud, and he thinks his injury makes him less of a man in your eyes, which means he will not come to you. If you love Darcy, it will be up to you to go to him."

"I... I doubt I shall ever be in his company again."

"That is where you are wrong. At this very minute, Darcy is a guest at Lord Beauford's cottage. If you still have feelings for him, I urge you to speak to him tonight. He will likely leave in the morning."

When Elizabeth did not reply, he turned to Mrs. Gardiner. "Thank you for allowing me to speak to your niece."

Mrs. Gardiner, who had been silently digesting everything that was said, stood and walked with him to the door. "I believe you have given her much to consider, my lord."

Richard donned his hat and glanced back at Elizabeth, saying quietly, "If my visit accomplishes what I set out to do—reunite a man and woman who love one another—I shall be satisfied."

"Let us pray it will," Mrs. Gardiner replied. "Now, I forgot to ask if you have a place to stay?"

"I am well acquainted with Lord Beauford, so I will have no trouble lodging there tonight. Good evening, Mrs. Gardiner."

With that said, Richard hurried towards his waiting coach.

Chapter 18

The Gardiners' cottage

After Richard's departure, Mrs. Gardiner turned to find Elizabeth standing at the windows and staring at Lord Beauford's cottage in the distance. Darkness was fast approaching, and the torches that had been strategically placed throughout the yard and along the path to the gazebo were already lit.

It appeared as though the weight of the world was on her niece's shoulders. Madeline Gardiner crossed the room to slide a comforting arm around her waist.

"Since you asked me to stay and hear all that was said, I feel free to offer my advice." When Elizabeth did not reply, she continued. "I agree with Lord Matlock. You should go to Lord Beauford's cottage tonight and speak to Mr. Darcy."

"I... I brought nothing suitable to wear. If I were to wear one of my usual gowns, it would embarrass him as well as me."

"Lizzy, I doubt Mr. Darcy will notice if your gown is appropriate."

"Perhaps not, but the others will."

"Then do not go to the front entrance. Go down to the beach and up the path from the gazebo. Once you reach the terrace, pass a note to a maid or footman and ask them to give it to

Lord Matlock. Once that gentleman knows you are there, he will make certain his cousin knows."

"But I have no idea what to say to him."

"Lizzy, are you still in love with Mr. Darcy?"

A tear slid down Elizabeth's cheek as she nodded.

"Then tell him." She took hold of Elizabeth's arms. "Now, go back upstairs, change your clothes and put the man you love out of his misery."

A kiss on the forehead and a gentle nudge in the direction of the door left Elizabeth little room to argue.

Lord Beauford's cottage

Richard wished the trip from the Gardiners' cottage to Lord Beauford's was not quite so short, for he still had not devised an excuse to give his cousin regarding his presence. He thought of telling him the truth, but not wanting to wound William's heart anew if Miss Bennet's stubbornness won out over her feelings, he decided against it. Hoping to avoid seeing William until he could change clothes and join the party downstairs, he felt fortunate that Lord Beauford happened by as the footman opened the door.

"Lord Matlock!" that gentleman said loudly, "What a surprise to see you here!"

Richard bowed and answered with his usual bravado, "My cousin insisted I would be welcome at the wedding, and I took him at his word."

"Of course, you are welcome, but I fear you have missed the ceremony. It was this morning."

"Unfortunately, I was delayed along the way."

"Well, dinner has already been served, but the dancing is about to begin. Would you like a tray of sandwiches sent to your room whilst you change clothes?"

"That would be perfect," Richard said. Then, he looked around cautiously. "May I ask where Darcy is at present?"

"To my knowledge, he returned to his room after dinner and

has not yet come down." Lord Beauford motioned to a footman. "Show Lord Matlock to one of our empty guest rooms, then tell Cook that I requested sandwiches be sent to his room as soon as possible."

As the footman motioned towards the stairs, Lord Beauford said, "Matlock, ring for a servant if you find yourself in need of anything. If not, I hope to find you dancing by the time the third set is called."

"Thank you," Richard replied. Then he followed the footman up the grand staircase.

By the time Richard had changed clothes, the music was playing, so he quickly devoured a sandwich and covered the dish again, intending to eat the rest before he retired. Satisfied with his reflection in the full-length mirror, he headed towards the grand staircase.

At the landing above the foyer, he ran straight into William, whose room was on another hall.

"Richard? What are you doing here?" William asked.

"Am I not allowed to attend the wedding of an acquaintance?"

Immediately suspicious, as they began down the stairs, William said, "Yes, but the ceremony was this morning, and furthermore, you declined my offer to accompany me."

"If you must know, I missed the wedding because of delays on the road. And the reason I declined the offer to accompany you was that it came before—" Richard hesitated as he struggled to come up with an answer.

"Before what?"

"Your offer came before I received a post from Isabelle asking if I had located you. She was so worried that I thought perhaps I should make certain you were still well."

"Why would your wife be so concerned about me?"

"Isabelle happens to care about you, Darcy. Naturally, after she learned I was going to London to talk with you, she began to fret as women are wont to do."

William's face reflected his doubts, and he seemed about to say more when they reached the foyer where, luckily for Richard, they were instantly confronted by Lady Gwendolyn.

"Mr. Darcy, I have been looking all over for you!" she declared. Then, realizing who stood beside him, she added, "Colonel Fitzwilliam, if I am not mistaken! I have not seen you since your last visit to my brother's house at Cambridge."

Though Richard pasted a smile on his face, he gave William a questioning look. "And who might your brother be?"

"Lord Tolbert," William curtly answered for her. "You recall Lady Gwendolyn, do you not?"

"I do, but this lady looks nothing like the child I remember."

"I would hope not, Colonel Fitzwilliam," Gwendolyn said.

"Actually, my cousin is Lord Matlock now," William said. "His father and brother have both passed, and the title fell to him."

"I am sorry for your loss," Gwendolyn replied. Then, though wanting William all to herself, she prevaricated, "I am very pleased you came."

"It was a surprise for Darcy," Richard stated.

"My cousin is full of surprises," William added dryly.

Gwendolyn took hold of William's arm. "I hope you do not mind if I steal your cousin for a while. Since he does not dance, he promised to take me for a walk. Now that the storm is over, the moon is bright, and except for an occasional cloud, we should be able to see our way quite clearly on the beach."

Astonished to think his cousin might be interested in this woman, Richard studied Darcy, who immediately began to address Lady Gwendolyn's assertion.

"I never said I would walk on the beach. It is impossible for me to walk on the sand without enduring severe and lasting pain; besides, it would not do for us to be seen walking in the dark unchaperoned."

"Nonsense!" Gwendolyn declared with a laugh. "I am a grown woman, not a debutante! That type of gossip ceased to concern me years ago. At least walk with me to the gazebo. The torches make the path bright enough that no one should find that scandalous."

Feeling powerless to refuse, William said, "If you will excuse us, Richard."

Richard nodded and watched his cousin escort Lady Gwendolyn through one of the doors leading to the terrace. With no idea how to prevent it, he hurried to follow, taking up watch where he could keep an eye on the now ghostly figures walking towards the gazebo.

As he observed them, one thought kept repeating in his head. *If Miss Bennet sees them, what will she think?*

The downpour had passed, leaving a large moon weaving in and out of fast-moving clouds. Unwilling to take a lantern for fear of being seen, Elizabeth carefully made her way to the back of her uncle's property, stopping often to await the moon's reappearance. Once at the beach, she kept close to the seawall and hurried towards Lord Beauford's gazebo.

When she reached that goal, she realised there were no torches that far from the house, and the gazebo was in complete darkness. Bracing herself, the next time the moon appeared she said a prayer and hurried up the steps at the seawall to the walkway leading towards the cottage. She reached as far as the white tent when voices compelled her to stop. They were coming towards her, so Elizabeth rushed behind one of the tent posts where the sides of the tent had been gathered and tied.

Once the voices were closer, she recognised that one belonged to Fitzwilliam. It was the other voice, however, that wounded her. To know that William was walking in the moonlight with another woman was so painful that she had to will the tears filling her eyes not to fall, lest they trigger the sob now rising in her chest.

The music from the ballroom wafted through the rain-scrubbed air, prompting Gwendolyn to say, "I do not know why you refuse to dance, Mr. Darcy. I believe you could, at least for one set, if you tried."

"I danced once after the accident, and it was a disaster," William replied as they continued to walk. "And I see no reason to keep trying when it is not something I enjoy."

Wrapping her arm more tightly around William's, Gwendolyn laid her head against his shoulder, saying seductively, "Perhaps all you needed was to meet the right woman—the one who could inspire you to dance again."

"There was only one woman capable of that."

Gwendolyn stopped abruptly. "You must miss your wife terribly," she said, hoping to discover the truth.

"Sadly, I do not. My aunt pressed me to marry Lady Cornelia. It was she who chose her and I found out why only hours after the ceremony."

"Forgive me, but almost all of London knew Lady Cornelia was a lady in name only."

"Everyone but me, it seems," William replied sombrely. "Admittedly, I should have been more guarded, but I had barely recovered from the accident and was preoccupied with demons of my own."

"I may be being too personal, but if you have not mourned your wife all these years, what kept you from marrying again?"

"The woman I loved was lost to me."

Not one to give up easily, Gwendolyn ventured, "Have you considered marrying someone who is merely a friend? Often marriages between friends fare better than great love matches."

"Once you love with all your heart, you cannot settle for less."

Astonished, she murmured, "All these years I have been mistaken; I never took you for a romantic. The woman you love is indeed fortunate."

"Eliz—" Halting when he realised what he was about to say, William began again. "She has no idea how much I still love her."

"Surely you are not afraid to reveal her Christian name. I doubt I could guess her identity, even if we were acquainted."

William stared into the darkness. At length he murmured, "Elizabeth. Her name is Elizabeth."

With all hopes dashed, Gwendolyn forced herself to smile. "I hope one day you and Elizabeth are given another chance. Now I believe it is time I returned to the ball. Perhaps somewhere in the crowd tonight is a man searching for a woman like me."

"I shall escort you back to the house."

"There is no need to aggravate your leg by making you walk more than necessary. The night is beautiful, and you enjoy solitude. Why not walk on to the gazebo, rest and enjoy listening to the waves crash against the shore."

William brought her hand to his lips for a kiss. "Good evening, Lady Gwendolyn."

This time her smile was genuine. "Good evening, Mr. Darcy."

Finding himself alone, William looked towards the beach just as the moon broke through the clouds, bathing the gazebo in moonlight. Once he reached that structure, the musicians struck up a waltz, and Gwendolyn's words came back to taunt him.

I believe you could dance if you tried.

Something inside urged him on, and he bowed as though addressing a partner before beginning an ungainly waltz. He had completed several turns about the gazebo when a voice broke the stillness of the night.

"For someone who never liked to dance, I think you do very well."

Halting awkwardly, William was stunned to see a woman in a pale-blue gown at the entrance to the gazebo. Though her long, dark hair was being whipped about by the wind, her face was hidden in the shadows. Then, in a flash, the moon re-emerged, and William froze.

Dear God! Are memories of Elizabeth not enough to torment me? Am I to be plagued by hallucinations as well?

Elizabeth took a step forward. "Forgive me if I startled you."

"This cannot be," William said. "I am going mad."

Hearing this, Elizabeth hurried to say, "You are not mad, Fitzwilliam. My uncle owns the cottage on the hill above. I was visiting my aunt, and Lord Matlock happened to—"

The mention of Lord Matlock's name seemed to rouse William from his trance. "I should have known Richard was involved," he interrupted. "My cousin thinks he is in charge of everyone's life."

"Actually, I am deeply indebted that he interjected himself into my life. Not only did he deliver a letter of apology that Lady Marianne asked him to give me, but he apologised for any offenses his family may have caused."

William's head dropped. "I blame myself for my daughter's misdeeds. I should have taught her that the *ton's* views should not influence her."

"Is there anything you will not accept the blame for?"

William's head came up. "Excuse me?"

"You and I have been so foolish, Fitzwilliam," Elizabeth continued. "As Lord Matlock pointed out to me, we have allowed misunderstandings to keep us apart all these years. It was he who said we should speak to one another and stop supposing we know what the other thinks. His advice is what brought me here."

"Elizabeth, anything you wish to know, you have only to ask."

Steeling herself to keep her voice from trembling, she said, "I confess that I was eavesdropping, when you spoke with—"

"Lady Gwendolyn?" William interjected. At Elizabeth's nod, he added, "She is merely the sister of a friend from Cambridge."

By now Elizabeth's heart was beating so fast she could barely get a breath. Gathering her courage she spoke with hurried eagerness, "Am I... am I the woman you mentioned? The one you still love?"

The pull of soul on body drew William a few steps closer. "I have loved none but you, Elizabeth. I always will."

Overwhelmed at his declaration, Elizabeth closed her eyes, giving William time to reach her. As his hands surrounded her waist, she looked up to him.

"What you said to Lady Gwendolyn was true. Until this moment, I never knew how much you loved me. Moreover, I believe you have no idea how much I love you."

Suddenly Elizabeth was surrounded by arms akin to steel. Once William's hungry lips found and captured hers, she began to respond, and her very first kiss became more passionate than she ever imagined it could be.

At length, William groaned, broke the kiss and burying one hand in her curls, settled her head against his chest. "Can this be happening?" he whispered. "If this is not real... if this is but a dream—"

Elizabeth murmured, "I am real, Fitzwilliam, and my heart is yours. It shall forever be yours."

An even more passionate kiss sealed her vow.

At the house

When Richard saw Lady Gwendolyn coming up the path alone, he hurried to her. "What have you done with my cousin, my lady?"

Gwendolyn laughed. "You need not worry. He went on to the gazebo, and he is well, though the thought of shaking some sense into him did cross my mind."

"Whatever do you mean?"

"I went to a lot of trouble to obtain an invitation to this wedding because I was assured that Mr. Darcy was still unmarried. I had my heart set on convincing him that he should marry me." When Richard remained silent, she continued. "Despite all my manoeuvrings, your cousin politely let me know that he is in love with another woman. Apparently, he has been for years."

Richard smiled. "I could have saved you the trouble, had you asked."

She sighed. "Unfortunately, all the best prospects are either married already or hopelessly in love with other women."

"Eventually, you will find the right man, my lady," Richard said as he peered over her head towards the gazebo. "Now I believe I shall see if my cousin would like some company."

"You are the kind of person everyone needs. Darcy is indeed fortunate to have such a cousin."

"I try," Richard said. Then, performing a quick bow, he said, "If you will please excuse me, Lady Gwendolyn."

In seconds, he was halfway to the gazebo.

William took a step back, saying breathlessly, "Elizabeth, if we do not stop, I shall not be able to call myself a gentleman in the morning."

She smiled. "All I care is that you are *mine* in the morning. Nothing more."

William moaned and rolled his eyes, which made Elizabeth laugh.

"I am serious!" he declared. "Let us sit down."

Directing her to the bench that ran around the circumference of the structure, he helped her to sit and then sat beside her. Bringing one of her hands to his lips for a soft kiss, he said, "One week should be sufficient."

A look of puzzlement crossed Elizabeth's face. "I do not understand."

"A week is the earliest we can marry. It will take a day for us to return to London. Once there, obtaining a special license from my uncle, the bishop, should take three days. We may marry the day following."

"Fitzwilliam—"

"William," he interrupted.

"William, we cannot possibly be married in so short a time."

"You will not have to lift a finger. I will arrange for the church, have my staff prepare the wedding breakfast, pay a modiste an outrageous sum to create your wedding gown as quickly as possible, and bring your family to London."

"What about Georgiana and her family? My family may be able to come, but how fast can one can travel from Edinburgh?"

William looked so crushed that she felt sorry for him. "We shall just have to see how things work out before choosing a date."

"Pray do not ask me to wait a day longer than is absolutely necessary," he pleaded.

Elizabeth framed his beloved face with her hands. "My darling, you must not imagine it is any easier for me to wait."

Instantly, she was pulled onto his lap. One of his hands caressed her body whilst the other directed her mouth back to his.

In the darkness, a loud cough resonated.

Richard was pleased to discover his cousin and Miss Bennet had found each other. Still, considering the consequences of someone else witnessing their affection, he knew it was time to send the lady in question back to her family. Subsequently, he decided to announce his presence to the lovestruck couple by coughing loudly. He repeated the exercise several times before the sound penetrated the couple's sensibilities.

When a startled William stood, bringing Elizabeth to her feet with him, Richard almost laughed aloud at his expression as he searched the darkness for the intruder. Suddenly, the moon illuminated the entire area, and his presence was revealed.

"Richard! You gave me a good fright!" William declared angrily.

"As well I should, Cousin. I realise you and Miss Bennet have years to catch up on, but you do not have to do it all at once. Do you not think it time she returned to her aunt and shared the good news? No doubt Mrs. Gardiner wonders what has happened to her."

"Yes, of course," William acknowledged. Turning to Elizabeth, he said, "I shall walk you back to your uncle's cottage."

"No, Darcy," Richard declared. "Your knee will give you fits if you walk that far in the sand. I shall escort Miss Bennet back to the Gardiners' cottage whilst you return to your room. I imagine you wish to return to London as soon as possible, so you need the rest."

Unconsciously, William still held Elizabeth's hands so tightly she could not have left had she wished. Noting this, Richard added, "Now would be a good time, Cousin."

Flustered, William said, "He is right, my love. I want you to return to London tomorrow with me, so you must get your rest, as well. I shall call first thing in the morning and speak to your aunt."

Elizabeth glanced shyly at Richard. "May I have one last kiss to remind me of our joy before I sleep?"

With no regard for his cousin, William pulled Elizabeth into his arms, rewarding her request with another fierce kiss. He followed that with a chaste kiss on her forehead before surrendering her to Richard.

"I trust you to keep her safe."

Richard smiled. "I believe my years in His Majesty's service qualifies me for the job." To Elizabeth he said, "Shall we, Miss Bennet?"

Elizabeth took Lord Matlock's proffered arm and, with a last yearning look at William, headed towards her aunt's cottage.

Chapter 19

London
The Cowan residence
A fortnight later

Jane entered the bedroom to find Elizabeth sitting on the side of the bed. "Lizzy, you are not yet fully dressed, and Mr. Darcy will be here at any moment," she gently chided.

When Elizabeth turned, the expression on her face melted Jane's heart. Crossing the room, she sat down on the bed and slid an arm around her sister's shoulder. "What is troubling you? Are you having second thoughts about marrying Mr. Darcy?"

"No, not at all. It is just—Georgiana should arrive any day now, and I am anxious about seeing her again."

"I do not see why you should be. You conducted your meeting with Marianne admirably."

"That is because Marianne was so contrite that she cried and apologised repeatedly. I ended up crying with her, and there were even tears in William's eyes by the time she and I embraced."

"As I recall, you once said Georgiana was not at all as Mr. Wickham described her. You said she was not proud, but merely shy."

"Yes, but now she is a grown woman with children of her own."

"You have a special way with children that will make you a valued aunt. That is all the more reason she will love you." Standing, Jane walked to the dresser and opened a drawer. "Now I shall find stockings to match your gown whilst you decide which shoes to wear."

"That brings up an entirely new conundrum. William has purchased so many shoes that I have too many choices. I can rule out the ecru-coloured, embroidered silk with silver buckles which are for special occasions, but should I choose slippers or half-boots?"

"It rained earlier, so I would choose the boots," Jane answered. "Oh, and by the way, another package was delivered this morning from Madam Dupree's shop. I laid it on the dining room table and forgot to bring it up."

"I have told William I do not need so many clothes and shoes, but he will not listen. Once the modiste and Mr. Moore[5] had my measurements, he went a bit mad. I believe he goes to the shops every morning just to see what else he can find."

"Mr. Darcy certainly has the means, and he has waited so long for this, Lizzy. You should not deny him these small indulgences," Jane cautioned. "If he wishes to shower you with gifts, let him. Besides, I imagine he knows more about what his wife will need than you do."

Elizabeth sighed. "I suppose you are right."

"I am," Jane said, giving her sister a sympathetic look. "Now I shall return downstairs for the package whilst you pull on these stockings."

It was not long before Jane returned, carrying the largest package Elizabeth had received thus far. "I do not know what it contains, but it is quite heavy."

---

5   *Moore Brothers* - *It was said that in the later 19th century 'in hundreds of houses the shoe-binders, the closers and finishers were busy week in week out'. The business with the longest history is Moore Brothers, whose origins can be found in William Moore, boot and shoemaker in 1822 and 1830.*
    https://janeaustensworld.wordpress.com/tag/19th-century-shoemaker-shops/

"Open it, please," Elizabeth said, as she busily pulled blue half-boots over the stockings.

When Elizabeth turned, Jane was holding up a full-length wool cape lined with a thin layer of fur. The wool had been dyed a royal blue, whilst the fur was the original reddish-brown.

"My goodness!" Jane exclaimed as she ran her hands over the lining. "If I am not badly mistaken, this is fox!"

"One of Madam Dupree's staff was working on this cape the first time I visited her shop," Elizabeth replied as Jane helped her try it on. "I heard her tell William it was part of a trousseau for someone who resides in Scotland and is to be married the month after next. Madam Dupree told him the lady is about my height and figure, and it would be no problem to resize everything to fit me. Now, should that poor woman return early, she may find her trousseau unfinished."

"The cape is beautiful, but I cannot imagine ever needing something so weighty," Jane said.

"William insists the winters in Derbyshire are much colder than they are here."

Jane pulled more items from the paper packaging. "And here is the fur muff and hat to match," she said, handing them to Elizabeth, who was examining herself in a full-length mirror.

Placing the hat on her head and burying her hands in the muff, Elizabeth asked, "How do I look?"

"Just as elegant as the women who occupy the expensive boxes at the theatre."

"Do you know what I find odd?" At the shake of her sister's head, Elizabeth continued. "I feel as though I am the same girl who would rather climb a tree to read a book than dress for a ball."

"I pray that part of you never changes, Lizzy," Jane said wistfully. "I could not bear it if it did."

"I am four and thirty," Elizabeth said with a chuckle, "so the prospect of that ever happening is growing dim." Both laughed before Elizabeth continued. "No, I fear it is poor William who will suffer my eccentricity from here on. I pray he is not too shocked once he learns my true nature."

"I believe Mr. Darcy knows your nature much better than you realise," Jane said. "I remember when we were at Netherfield, he could not keep his eyes off you. Do you recall me saying I thought he was enamoured of you?"

"I do, but I was convinced he was looking to find fault."

"Which proves my point!" Jane replied with a smirk. "I can interpret Mr. Darcy's feelings much better than you—at least when it comes to his feelings for you!"

Elizabeth turned back to the mirror. "In any case, I plan to make him so deliriously happy he shall never notice my faults."

Jane walked over to slip her arms around Elizabeth. Giving her a hug, Jane said, "If the way he looks at you is any indication, you already have."

Suddenly, there was a knock on the door. "Excuse me, ma'am, but Mr. Darcy's coach has arrived," a maid announced.

"We will be right down," Jane replied.

Elizabeth was not surprised to find that Marianne had accompanied her father, for ever since her apology she had done everything possible to let Elizabeth know she was looking forward to having her join their family. Much to William's chagrin, the result was that Marianne insisted on spending as much time as possible with Elizabeth prior to the wedding. Although happy that his daughter and fiancée were growing close, he made it clear to Elizabeth that he had hoped to be alone with her in the days leading up to their wedding, which his daughter's company now made impossible.

As Elizabeth descended the stairs, her eyes sought William. He was standing behind Marianne with so obvious an expression of longing that her heart began to ache with the same yearning. She knew exactly how he felt, having spent considerable time and effort attempting to suppress that same expression, lest anyone guess how truly love-sick she was.

The moment her feet touched the marble floor, Marianne

rushed forward to give her a hug. Though only one day had passed since they had seen one another, she said, "I missed you."

"I missed you, too," Elizabeth replied.

"I was telling Aunt Georgiana—" Marianne stopped, then began more animatedly, "I forgot! You do not know! Aunt Georgiana and her family arrived yesterday evening. She and I talked for hours last night, and she wishes to accompany us to the modiste for your fitting. I hope you do not mind that I asked her to come! Papa said we should let her sleep late, so I left word for Mrs. Barnes to wake her after we had left. Once we return to Darcy House, she should be dressed and ready to accompany us."

"Of course, I do not mind," Elizabeth replied. Then, she smiled affectionately at her intended. "How are you faring this morning, William?"

"I am very well," he answered in the deep baritone she loved. Stepping forward, he took her hands and brought them to his lips for soft kisses. "Seeing you always raises my spirits."

The unmistakable love shining in his light-blue eyes instantly darkened with desire, and Elizabeth thought it wise to change the subject. "Tell me, do you plan to accompany us to the modiste?"

"Unfortunately, I cannot. Isabelle has questions about the wedding breakfast, so after you greet Georgiana and her family, I shall be off to Matlock House. I hope to be home by the time you return. You do intend to stay for dinner, do you not?"

"Yes."

"Excellent!" William said. "Then I suggest we be on our way."

As her father escorted Elizabeth towards the door, Marianne whispered to Jane, "I have never seen Papa so happy! Having Elizabeth in his life has changed him completely. It is as though I never really knew him until now." She shook her head. "I shall forever be grateful that I witnessed this transformation whilst I was still at home."

"Elizabeth has told me how thrilled she is that you and she have grown so close. She will be a wonderful, caring mother, if you allow it."

"I have often longed for a mother, and I intend to make the most of having one," Marianne replied. Then, giving Jane a wink, she added, "Papa will just have to share her with me."

Chuckling, she followed William and Elizabeth to the coach.

Darcy House

The second William and Elizabeth entered Darcy House a tall, willowy, blonde woman rushed from the library towards them. Given that she looked much as she had years before, Elizabeth recognised Georgiana right away.

She enveloped Elizabeth in an embrace. "Oh, Elizabeth! When Brother wrote that he was getting married and you were the one who had stolen his heart, I could not have been more pleased."

Her sister-to-be began to cry, which made Elizabeth begin to weep with her answer, "We met so long ago that I wondered if you would remember me."

"You took the time to draw an insecure, shy girl into your conversation. One never forgets kindness like that. Moreover, that was the first time I had ever seen William act as though he was in love, so meeting you was memorable."

Elizabeth glanced at William, who had coloured and was staring at the carpet. "To be honest, that was also the first time *I* was in love." William's head came up, and their eyes met. "All these years he and I have loved each other without knowing the other felt the same way."

"Brother told me everything in his letter, and I believe your marriage will be even more precious because of what you both endured."

At that moment, a handsome, sandy-haired man appeared in the library doorway. When he began walking towards them, Georgiana stepped aside. "Elizabeth, I would like to introduce my husband, Gregory Langston." To him she said, "Gregory, this is Fitzwilliam's fiancée, Miss Elizabeth Bennet."

"I am very pleased to meet you, Miss Bennet," he said with a bow. "My wife has talked of nothing but you since she received William's letter."

"The pleasure is mine, Mr. Langston," Elizabeth said.

"Gregory," he replied.

"Gregory," Elizabeth repeated with a smile. "I do hope you are not already weary of hearing my name."

"On the contrary, I am as thrilled as Georgiana that my brother is to marry." He tilted his head towards William. "I have been telling this fellow for years that he is too young to be on the shelf."

"And I said that, given the right woman, I would marry again," William answered.

"Touché!" Langston replied.

"We are all thankful that you and Papa found each other again," Marianne declared.

"And I am thankful that in two days' time, I will not only gain a husband, but a daughter, a sister, a brother and their children in the bargain. By the way, where are the children?"

"They were so tired from the journey that I found them asleep in the playroom after they had eaten," Georgiana replied. "Once they get their rest, I fear they will be so rambunctious that they will test everyone's patience, especially William's."

"Actually, I have missed the sounds of children laughing."

"What about the sounds of children arguing?" Georgiana asked, tongue-in-cheek.

"Even that," William said, giving his sister a wink.

Then, looking longingly at Elizabeth, he said, "I should be on my way. A carriage is standing by for your use whenever you decide to leave for the shops."

He appeared to want to say more, so Marianne declared, "Aunt Georgiana, shall we look in on the children before we leave? Uncle Gregory, would you like to join us?"

Georgiana took Marianne's meaning. Turning to Gregory, she said, "Yes, please join us, sweetheart."

Gregory was about to demur when Georgiana tilted her head towards the grand staircase. "Of course!" he declared and followed his wife up the stairs.

As soon as the others had disappeared, William guided Elizabeth into the library and closed the doors. Instantly drawing her into his embrace, he kissed her with such passion it took her breath away. When her knees began to buckle, he ended the kiss, holding her tightly against his chest.

"Forgive me," he murmured into her hair. "I am a beast to kiss you that way. My only excuse is that we have been apart so long I have been starving for you."

"Why should you apologise when I returned your kiss just as fervently?"

Elizabeth's words resulted in another fiery kiss. Once William was able to pull away, he murmured, "Only a little while longer, and we will not have to steal moments like this. Oh, Elizabeth, you have no idea how it excites me to know you desire me."

"On the contrary, I have a very good idea."

It was several more minutes before footsteps in the hallway broke through William and Elizabeth's sensibilities. Taking a step back, William took great gulps of air to slow his racing heart, whilst Elizabeth rushed to a large mirror on the wall.

"Is my hair in place?" she asked, touching the upswept chignon Jane's maid had created.

William walked to where she stood. Grasping her arms gently from behind, he placed a searing kiss on the back of her neck. "Everything is as it should be. You look beautiful."

She smiled at him in the mirror. "You need to leave before Marianne and Georgiana discover you are still here and wonder what we have been up to."

He turned her to face him. "Promise that you will try to think of an excuse for us to be alone after dinner."

"I will do my best." Instead of being placated, William searched her eyes until she said, "I promise."

A hasty kiss proved that to be the correct answer. Taking her hand, William escorted her back to the foyer. Once there, sounds of voices on the floor above confirmed there was no time left for more goodbyes. William rushed out the front door, and a footman closed it just as Georgiana and Marianne appeared on the landing.

"You look flushed, Elizabeth," Georgiana said as she and Marianne began to descend the stairs. "Do you feel well?"

"I am fine," Elizabeth replied, pasting on a smile.

Whilst Georgiana and Marianne spoke with the footman regarding the carriage, she savoured the memory of their kisses and considered her current state of bliss.

Until William kissed me, I never knew it was possible to feel this fine.

Matlock House

The instant he arrived at the townhouse William was shown to the front drawing room to await his cousin. His yearning for Elizabeth made it almost impossible to sit still; consequently, he was pacing the floor when Richard entered the room.

"Darcy! What took you so long? I expected you hours ago."

"I thought you understood I intended to fetch Elizabeth this morning and take her to meet Georgiana and Gregory before coming here."

"To be truthful, I do not recall you saying that, but ever since Isabelle and the children arrived in Town, it has been pure bedlam here. Two of the maids are assisting with the children, but they are of no use when it comes to their lessons. Thanks to you, we need to hire another governess, and I hope we are successful whilst we are in London." William started to reply, but Richard hurried to add, "I am just teasing, Cousin. I am delighted that you and Miss Bennet are to wed."

"Speaking of my fiancée, I wish to see her when she returns from the modiste, so I would like to conclude our business quickly and return to Darcy House."

Richard reached into his coat and drew out a sheet of paper. "Isabelle compiled this list of people who were invited to the wedding and—"

William interrupted. "I hope she remembered we want a small affair with only family and close friends."

"Darcy, you have been in society long enough to know a small affair is never a *small* affair." William rolled his eyes, and Richard added, "Isabelle wants you to examine the list and tell her if there is anyone we may have forgotten. If there is, we will have any additional invitations hand-delivered, since the wedding is so close."

Suddenly a maid appeared in the doorway. "Lord Matlock, your wife asked me to fetch you right away. You are to go straight to the classroom."

Richard sighed. "Tell her I shall be right there." Then he handed the list to William. "God only knows what calamity has befallen us now. Read over the list, and I will return as soon as may be to see if you wish to make any additions."

Before William had time to reply, Richard disappeared. Whilst he was still staring in the direction his cousin had gone, a voice called, "Psst! Cousin Darcy!"

Recognising the voice as Ellen's, William looked about but did not see her. "Where are you?"

"Behind the curtains."

William crossed to the wall of windows where heavy curtains had been drawn against the sun. Seeing nothing amiss, his eyes followed the line where the curtains met the carpet until he spied the tips of a pair of green leather shoes. Pulling that curtain aside, he found Ellen and stooped to speak to her.

"Why not show your face instead of forcing me to find you?"

"I wanted to know if you could find me without much trouble."

"Why are you hiding?"

"Papa told Mama you were coming, and I asked if I might speak to you. Papa said I would have to wait because you were too busy. But if I wait too long, he and Mama may make another mistake."

"What kind of mistake?"

"Evelyn, Emily and I agree that, with the exception of Miss Bennet, all our governesses have been complete failures."

William suppressed a smile. "And how would speaking to me prevent them from hiring another *failure*?"

"We want Miss Bennet to help them find someone exactly like her. Will you ask her?"

"I know Miss Bennet will appreciate your confidence in her ability, but she is very busy at present preparing for our wedding. Then, we leave on our honeymoon right after the ceremony."

"I know *that*," Ellen said with great exasperation. "But we are perfectly willing to wait, if only she will help Papa find a new governess when you are done with your honeymoon."

"That is very thoughtful of you," William replied, no longer able to hold back a smile. "I shall certainly inform Miss Bennet, but you do know your parents may not want to wait that long to hire someone."

Ellen sighed heavily. "Given their previous choices, I do not know why not."

Not able to argue with her logic, William said, "Are you ready to come out of hiding now?"

Ellen shook her head. "I think I shall stay hidden a while longer. If I am not mistaken, Mama sent for Papa because she has discovered that Emily painted Evelyn's hair green whilst she was trying to paint the chair Evelyn was using. And, of course, I will get the blame."

William pursed his lips so as not to laugh. "Why would they blame you?"

"Because I am the only one tall enough to stand on a chair and open the latch at the top of the closet where the paints are stored. Emily begged me to bring out the paints. How was I to know she would paint furniture instead of a picture?"

The sound of Richard's voice coming down the hallway motivated Ellen to rush behind the curtain again. Holding out her little finger, she said, "Swear you will not tell Papa you saw me."

William linked his finger with hers. "I swear."

Chapter 20

Darcy House
Their wedding day

Upon hearing of their coming nuptials, Lord Beauford offered the use of his Southend cottage to William and Elizabeth for their honeymoon. Since the cottage would always hold a special place in their hearts, the offer was accepted. William's plans included visiting different towns along the east coast over the course of an entire month as they wound their way northward towards Pemberley. However, when asked where she wished to go after Southend, Elizabeth had delighted William by saying, "There is no place on earth I would rather go than to Pemberley."

Once their itinerary had been decided, Elizabeth was encouraged to move into Darcy House before the wedding to facilitate their departure after the wedding breakfast, whilst William moved into Matlock House. Both transfers had been achieved in the time that remained, giving Elizabeth a chance to get to know Georgiana and her family better. William had also suggested she invite Mary and Kitty and their families to stay at Darcy House, but her sisters thought it best if Elizabeth spent the time getting to know the Langstons, who did not often visit England. Subsequently, they stayed with Jane, as they had in the past.

On her brother's wedding day, Georgiana rose early to make certain her children were fed, and that their maids had no questions regarding the children's attire before she dressed. They were to stay at Darcy House during the ceremony and she and Gregory would collect them before going to the wedding breakfast being held at Matlock House. She had thought of letting the maids keep them the entire day, but Elizabeth insisted on all her nieces and nephews attending the breakfast. Her exact words were: "I should like to have all of my family present—young and old—even though those of the *ton* may find it odd."

After her maid dressed her and styled her hair, Georgiana peeked into Elizabeth's dressing room to see how her sister-to-be was progressing. She was astounded to find Elizabeth standing in front of a full-length mirror, already fully dressed but for her shoes. The modiste had done an excellent job of creating the perfect wedding gown for Elizabeth. It was made from a delicate, white muslin completely covered in embroidered flowers in various shades of yellow. The flowers were connected by tiny green leaves and vines. The bodice and puffed sleeves were trimmed with a wide band of white Chantilly lace with thin, yellow ribbons interwoven along the bottom edge. Half-way down the full skirt, rows of the same lace and ribbons began and continued every few inches until they reached the hem.

"Oh, Elizabeth," Georgiana murmured reverently, "you look stunning. I have never seen a lovelier bride, and your hair is simply magnificent."

Since William despised bonnets, Elizabeth's dark tresses had been swept into a chignon that began at the crown of her head and continued to the nape of her neck. Narrow braids of her hair and yellow ribbons weaved in and out of the chignon and were secured in the middle by a nosegay of white rosebuds and greenery.

"I cannot take credit for any of this; I hardly recognise myself. Madam Dupree designed my gown and finished it in record time," Elizabeth replied. "Moreover, the lady's maid that William hired at Lady Matlock's recommendation is nothing short of a genius when it comes to styling hair."

"Where *is* O'Malley?"

"Since this was her first time to style my hair, she said she was too nervous to eat before she came. Once she finished, I sent her straight downstairs to break her fast. Frankly, I have no idea why anyone with her talent would be nervous."

"She is young to be a lady's maid," Georgiana said, recalling the plain, round-faced woman. "That could be the source of her nervousness."

Elizabeth had picked up a hand mirror and was admiring the chignon in the full-length glass behind her when Georgiana said, "I just realised you are not wearing any jewellery."

"William said I was not to worry about jewellery. He said he would see to that."

"Well, if that is the case, he had better arrive soon! We must all be at St. George's in a little more than an hour."

As though on cue, Mrs. Barnes appeared at the dressing room door. "Miss Bennet, Mr. Darcy is waiting for you in the sitting room," she said with a motherly smile.

"The groom cannot see the bride before the wedding!" Georgiana declared.

"I told him as much," the housekeeper replied, "but he insisted that he must see Miss Bennet now."

"I am certain he has brought the jewellery," Elizabeth said. "Pray tell him I shall be right there." As Mrs. Barnes departed, she turned to Georgiana. "Please hand me my dressing gown, and I shall use it to cover my dress."

"William could have passed the jewellery to me, and I could have given it to you," Georgiana muttered as she helped Elizabeth into a white, satin dressing gown that Mrs. Dupree had sent over the day before. It had arrived, along with several silk nightgowns and their matching robes.

Once the belt was tied, Elizabeth clasped Georgiana's hands. "Please do not be upset with your brother. William is a romantic, so naturally *he* wants to present the jewellery to me."

With that, Elizabeth rushed out of the dressing room bare-foot, leaving Georgiana contemplating her words. Slowly a smile crossed her face. "I will give you that, Elizabeth. You have managed to turn my taciturn brother into quite a romantic."

A sitting room

When Elizabeth walked into the room, her beauty rendered William speechless.

Smiling lovingly, she went to him. "You wished to see me, sweetheart?"

"I... I did," William managed to reply. "But first I must tell you how beautiful you are."

"Barefoot and in a robe?" she asked with a chuckle.

"I assume you are wearing it over your wedding gown?" Elizabeth nodded. "Turn around," he directed. She complied, causing him to add, "I have never seen your hair look more enchanting."

"I believe the lady's maid you hired is going to be worth every penny of her salary," she replied with a blush.

"She already is."

William wore a dark-blue suit, a white shirt with ruffles at the cuffs, and a silver waistcoat embroidered with dark blue threads. In his starched, white cravat, a stickpin consisting of a single diamond surrounded by blue sapphires sparkled whenever he moved. His carefully chosen clothes enhanced his blue eyes and the silver in his hair to perfection.

"You look very handsome," she announced. "If it were in my power, I would double your valet's pay."

"I pay Mr. Jackson very well," he quipped with a wink. "It is unfortunate that my trip to Southend proved too strenuous for Mr. Martin, but it was past time he enjoyed his retirement. Mr. Jackson shall accompany us on our trip," William said, speaking of the valet he had just hired, "as will O'Malley, so everything worked out for the best."

"I agree."

"Now, as to why I am here at this late hour." William pulled a black velvet box from inside his coat. "I wish to continue a family tradition my father began.

"As Father explained, shortly before his wedding he thought to have a necklace designed for my mother to celebrate their marriage. He was not certain the jeweller could finish it before the ceremony, but the man hand-delivered it in time for Mother to wear it with her wedding gown. Not long before her death, Mother called me into her bedroom and handed this box to me. She said she hoped I would present the necklace to the woman I love on our wedding day. It has remained in the safe ever since."

Elizabeth realised that left unsaid was the fact that he had not given it to Lady Cornelia. Her eyes grew wide as she watched him open the box and bring out a gold heart on an intricately woven gold chain. One side of the heart was completely covered in pavé diamonds, whilst the other was inscribed with the words *Forever and a Day*.

"Oh, William!" Elizabeth murmured. "It is the most beautiful thing I have ever seen."

"It was my mother's favourite, and I hoped it might become yours."

"It already is," she said as he fastened it around her neck.

"There are matching earrings."

After presenting Elizabeth with the earrings, he watched her cross to the mirror over the mantel to put them on.

Turning, she asked, "Do you approve?"

William's light blue eyes locked with hers as he walked across the room. Then gentle fingers began to glide down the side of her face and neck, continuing until they rested lightly atop her shoulder. "As exquisite as they are, they add nothing to your beauty, my love."

Suddenly feeling inadequate, Elizabeth blushed and lowered her eyes. Instantly her face was framed in his hands. "I abhor deceit of any kind, Elizabeth. If I say you are beautiful, it is because you are." Then his mouth captured hers in a kiss ardent enough to validate his words.

It was at that moment Georgiana opened the door. Embarrassed, she turned her back, saying, "Brother, I hate to intrude, but Elizabeth must finish dressing if we are to get to the church on time."

Reluctantly breaking the kiss, William beamed at his intended. "As much as I hate to agree with my sister, in this case, she is correct. I shall leave you in her capable hands, and the next time we meet, it shall be at the altar."

"Until then, my love."

That endearment garnered her another kiss before William walked out the door, and Elizabeth hurried to the doorway to gaze upon his retreating form.

Recalling how in love she had been on her own wedding day, Georgiana's eyes filled with tears.

When at last she was able to speak past the lump in her throat, she said, "Come, Elizabeth! We do not want to keep my wonderful brother waiting. Let us find your shoes, gather Marianne and Gregory, and be off to the church."

The ceremony

The wedding day of Fitzwilliam George Andrew Darcy of Pemberley, Derbyshire and Miss Elizabeth Rose Bennet of Hertfordshire proved the perfect opportunity for the residents of London who had been shuttered behind closed doors to come out of hiding. For the wealthy who had escaped to their country estates, it was a reason to return to Town.

Having endured the closure of theatres, museums, art galleries, parks and all public venues in order to facilitate the end of the dread disease that recently swept across their town, even the poorest were eager spectators at the social event of the season. After filling the rear pews of the sanctuary to watch, not only did they discover that the elusive Mr. Darcy was still a fine specimen of a man, but his new bride proved to be as beautiful as the rumours had implied.

At William's insistence, the presiding clergyman kept the ceremony as brief as possible, and the wedding seemed to take far less time than it took for Mr. Gardiner to escort Elizabeth down the long centre aisle to music selected by William and performed by the church's organist. None of the spectators had reason to complain, however, because the wait gave them ample time to examine both the groom and the bride.

Ere long, William and Elizabeth had said their vows, were pronounced man and wife and he had slipped Lady Anne's wedding ring on her finger. After signing the registry, family and friends rushed to congratulate them. Elizabeth had managed not to cry until she was surrounded by her sisters and Aunt Gardiner, who were all crying with happiness.

"Oh, Lizzy," Jane said, embracing her first. "After praying all these years for God to send along a man whom you could esteem, I am so happy He returned to you the one man you never stopped loving."

"I am fortunate," Elizabeth replied, glancing adoringly at her husband, "for no one could ever have taken William's place in my heart."

Kitty hugged her next, wishing her every happiness, before Mary stepped forward to do the same. Then Aunt Gardiner embraced her saying, "It is my belief that God, in His infinite wisdom, honoured your persistent love for one another by arranging this reunion. He knows that after enduring so much sorrow, each joy you and your husband experience will be cherished all the more."

"I intend to thank Him by living every day to the fullest. I shall never take William for granted," Elizabeth replied.

After receiving congratulations from Marianne, Georgiana and Isabelle, her former charges were brought forward to offer their good wishes. Whilst Emily and Evelyn seemed very happy to see her, Ellen was not as enthusiastic. Having received kisses on the cheek and wishes of joy from the younger girls but none from Ellen, Elizabeth gently pulled her aside.

"I have missed you very much, Ellen."

The child looked away when she answered. "I cannot imagine why, since you were busy planning your wedding."

"It is true I was busy, but I thought of you often, and each time I did, I wondered how you were. Are you still teaching your sisters?"

"I am, but Papa has hired a new governess; she arrives next month."

"I hope you will give her the chance to find out how smart and helpful you are."

Ellen shrugged.

"Are you disappointed that your cousin and I married?"

Ellen's head dropped. "No. It is just... I overheard Papa tell Mama that now that my cousin is married, he will seldom visit. He said Cousin Darcy would be too busy working on a progeny—whatever that means."

Elizabeth stifled a laugh. "Your Papa is mistaken. William and I plan to visit often, and we want to have your family visit Pemberley for at least a week very soon."

Ellen looked up, meeting her eyes. "I am glad that my cousin married you and not Aunt Amy. She has a horrid temper!" She glanced around Elizabeth to look at William. "I can clearly see he is happy, which makes me happy. After all, he is my best cousin."

Elizabeth tried not to smile as she pulled Ellen into an embrace. "I am happy that you approve." Then, holding her at arm's length, she added, "Just think! Now you and I are cousins, too!"

Ellen offered a wry smile. "I think I shall like that better than having you as our governess, for that means you can never leave."

"I like it better, too."

"It will be our secret," Ellen said, looking around. Seeing no one looking, she held out her little finger. "Link your finger with mine."

Elizabeth did as she was instructed.

"Now say, 'I swear!'" Ellen ordered.

"I swear!"

Ellen smile broadened. "Now neither of us can tell."

Not long afterward, William and Elizabeth were swept out a side door and into the carriage that was to transport them to the wedding breakfast. The top was down and the carriage and horses were decorated with flowers, ribbons and bows befitting a newly married couple; thus, it followed that as they made their way from St. George's to Matlock House, they were applauded and cheered by those they passed.

Wondering whether her reticent husband was perturbed by the attention, Elizabeth dismissed her doubt when she turned to find William smiling from ear to ear. Once he caught her watching, he did something totally out of character—he leaned over and kissed her. A huge cheer went up from the spectators, and William whispered, "I love you, Mrs. Darcy."

"I love you, Mr. Darcy."

Another kiss followed, prompting even louder cheers.

The wedding breakfast

If the members of the *ton* in attendance considered the inclusion of so many children at the breakfast inappropriate, they kept that opinion to themselves. It was obvious that the bride and groom were delighted to have them there, and even Lord and Lady Matlock smiled happily at every spilled cup of tea and dropped biscuit. It would not do to risk losing the good opinion of Lady Gordon, either. That matron was one of a select few who could dictate whether one was accepted into the highest echelons of the *ton*... or not.

Of course, the true attraction for those in society was the unknown woman who had managed to coax Fitzwilliam Darcy back to the altar. Many of the women were green with envy, since they had tried to catch his eye as debutantes years before. Then, when their own offspring began to debut, they had promoted their daughters as potential wives for the still-eligible Mr. Darcy—to no avail. That at Elizabeth's age—she was rumoured to be in her mid-thirties—the men of the *ton* openly admired her slim figure, silky hair, and striking eyes only added to their resentment.

As for the object of their jealousy, Elizabeth was oblivious to all save her handsome husband. She had never been in company with William at a gathering of the *ton* and was astounded at how openly some women flirted with him—even in front of their own spouses. She tried to stay at William's side, as was his desire, but on occasion found herself whisked away to greet a guest. After one such incident, Elizabeth was once again making her way towards William when Lady Gordon took hold of her arm, stopping her progress.

"Mrs. Darcy!" Lady Gordon declared. "You have no idea how pleased I am that Mr. Darcy had sense enough to choose you for his wife. I told him so just moments ago."

Elizabeth smiled. "How kind of you."

"Kind?" Lady Gordon crowed. "Kindness had nothing to do with it, my dear! I simply knew you were exactly what he needed in a wife. You and he belong together, just as certainly as he and my Amy did not! I have a gift for matchmaking, you know. It was I who told Isabelle that she should marry Colonel Fitzwilliam whilst he was still available." She laughed heartily. "When your daughters are old enough to be out, I hope I will be able to advise them."

Elizabeth had stopped listening when she saw a gentleman who looked about the same age as her husband approach William. That gentleman was unremarkable, but on his arm was a very handsome young woman with dark-auburn hair, grey eyes and a very ample bosom, liberally displayed. Overhearing the word Cambridge, she assumed he and William were once classmates. Full curious to know if the woman, who looked not a day over twenty, was the man's wife or his daughter, Elizabeth strained to hear their conversation. Unfortunately, additional guests congregated between her and William, and she could not. Not wishing to insult Lady Gordon by walking on, Elizabeth was left puzzled.

Lady Gordon noticed what had caught Elizabeth's interest, and instead of being upset, she seemed to understand completely. Leaning close, she said, "That is Lord Cummings talking to your husband, and the child on his arm is his new wife. Cummings is one and forty, if a day, and when it comes to female companionship, he has always robbed the cradle. My opinion is he cannot hold a decent conversation with anyone older than twenty. I was surprised, however, to hear that he had wed this one, although it is rumoured she was already with child." Elizabeth's eyes grew wide, so she added, "You should thank God every day that Mr. Darcy has never valued simple-minded women."

Elizabeth could not hold back a smile.

Suddenly, Lady Gordon declared, "But why am I telling you this? You must go over there right this minute and let Cummings see the mistake he made by marrying someone young enough to be his daughter."

As she gently pushed Elizabeth in William's direction, he turned. Devilishly handsome when he smiled, he did just that when he spied her. "There you are!" he said, holding out one hand. He waited for her to grasp it before adding, "I wondered where you had gone."

Elizabeth gave him a brilliant smile in return as he pulled her to his side and brought her hand to his lips for a kiss saying, "Lord Cummings, may I present my wife, Elizabeth." As Cummings bowed, William added, "Elizabeth, this is a former classmate of mine from Cambridge, Lord Cummings, and this is his wife, Lady Mary. They were recently married, too."

Acknowledgements were made and the conversation turned to determining how many years had passed since William and Lord Cummings had last seen each other, whilst Elizabeth and the child bride stuck to exchanging smiles.

After a few minutes, Lord Cummings said, "Fitzwilliam, you and Mrs. Darcy must visit our estate in Bath the instant Mary and I return."

"I thought your family's estate was in Yorkshire," William said.

"It was, but I had to sell it in order to buy another in Bath.

I like to gamble, you see, and Mary loves to dance. In Bath, one can pursue both activities."

"I am afraid we cannot make any commitments, for following our honeymoon Elizabeth and I want to enjoy the beauty of Pemberley for at least a year whilst we settle into married life."

"How dull!" Lady Cummings declared. "I told Lord Cummings before I agreed to marry him that I had to live where there is plenty to entertain, else I would turn into a shrew."

Lord Cummings grimaced, but quickly replaced it with a faux smile. "Luckily, Mary married me instead of you. Am I right, Darcy?"

Lady Mary began arguing with her husband, which gave William time to whisper to Elizabeth, "I am the lucky one." Elizabeth had to refrain from laughing out loud.

"What did you say, old boy?" Lord Cummings asked as Lady Mary finally quieted. "I fear I am getting hard of hearing."

"I said Lady Mary was indeed fortunate to have married you."

"Yes, well, we had best hurry if we wish to have something to eat before the breakfast ends. Come, my dear."

As Lord and Lady Cummings went towards the sideboards filled with food, Georgiana suddenly appeared. "Brother, may I have a word with you in private?"

"Of course." To Elizabeth he said, "I shall not be long."

As William and his sister walked away, his London physician, Dr. Graham, crossed the room to Elizabeth. They had been introduced at the beginning of the breakfast but had not had time to converse.

"Mrs. Darcy, allow me to tell you how pleased I am that you married my most *impatient* patient," he said with a chuckle. "It is my belief that happiness can help to keep pain at bay, and I am sure your love will act as a balm for Fitzwilliam."

"I agree, Dr. Graham. However, I intend to do more than make him happy. I plan to do everything in my power to discover new ways to help William manage the pain. After all, there are new discoveries every day. Surely, someone will devise a way to help him, if they have not already."

"Your husband is very fortunate to have found you, Mrs. Darcy. Rarely do the wives, and I might add, the husbands of my patients take it upon themselves to find ways to help their spouses."

"I would travel the world if I thought I could find a way to ease his pain."

"I believe you would. Moreover, your enquiry has reminded me that one of my colleagues, Dr. Jansen, has just returned after a year of studying medical advances in the Netherlands. His ancestors, many of whom were physicians in centuries past, come from there, and some of his relations still practice medicine there. One ancestor, Willem ten Rhyne,[6] visited Nagasaki in Japan in the latter part of the seventeenth century and brought the ancient Chinese practice of acupuncture back to his post in the Dutch East Indies and eventually it spread to his homeland. Dr. Jansen is especially interested in the use of acupuncture to alleviate pain."

"Acupuncture?" Elizabeth repeated. "What is that?"

"According to Jansen, the Chinese use the term *Zhēn jiǔ*. *Zhēn* literally means needle. I understand it involves inserting thin needles in various places on the body. At present, that is the extent of my knowledge regarding the practice, but Janson is preparing a paper to present at our next conference in London regarding acupuncture."

"I would love to correspond with Dr. Jansen about the possibility of using this treatment for William. Will you give him our address and ask him to write to me?"

"To you, not Fitzwilliam?"

"Yes. Until I am certain it could help, I do not wish to raise his hopes."

---

6 **Willem ten Rhijne** *(1647, Deventer – 1 June 1700, Batavia) was a Dutch doctor and botanist who was employed by the Dutch East India Company in 1673. In summer 1674 he was dispatched to the trading post Dejima in Japan. While giving medical instructions and taking care of high-ranking Japanese patients, ten Rhijne collected materials on Asian medicine, especially on acupuncture and moxibustion. In autumn 1676 he returned to Batavia where he continued to serve as a physician. In 1683 he published a book entitled "Dissertatio de Arthritide: Mantissa Schematica: De Acupunctura: Et Orationes Tres". His treatise on the art of needling which he called acupunctura was the first Western detailed study on that matter. https://en.wikipedia.org/wiki/Willem_ten_Rhijne*

Dr. Graham smiled. "I understand. And, yes, I will ask Dr. Jansen to write to you."

Elizabeth was beaming when she thanked Dr. Graham.

"You are most welcome," he replied. "Now, I believe I shall see if there is any wedding cake left."

As the physician walked away, William returned. Having overheard her last statement, he was curious. "Why were you thanking my doctor, Elizabeth?"

"I thanked him for saving your life so that we could be married today."

William smiled. "Perhaps I need to thank him, too. Come! Let us find him. Then you and I must be on our way if we are to reach Southend before dark."

Chapter 21

Darcy House

Elizabeth understood she and William would return to Darcy House to transfer to one of his coaches for the long trip to Southend. Their servants and luggage should have departed hours before, and everything was to be in place when they reached Lord Beauford's cottage. She had no idea that Georgiana had, with William's blessing, changed their plans, for she was still reflecting on the disparities between herself and Lady Cummings.

Not usually one to envy others, Elizabeth conceded that the beautiful woman on Cummings' arm had managed to set off doubts she thought she had conquered. Consequently, whilst they made the short trip to Darcy House, Elizabeth wished to discover William's opinion of the match.

"I understand you graduated Cambridge with Lord Cummings, is that correct?"

"Yes."

"Does it follow, then, that you and he are about the same age?"

"If I remember correctly, he is a half-year older," William answered. "Why do you ask?"

"You look much younger."

"I dare say that if Cummings would lose weight and drink less he might not look as old."

"True," Elizabeth said. She sat silent for a time, then ventured, "Lady Cummings is a very beautiful woman."

"Is she?" William said, seemingly oblivious of the motive behind Elizabeth's statement. "I confess I did not pay her much notice."

"Truly? The other men in the room certainly did."

All of a sudden, it dawned on William that insecurity might be behind her interest in Lady Cummings. Moreover, from the look that crossed his face, Elizabeth realised he had figured out her purpose in broaching the subject.

Giving her an adoring smile, he said, "Elizabeth, I am quite aware that, even at my age and despite my disability, due to my rank and wealth, I could likely have my choice of this year's debutantes. Nonetheless, I have no wish to marry someone barely older than Marianne, nor could someone with nothing more to offer than the ability to crochet a pillow, paint a table or decorate my arm hold my interest."

"Not even if they could provide an heir?"

"Not even then."

Elizabeth felt the weight of the world lift from her shoulders.

"Make no mistake. Not only do I consider you the most beautiful woman of my acquaintance, I recognised shortly after we met that no woman could ever satisfy my soul, save you."

By the time he had finished speaking, tears were brimming in Elizabeth's eyes, so he leaned in and kissed her softly. "Now, no more talk about Lady Cummings. Hopefully, we will never be in her company again, for I do not think I could survive her prattle for more than a minute."

"So she *is* indeed fortunate to have married Lord Cummings and not you," Elizabeth replied wryly.

William laughed. "Unfortunately, I cannot say the same for my friend!"

When the carriage began slowing to a stop in front of Darcy House, Elizabeth asked, "Why are we stopping here? I thought we would continue to the rear where the coach awaits."

"I have something to show you," William said as he helped her from the carriage.

When Elizabeth entered the foyer, her mouth fell open. The entire entrance hall was covered with dozens of roses in vases, baskets and various other containers, whilst greenery and additional roses wound around and through the railings of the grand staircase. The scent was intoxicating.

Reverently, Elizabeth murmured, "William, what have you done?"

Her husband, who had stopped a few steps back to watch her reaction, came up behind her. Circling her waist, he leaned down to place a kiss on her neck. "I hoped you would like it, but this was all Georgiana's idea. Most of the flowers came from our conservatory; Richard and Lady Gordon provided the rest."

"They are gorgeous!"

"Moreover, we are not going on to Southend until morning."

"We are not?"

"No. My sister feared we would both be exhausted by the time we reached the cottage, so she suggested we stay here tonight and leave in the morning. She, her family and Marianne removed themselves to Matlock House to give us privacy. I also asked Mrs. Barnes to have all the maids and footmen stay below stairs until morning. Other than my valet and your maid, no servants will be upstairs unless we ring for them."

"So, Jackson and O'Malley have not gone ahead?"

"No. They will travel when we do."

Suddenly, Mr. and Mrs. Barnes walked into the foyer looking very satisfied with themselves. "Welcome back to Darcy House, Mrs. Darcy," they said in unison.

"Thank you," Elizabeth replied. "This—" she waved an arm around the room, "is beautiful and so thoughtful."

"I did my best to follow Mrs. Langston's instructions," the housekeeper replied, beaming. "I hope you will be just as pleased when you see the upstairs."

"I am certain we will," William replied.

"Cook has prepared pheasant for dinner, along with other family favourites. For dessert she made the apple tart you prefer, Mr. Darcy, and there is a tray of refreshments already in the sitting room and a pot of hot tea, just in case you are hungry now."

"Please thank Mrs. Colton for her thoughtfulness."

"Of course. Now, pray excuse us. Please ring if there is anything else we can do for you."

"Thank you, Barnes," William said.

William waited patiently until the butler and housekeeper exited the foyer, then said solemnly, "Would that I could sweep you into my arms and carry you up the stairs, Elizabeth."

Throwing her arms around him, Elizabeth rested her head against his chest. "Oh, my darling, it matters not a jot that you cannot pick me up. I asked for nothing more in this life than to be your wife, and I am satisfied beyond measure."

"You always know what to say to sooth old doubts," he whispered into her hair.

"Perhaps that is because we are kindred spirits."

Their next kiss escalated quickly as long-suppressed yearnings broke free. Forgetting where they were, William's hands began to roam over her back before sliding down to cup her bottom and pull her tightly against the evidence of his desire. The sound of a door closing somewhere in the house brought him back to his senses, and he stepped back.

Taking her hand, he said, "Come, my darling. Let us see what awaits us upstairs."

Upon entering their sitting room, they found it also full of roses, and a trail of petals led across the room to her bedroom door. Giving William a hesitant smile, Elizabeth crossed to the door and opened it. Upon stepping inside, she discovered that not only did the petals lead straight to the bed, they covered the entire counterpane.

William, who followed right behind her, chuckled. "Georgiana must be convinced that roses are the key to a woman's heart."

"Whilst roses are certainly a symbol of love," Elizabeth said, turning to him, "you have held the key to my heart all these years without the gift of a single flower."

Instantly capturing her in his arms again, William rested his head atop hers. "If only I had known."

"Regrets may haunt us from time to time," Elizabeth murmured, "but from this day forward, let us strive to think only of our future."

William placed a kiss in her hair. "You are so wise."

Soon his lips found hers again, and the passion unleashed downstairs promptly resurfaced, though now it burned even hotter. Then, out of the blue, William stepped back, breathless, and closed his eyes.

"Is something wrong, sweetheart?" Elizabeth asked.

When his eyes opened, they begged for understanding. "I do not know how to say this delicately, but if we continue in this manner, I will not be able to wait until dark to make you mine."

"Do you think I would object?" A confused expression crossed his face, so Elizabeth added with an elfin smile, "Be it day or night, we *are* man and wife now."

"You will not be embarrassed if there is talk amongst the servants? Most know better than to gossip, but I cannot speak for them all."

"After what we have been through, I refuse to care what anyone thinks. We belong to each other, and if we wish to consummate our marriage this instant, what business is it of anyone else?" Then she smiled conspiratorially. "Besides, what is the worst they can say? That we loved each other too dearly to wait?"

William growled playfully and leaned down to kiss her. "You have no idea how hearing you say that pleases me."

"I have only begun to please you, my husband."

It was several kisses later before they separated to change out of their wedding attire.

Elizabeth's dressing room

According to Aunt Gardiner, Madam Dupree catered not only to the *ton*, but in another shop in a less fashionable area of town, she created scandalous attire for wealthy courtesans and those ladies who plied their trade in the finest brothels in London. According to the gossip, her nightgowns were particularly shocking.

Elizabeth was uncertain whether the rumours were true until the last package from Madam Dupree arrived two days before the wedding. Not only were the gowns and robes enclosed made of the finest silks, satins and lace, they were designed to expose much more of the female body than those displayed at the shop on Bond Street. In truth, Elizabeth speculated that Madam Dupree may have confused her order with one meant for a more *colourful* client once Georgiana began to hold them up for inspection.

She had tried not to blush as her new sister-to-be exclaimed over each item, but if she failed, Georgiana was too polite to tease her about it. Consequently, with no time to look for different nightwear, Elizabeth had quickly forgotten about the gowns... until now.

After O'Malley had let down her hair and brushed it out, she helped her don one of the nightgowns—a light-blue silk covered in lace. Trying not to appear embarrassed at how exposed she felt, Elizabeth quickly dismissed the maid.

Now standing at the full-length mirror in her dressing room, her dark locks flowing over her shoulders and down her back, Elizabeth examined herself with a critical eye. Reaching for one of the white rose buds O'Malley had just removed from her hair, Elizabeth placed it in a wave over one ear. Feeling foolish, she plucked it out and tossed it back on the table.

Flowers in your hair will not make you look any younger!

Then her eyes travelled to the main source of her disquiet. Having never worn anything so immodest, Elizabeth was mortified to find the bodice was made entirely of delicate, white, openwork lace. Not only were the dark circles of her breasts displayed, but each taut nipple had managed to find the perfect hole to slip through. Sighing, she reached for the matching silk robe and pulled it on over the gown. Grasping the sides, she drew them together to hide the bodice.

"I had rather you remove the robe."

Whirling around, Elizabeth was stunned to find her husband leaning against the doorframe. He looked extraordinarily handsome in a black silk robe that revealed his chest was covered with fine hair. His thick black hair was tousled just enough that some of the locks fell across his forehead, whilst straight, white teeth cut a swath across his tanned face when, at length, he smiled. Dazed, Elizabeth forgot to reply.

William walked over to push the robe from off her shoulders and watched it float to the floor.

Slowly, he examined Elizabeth, his eyes travelling to her toes before coming back to her bosom. At the sight of her proud nipples, the fire already burning in his belly began to blaze out of control. Grasping a single lock of silky hair that had come to rest over one perfect breast, he let it slip through his fingers.

"Have I told you today that you are the love of my life, Elizabeth, and that I shall love you forever?"

"Yes, but I will never tire of hearing it."

William hesitated. "Will you join me on the balcony for a glass of champagne? Mr. Barnes went to the trouble of chilling the wine, and it seems a shame not to partake of it."

Elizabeth nodded, and he led her through the French doors.

The sky was now overcast and dark clouds were gathering in the distance. Following the direction of Elizabeth's gaze, William said, "The storm should reach us in an hour or so, but we are safe here."

A lantern had already been lit against the waning sunlight and had been placed in the middle of a table next to the champagne. Elizabeth watched William open the bottle and pour two glasses. Handing one to her, he held up the other.

"To us! May our marriage be blessed with love, laughter and the joy of children."

Elizabeth tapped his glass with hers. "To love, laughter and the joy of children!" The bubbles in the champagne tickled her nose, making her giggle. "I think I rather like this, William. Is champagne very expensive?"

"*This* champagne is," William replied with a wink, "but I think we can manage to enjoy it often."

The sound of thunder drew Elizabeth's attention back to the storm, where lightning had begun to light up the sky. "I love watching storms from a distance, and the view from here is breath-taking."

"*You* are breath-taking," William replied, setting his glass down to pull her into his arms. "Do you have any idea how many times I stood on this very spot, gazing at the stars and wondering if you were seeing them, too? I could not help but wonder where you were and if you were happy. It happened so often that, in truth, I find it difficult to believe that you *are* in my arms now."

"Would you believe me if I told you that in my prayers, I asked God to bring me to mind whenever you gazed at the stars? I was so selfish that I cared not if you were happily married with two dozen children; I just wanted you to remember me with some degree of regret."

William stroked her face gently with his knuckles. "There was hardly a day that passed when you did not cross my mind."

"I often wondered what God thought of my audacity. Still, now that He has brought us together, I choose to believe He honoured my undying love for you."

"Our undying love for each other," William corrected.

"For each other," Elizabeth acknowledged. "You and I are so

blessed to be given another chance, and I plan to do all in my power to make you happy."

"You already have. My only prayer is that my injury does not become a burden for you."

"Oh, my darling, your injury will never define who you are! You are defined by your character, and you are the most honourable man I have ever known, and the only man who has ever owned my heart. I have never confessed this to anyone, not even Jane, but when we were the most at odds in the earliest days of our acquaintance, my heart desired you. Against my will, mind you, but, nonetheless, it did."

Her declaration moved William to capture her lips in another, all-consuming kiss. Then, picking up the candlestick, he led her back into the bedroom. He placed the candlestick on the table beside the bed and resumed his kisses. As passion removed all restraint, his hands captured her breasts through the soft fabric of the gown. When Elizabeth moaned her approval, he grasped the hem of the garment and brought it up and over her head. Tossing it aside, he stood frozen in place, mesmerised by her beauty.

Just as she began to feel self-conscious, he murmured, "I have seen countless nudes in museums throughout Britain and Europe, my darling, but none compare to you."

Unable to restrain himself any longer, William grasped the counterpane and tossed it aside before helping Elizabeth into bed. After slipping to the middle of the mattress, she watched wide-eyed as he discarded his robe and joined her. Once by her side, he captured her mouth anew, with each kiss increasing his passion until he rolled to lie atop her. Continuing his quest, he began placing kisses across her ear, where he whispered words of endearment, then down her neck to her shoulders.

Once there, he nipped the soft, fragrant skin before continuing to her breasts. Capturing one taut mound in his mouth, he suckled it before teasing the firm nipple with his tongue. Then, gripping it lightly between his teeth, he gently tugged, making Elizabeth moan. Letting go, he kissed that dark circle before moving to the other and repeating his actions.

Elizabeth writhed beneath him, so he slid one hand between her legs and felt them open wide. Her moans increased with his every stroke, every caress.

"Are you ready, sweetheart?"

"Yes, my love."

More than ready, William positioned himself and slid inside, claiming her as his own.

Though she flinched at the beginning, the steady rhythm of William's movements began to create a feeling of pleasure such as Elizabeth had never known. It continued to build until she felt she might die if he were to stop. Then, suddenly, it was as though she had reached the peak of a mountain and, just as quickly, had fallen off the other side. Calling out William's name as she dropped over the edge, she floated back to earth in a state of exquisite bliss.

Continuing until he reached satisfaction a few strokes later, William collapsed, breathing heavily. Then, lifting his head to look into her eyes, his expression fell when he saw the tears in them. "Please forgive me for making you cry."

Elizabeth lifted her head to kiss his lips before letting it drop back on the pillow. "There is nothing to forgive, my darling husband. These are tears of joy. There was a little pain at first, but just as my aunt said would happen, it was quickly forgotten in the love we shared afterwards. At this moment I could not be more perfectly and incandescently happy."

William's anxious expression changed to joy. "Neither could I." Then, taking Elizabeth with him as he rolled onto his side so that they faced each other, he added, "I need to take the weight off my knee."

In her euphoria, Elizabeth had completely forgotten his injury. "Are *you* in pain?"

"To be truthful, the only time I was not aware of the pain was when I claimed you."

Slipping a hand behind her husband's head, she grasped the long hair at the nape and pulled his mouth back to hers. Kissing him firmly she declared, "We should repeat it often, then."

William could not hold back a smile. "If you are looking for an argument, sweetheart, you will get none from me."

Settling her head against his chest, Elizabeth recalled what her mother once told her once about the marriage bed. "William, will you be able to... to—"

"To what, Elizabeth?"

She let go a sigh. "To *perform* again soon?"

"*Performing* will not be a problem, Elizabeth." William smiled. "But since this is your first experience, I felt I should not impose on you again today."

"You would not be imposing," she insisted.

"You have no idea how much that pleases me."

Suddenly, it occurred to Elizabeth that this was not her husband's first experience. After all, he was forty years old and had been married before. That realisation rendered her completely silent, and it did not take long for William to notice.

"Tell me what you are thinking, Elizabeth."

He felt her take a deep breath and let it go. "It is nothing to speak of now."

"We vowed never to have any secrets between us."

She sighed. "Your relationship with Lady Cornelia, was it—"

"We had no relationship," William interjected. "After I learned on our wedding day that Cornelia was carrying another man's child, I could not stand to be in the same room with her, much less share a bed." He rolled over so that Elizabeth was beneath him once more. "Pray believe me. All the love in my heart has always belonged to you."

Elizabeth framed his face with her hands. "I believe you."

It was a good deal later before they took advantage of the hot water Mr. Barnes had delivered to the master's dressing room at Jackson's request.

After taking pleasure in the huge copper tub until the water was cold, they donned their robes again and rang for dinner to be brought to the sitting room.

By the time the clock on the mantel in the adjoining sitting room chimed midnight, William had fallen fast asleep.

Not so Elizabeth. She lay on her side, cocooned in her husband's arms, listening to the sound of his heartbeat. It seemed to match the rhythm of the steady rain that now pitter-pattered on the floor of the balcony. The rain had begun in earnest whilst they were eating, and she had asked William to leave the doors open so she could smell the fresh air it would leave in its wake.

Reliving all that had happened since that morning, Elizabeth felt her heart might actually burst with all the love it held for the man lying beside her. Gently placing a kiss on the hard planes of William's chest, she smiled to recall questioning his ability to love her again. Not only had he performed—once more in the copper tub and again when they returned to bed—he had done so with as much vigour as his first performance.

Pulling back to study William's peaceful mien, she whispered softly, "My darling husband, if you only knew how much I love you. You own my heart. You always have; you always will."

Kissing two fingers, she pressed them against his lips. Satisfied, she snuggled closer to him and closed her eyes. It was not long until the rain encouraged her to join her husband in slumber.

Chapter 22

Three months later

If ever there was an ideal place for a secluded honeymoon, it was Lord Beauford's cottage in Southend. With no one but the servants at the cottage and the old couple who worked for the Gardiners across the lane, William and Elizabeth had the entire property on that secluded road, including the beach, entirely to themselves.

Most evenings were spent either at the gazebo, eating dinner whilst listening to the waves crash on the sand, or lying under the stars on the balcony of their bedroom. Nonetheless, both William and Elizabeth were eager to return to Pemberley once the week was over.

Pemberley had proved even more beautiful than Elizabeth recalled from her short visit years before. From the beginning, she treasured her early morning walks about the estate. Until Dr. Jansen arrived a few weeks later at Elizabeth's request, William managed estate business during her morning constitutional; however, after the doctor applied acupuncture to William's knee several times in succession, he began to join her for a portion of her walk around the gardens.

Subsequent treatments had proved so beneficial that by the time the good doctor returned to London, William was in much less pain. Dr. Jansen promised to relate to the physicians he was training in the procedure William's offer to provide an office in Lambton, complete with everything needed for a traditional practice, along with acupuncture. Praying that someone would accept, William and Elizabeth had sent Dr. Jansen back to London with renewed hope for a more permanent solution to alleviating the pain he dealt with daily.

Marianne had returned to Pemberley four weeks after the wedding, and as she and Elizabeth spent more time together, they became steadfast companions. Though on occasion William missed having Elizabeth solely to himself, he was grateful that Marianne had taken Elizabeth to heart as a mother. Often coming upon them sitting side by side conversing animatedly, he had marvelled at the change in his daughter's manner until recalling how Elizabeth had completely changed his life as well. Scenes such as those filled his heart with gratitude for the woman who had accepted his hand.

Life could not have been more perfect as Christmas approached. The prospect of having all of Elizabeth's family, as well as Georgiana's, at Pemberley for the holiday gave William a sense of completeness he never imagined possible. Moreover, in the days leading up to their marriage, he had become cognisant of how much joy his wife experienced with her family about her. Consequently, he vowed never to let long periods pass without either hosting her relations or taking Elizabeth to visit them.

The event that finally persuaded them to leave Pemberley was the birth of Master Richard Edward David Fitzwilliam. They had waited almost two weeks before travelling to Matlock Manor to see him, in order to give Lady Matlock sufficient time to recover from the birth before receiving visitors. Their plan was to return to Pemberley just before Christmas Day in time to greet their guests.

Matlock Manor

Autumn had produced mild temperatures that lasted through November, with the first really cold spell arriving during the first week of December. The first snowflakes of the season began to fall just as William and Elizabeth walked out the back entrance of Matlock Manor near daybreak. As they progressed around the path that circled the pond, a smile crossed Elizabeth's face.

Never one to confine lovemaking to their bed or to the dark, William's passion had quickly eliminated all her reservations about when and where to practice marital delights, though Marianne's return to Pemberley had, of necessity, made them more cautious. Still, they were just as likely to enjoy intimacy in his study—with doors locked, of course—as in their bedroom. These trysts did not take the place of the bliss they experienced each night, nor did they replace William's habit of loving Elizabeth again before starting his day.

Trying not to blush at the memory of how vigorously he had taken her that morning, she decided to focus on his footsteps. William did not seem to be struggling to walk as he had in the past; still, once at the gazebo, she said, "I pray I did not ask too much by having you walk this far. Tell me truly. Are you in pain?"

"I cannot say there is no pain, but there is much less than when I was here before. I do, however, wonder at your wanting to walk so far in the cold."

"I wished to visit the gazebo. I have a special spot in my heart for this place, since it is here I first began to believe you might still love me."

William stopped to pull her into his arms for a gentle kiss. "I have not forgotten."

Elizabeth sighed. "I pray daily that one of Dr. Jansen's colleagues will accept your generous offer to relocate to Lambton. It would be a great comfort to have a doctor nearby since no one took Dr. Camryn's place after his death. If none accept, however, we must consider residing at the house in London the majority of the year. At least there you can avail yourself of Dr. Jansen's expertise."

"We shall just have to place these matters in God's hands, my love," William said, leaning in to claim her lips again.

The snowflakes had begun falling faster as they walked, but William had been certain the fox-lined cape, hat and muff he had purchased for Elizabeth in London would suffice until he straightened and noticed her cheeks were crimson.

"Sweetheart, are you warm enough?"

Elizabeth smiled. "I am. Why do you ask?"

"Your face has reddened. I fear you are too cold." Taking her arm, he said, "We should return to the house."

A melodious string of laughter stopped him in his tracks. "We will do no such thing," Elizabeth declared. "My face always takes on a rosy glow when I walk in brisk weather. Please, let us sit in the gazebo until I have rested; then we can return to the house."

"We both know that you mean 'until *I* have rested,'" William replied, not complying with her suggestion.

Elizabeth laughed. "Did it not occur to you that a woman carrying your child might wish to rest after walking so far?"

William froze, the steady blink of his eyes the only indication that he had heard. She waited anxiously until, at last, he stammered, "Are you... are you saying... you are with child?"

Elizabeth nodded enthusiastically.

Fixing his eyes on her stomach, William murmured reverently, "Are you certain?"

"According to every sign my sisters and Aunt Madeline said I should look for, I am. Moreover, I spoke to Dr. Jansen before he left Pemberley, and he believed it possible. He did advise me, however, that I must feel the quickening to be sure." Dropping the muff, she framed William's face with her hands. "I felt the quickening this morning, my love."

Abruptly enveloped in strong arms, Elizabeth felt William tremble as he held her. Concluding that her tender-hearted husband might be struggling not to cry, she was not surprised to find tears glistening in his eyes when he pulled back to look at her.

"Oh, Elizabeth! I had lost hope of ever hearing those words. Other than the day we were married, this is the happiest of my life."

"I am happy that you are pleased."

"Pleased?" William declared. "I am ecstatic."

"I have only one request, please."

"Anything, my darling!"

"I think we should keep this news a secret... at least until after Christmas. I do not wish to draw attention away from the Matlocks' new blessing. Besides," she snuggled into his chest, "I love that only you and I will know, if only for a little while."

William placed a kiss atop her head. "It will be our secret."

A short while later, he stooped to pick up the muff and held it for her to put on. "I will not have the mother of my child catch a cold. Let us return to the house, break our fast and have another look at Master Edward."

"It will be difficult holding the baby without imagining our child in my arms. Still, I am determined not to divulge our secret by crying when I do."

As they returned to the house, two pairs of eyes followed them from a balcony.

Marjorie and Marianne were breaking their fast on the balcony of Marjorie's bedroom when they caught sight of William and Elizabeth in the distance. Just as they did, William leaned down to give his wife a kiss.

"We have always been completely honest with each other," Marjorie said. "So, tell me. Are things as ideal between your parents as I have heard Papa say?"

"No," Marianne answered in jest. "They are even better. They never separate for very long and when they are together, they hold hands. And the way they look at one another..." Marianne sighed heavily. "Their marriage has made me realise what I want when I marry."

"My parents act the same way."

"That may be so, but I have never seen Papa so... *joyful* is the only word that suits. And, seeing him that happy makes me realise anew how selfish I had become. After all, I shall marry one day, and now that he has Mother, I will not have to worry about him being alone."

"Why do you call her 'Mother'?"

"It was not forced upon me, if that is what you infer. I was told I could call her 'Elizabeth,' but I had rather address her as 'Mother' out of respect. I never knew how much I missed having a mother until she married Papa. We can speak about anything, and Mother seems to know what I am going to say before I even open my mouth."

"That sounds a little frightening," Marjorie observed. "You will never get away with anything."

Marianne laughed. "It is not like that at all. It is just... it is uncanny how she understands the concerns of someone my age."

"Such as?"

"How to know if a gentleman is only flirting with me or is serious, how to get him to notice me without appearing immodest, or how to gently dissuade someone I may not care for from pursuing me. Such things as these."

"My mother has discussed those things with us in the past."

"If she did, I had forgotten. In any event, I can speak to my mother about anything, and she never gets ruffled. She explains without judging, which I have come to appreciate."

"I am pleased for you," Marjorie said. "It is good to have a mother, especially when one has questions."

"I think it good to have a mother at all times."

The nursery

Laying the sleeping infant in his bed, Lady Matlock smiled

at the nurse sitting in a chair beside it before joining her husband in the sitting room next door. Richard was at the window when she entered and she went straight to him.

"Finally, Edward is asleep," she announced wearily.

Sliding an arm around his wife's waist, Richard pulled Isabelle into his embrace and placed a gentle kiss on her forehead. "Your mother still insists that I hire a wet nurse so you may get more rest."

"Edward might be my last child, and I wish to feed him just as I did our girls. Besides, Mother is of the old school and believes all mothers should turn their children over to a wet nurse the second they are born. I do not want that for our son."

"No need to get upset, my love," Richard said. "The matter is entirely up to you. After all, you are the one who has to rise at all hours to feed him. I have to say, though, that if memory serves, none of the girls had to be fed as often or for as long as Edward."

"Your son is larger than our daughters when they were born."

"So, now he is *my* son," Richard said, smiling.

"He is very much *your* son," Isabelle replied with a wry grin. "Not only does he favour you, but his brows knit exactly like yours whenever his temper flares."

"A two-week-old babe does not possess a temper. He cries because he has no other way of communicating that he is hungry or wet."

"Would that I had only known that with my other children," Isabelle declared, bringing a hand to her heart impertinently.

"You are so amusing."

"I am not trying to amuse," Isabelle responded. "I can assure you that, even at his age, Edward has quite the temper, especially if he believes I have taken too long to meet his demands!"

"I will not listen," Richard interrupted with a chuckle. "If he does have a temper, he will have inherited it from your side of the family."

Isabelle smiled knowingly. "Of course, because obviously you have no temper."

"Obviously."

Suddenly, Richard's attention was drawn to something outside, and turned to get a better view. Isabelle turned to look, too. "What are you searching for?"

"Mr. Goings said that Darcy and Elizabeth walked out at dawn. I have not had an opportunity to see how well my cousin walks after a long stroll since Dr. Jansen began his treatments."

"What are the treatments called again?"

"Dr. Jansen calls it acupuncture."

"That sounds foreboding. What does it entail?"

"As Darcy explained it, the doctor places needles at certain points around the painful area and by manipulating them, the pain is relieved. Moreover, as I understand it, with constant use, the pain can often be kept at bay."

"I would think having needles stuck into one's body would cause more pain, not less."

"I agree, but Darcy swears by it. He also believes it could help my shoulder—the one I injured when my horse was shot out from under me during my last campaign. I am curious to see how well it has helped him."

"They only arrived last night, and there is plenty of time to observe Darcy's steps before they leave."

Richard turned back to his wife. "As always, you are correct. Now, would you care to join me in the dining room to break your fast? I am starved."

"You have not eaten?"

"I wanted to wait for you."

She smiled. "Then, yes. I would love to join you."

The nursery
That afternoon

Elizabeth had worried about returning to Matlock Manor as William's wife, but had been greatly relieved to discover that none of the servants seemed to notice, or if they did, they did not act as though they had. In fact, the discussion of governesses came from Ellen, who, along with her sisters, filed into the nursery to see their baby brother just after she and William entered the room.

Quickly crossing to where Elizabeth sat holding Edward, who was beginning to whimper, Ellen slid onto the settee next to her. Elizabeth leaned close. "I imagine that you are thrilled to finally have a baby brother."

Ellen's pained expression reminded Elizabeth so much of Lord Matlock that she struggled not to smile.

"I cannot say for certain. I have never had one before." Then Ellen lowered her voice. "I have found, though, that if you can get used to all the crying, Edward is not so bad. I tried to tell my sisters this, but I fear Evelyn is just not interested in getting to know him yet, and Emily is too young to understand. Whenever she is brought here to see Edward, she covers her ears."

Elizabeth glanced to where Ellen's sisters sat on a sofa beside their mother, who was conversing with Richard and William. Just as Ellen had said, Emily's hands were clasped over her ears.

Pursing her lips to keep from laughing, Elizabeth said, "I will wager that you are already quite a help to your mother. Babies are a lot of work."

Ellen sat up taller. "I try, but Mother is so particular about him that she would make even the most skilful nanny nervous." She leaned over to pull the blanket away from her brother's face for a better look. "I have not said anything to Papa or Mama, for I do not wish to worry them, but I think he looks odd without any hair."

"Many babies are bald when they are born, but in no time at all they have a full head of hair."

"Not my sisters!" Ellen argued. "I clearly remember they each had plenty of hair when they were born." She studied her brother more closely. "Perhaps it is just boys who have no hair at the beginning."

Amused, Elizabeth said, "You could be right." Then, she added, "Your mother told me that the new governess is doing a good job."

A heavy sigh escaped her companion. "I suppose they would

think so. She is entirely too quiet, if you ask me. Still, she is not as unbearable as some we had before you."

"That is good to know," Elizabeth replied. "Have you had a chance to show her how smart you are?"

Ellen shrugged. "I have tried, but she tells me to be quiet. Not once has she asked me to help Evelyn or Emily with their numbers or letters, either."

Making a mental note to ask Richard if she might speak with the governess before she left, Elizabeth answered, "I understand. She has not been here very long. Give her time."

Suddenly, William stood over them and Elizabeth turned the baby to give him a better view. Chucking the infant under his chin, he teased, "Someone has been eating well."

"Too well," Richard said, crossing the room to where they were. Looking extremely proud, he continued, "It is all Isabelle can do to keep him fed."

"Richard is just jealous that I spend so much time with the baby," Isabelle teased as she joined them.

"This is what you have to look forward to, Darcy," Richard replied. "Once a child is born, he or she will require all of your wife's attention."

"If ever I am so fortunate, I will not complain," William replied, giving Elizabeth a loving look.

"Spoken like a true gentleman," Isabelle said.

"Or a man just recently married. Just wait until Elizabeth has a child, and we shall see what he says then!"

Chapter 23

Pemberley
June 1827
A sitting room that evening

The halls of Pemberley were filled with servants dashing in one direction or another, however, the master of Pemberley took little notice of them. His attention was focused on the door to Elizabeth's bedroom, where the new Lambton physician, Dr. Porter, had been ensconced since noon, along with Jane Cowan, Madeline Gardiner, a midwife and some maids.

Though William prided himself on his self-control, Elizabeth had been in labour since before dawn, and his patience had vanished. He had begun pacing the floor in an endless pattern, despite knowing it would certainly aggravate his knee.

Edward Gardiner and Jonathan Cowan exchanged knowing looks, nodding imperceptibly. Having attempted several times to tell William that it was perfectly normal for a woman giving birth to be in labour for as long as a day, perhaps more, they had not been able to reassure the anxious father. As it was, for the past hour they could only watch silently as William coped with his fears in his own way.

Suddenly a shrill cry pierced the air, bringing his pacing to an abrupt halt. William stared at the bedroom door without blinking until the crying commenced again and did not stop. Instructed by Jane to make certain William waited until summoned, Jonathan rose and went to stand next to him.

Sliding an arm around his shoulder, he said, "Be patient. It will not be long now. Jane promised to give us a report as soon as she could."

Recollections of his mother's death shortly after Georgiana's birth, and even Cornelia's death during childbirth, had begun tormenting William the last month, and the arrival of Jane and Aunt Gardiner had been his salvation. The melancholy that had plagued him most of his adult life had attempted to supplant the joy he felt at the prospect of having a child with the love of his life, and he had struggled to keep Elizabeth totally unaware of the fear that gripped him. The effort had, however, taken a toll on his equanimity.

Elizabeth's sister and aunt had pointed out that Elizabeth was in much better health than Anne Darcy had been when Georgiana was born, and that all her sisters had delivered children successfully, and he found some solace in their reassurances. Still, a niggling doubt he could not conquer continued to torment him when he least expected it.

As it did now.

Suddenly the door to the bedroom opened and Jane rushed into the room. Though she looked weary, she was smiling.

"Congratulations, William! You have a beautiful, healthy son."

"Eliz... Elizabeth?" William stammered.

"Though she is exhausted, as would be expected, my sister is doing very well."

As relief washed over William, he closed his eyes.

"Dr. Porter asked me to tell you he will speak with you shortly. Meanwhile, Lizzy expressly requested that you wait until she is presentable to come in, so I will come for you once she is ready."

"Elizabeth could never be anything but beautiful to me."

Jane reached out to take his hand. "I know this has been

hard for you, but the wait will not be long now." Then, giving her husband a smile, she hurried back into the bedroom.

Mr. Gardiner had come to his feet when Jane entered the room, and now he slapped William on the back. "Well done! You survived the birth of your first child."

"I agree. You handled it remarkably well," Jonathan added.

William could not fully rejoice until he had seen the babe and Elizabeth. Still, he offered a small smile with his reply. "If you were privy to my thoughts, you would not be so quick to praise me. It broke my heart to hear Elizabeth suffering so terribly when there was nothing I could do to alleviate her pain."

"Any man worth his salt would relieve his wife of the pain if he could," Mr. Gardiner said. Then he chuckled. "I fear, though, that if it were left up to men to bear children, one child would be our limit!"

"Fortunately, women are stronger," Jonathan added.

Suddenly the bedroom door opened, and Dr. Porter emerged. The short, balding man smiled as he crossed the room to stand before William.

"Mr. Darcy, your wife has delivered a healthy son. She is doing remarkably well, considering she delivered a child who I wager will surpass you in height once he is grown."

"But... but you do expect Elizabeth to fully recover?"

"Most certainly. I will admit to being worried about bearing her first child at her age, but because of her habit of walking in the fresh air throughout her pregnancy, she delivered a healthy child with no more effort than a woman in her twenties might."

"Thank God," William murmured, the tension in his body diminishing for the first time in hours. "How can I ever repay you for taking such remarkable care of Elizabeth and our child?"

"My reward is in knowing that all went well. Besides," he teased, "you will receive a bill. By the way, Mrs. Darcy said she plans to nurse the babe, but I suggest having a wet-nurse on call in the event she becomes too tired. Moreover, I told her that she must stay abed until I say differently."

"Of course."

"Given your generous offer to stay here tonight, I will retire to the bedroom assigned to me and get some sleep. I will check on Mrs. Darcy and the child in the morning, but do not hesitate to wake me if I am needed before then."

The doctor extended a hand, and William grasped it. Dr. Porter glanced at his leg. "I imagine you have been on your feet for hours. What say you to an acupuncture treatment on your knee again tomorrow?"

"I think that an excellent idea. I wish to care for Elizabeth, and any pain would be a hindrance."

"It most certainly would," the doctor replied. Then he smiled. "Now. Do you not think it time you met your son?"

William flashed a rare, wide smile and rushed towards the bedroom. As he watched him vanish, Dr. Porter smiled. "This is what I love about my profession."

"What a joyful day this is!" Mr. Gardiner said as he approached the doctor. "My niece and nephew waited many years for such happiness."

"I have not known either of the Darcys very long, but their regard for one another is evident."

"It certainly is! My niece is fortunate to have married such a man."

"And I dare say that my brother is fortunate to have married such a woman," Jonathan observed. "Clearly, Lizzy and William's love was ordained by God. After all, He practically arranged their reunion."

"I am afraid I know nothing of their past, but they seem devoted to one another," Dr. Porter stated.

"They were close to an engagement fourteen years ago, but circumstances forced them to part," Jonathan replied. "Only recently crossing paths again, they were reconciled and decided to marry."

"What a remarkable account!" Dr. Porter declared. Then he stifled a yawn. "Please excuse me. I simply must retire."

Mr. Gardiner stretched. "I think I shall follow the good doctor and retire. Madeline will be along shortly, and she will want to share every detail." He laughed. "I hope I can stay awake long enough to hear it."

"I fear Jane will do the same," Jonathan said, "but I believe I shall wait for her here."

In the bedroom

Whilst the bed clothes were being changed, Aunt Gardiner helped Lizzy to wash and dress in a white nightgown with pink flowers embroidered along the neck. Then she pulled her niece's hair back, using a matching ribbon to secure it. After extracting a promise from Elizabeth to call if she were needed, Madeline Gardiner retired for the night.

Jane was busy replacing the burned-out candles in the room. Placing the newly filled candelabrum back on the bedside table, she looked at her sister, who lay propped up on pillows cradling her son.

"I added more candles so that William can see you and the babe more easily." She nodded to the Darcy cradle that had been brought out of storage and now rested on the floor beside the bed. "The cradle is ready. Moreover, the baby's nurse said that should you wish to leave the child with her tonight, she will be in the nursery."

"Our baby will sleep here tonight," Elizabeth answered wearily.

Jane reached to take her sister's hand and squeezed it. "I am so proud of you, Lizzy. You were so brave throughout the entire day."

"I would not have been half as brave had not you and Aunt Madeline been here."

"We are fortunate that we were able to get here ahead of the birth." Hearing the door open, she turned to see William come in. "Now, I shall leave so that your husband may meet his son in private."

As Jane passed, she gave William a smile. Returning the smile, he hurried to sit down on the bed beside Elizabeth. Leaning towards her outstretched fingers, he placed a soft kiss on her lips.

"It was agony being separated from you, Elizabeth. Forgive me for getting so upset that I was asked to leave. It was—" He dropped his head, sighing heavily. "I could not stand to see you suffer, when I could do nothing."

Elizabeth brought up a hand to caress his dear face. "There is no need to apologise for being tender-hearted, William. That is one of many reasons why I love you."

Clasping the hand, he placed a kiss on her palm. "I love you so much, Elizabeth Darcy."

A more ardent kiss followed before William turned his attention to the innocent cherub with a plethora of black curls asleep on Elizabeth's breast. Pulling the blanket aside for a better look, his heart swelled with pride as he began to run his fingers gently over the child's silky halo. His eyes glistening with tears, he murmured, "He is perfect."

Elizabeth smiled lovingly. "That is because he looks just like his father."

"*I* am hardly perfect, and those curls are not mine," William teased.

"You *are* perfect for me, and even if he inherited the curls from me, the colour is from you. Look, his eyes and nose are identical to yours, too!"

"His eyes are closed. I cannot tell."

"They were open immediately after he was born, and he studied me so seriously, it was as though you were looking back at me. All new-born babes have blue eyes, but I am certain his will lighten to the same shade as yours."

"I hoped he would inherit your lively, brown ones."

"Do not worry. I plan to raise Bennet Fitzwilliam George Darcy to be a very lively boy, no matter the colour of his eyes."

"You have enlivened my life and Marianne's so extraordinarily that I have no doubt that you will do the same for all our children."

"All?" Elizabeth teased. "How many do you imagine we shall have?"

"I shall leave the number entirely up to you. I should be deliriously happy with just you, Bennet and Marianne."

"Where *is* Marianne?"

"She was so exhausted that she fell asleep. I will wake her in a little while, but I wished to see you and our son alone first."

"I understand." Elizabeth turned Bennet so William could get a better look. "Is he not the most beautiful baby you have ever seen? Would you like to hold your son?"

"I... I have not held a babe this small since Georgiana was born," William replied nervously.

Elizabeth offered a sympathetic smile. "There is no better time to begin practicing than now."

Wrapping the blanket more securely about Bennet, she offered him to William. Carefully taking the babe, he stood and moved closer to the candles to admire him.

"He is as light as a feather."

Elizabeth chuckled. "Wait until you hold him a while. You may not think so."

Suddenly the door flew open and Marianne rushed in, talking animatedly. "I woke up and discovered the sitting room was empty. I realised the baby must have—"

She stopped speaking and crossed the room. For a moment, Marianne studied her new sibling in complete silence. Then her expression softened and she murmured, "So beautiful."

William caught Elizabeth's eye. "His mother and I were just saying that."

"So I have a brother?"

"You do."

"May I hold him?"

"Of course you may," William said. "Sit down, and I will put him in your arms."

Marianne did as her father asked, and soon the babe was sleeping in her arms. Overwhelmed, tears began to roll down her cheeks. "To think, without Mother I would never have had a brother." She looked to Elizabeth. "Thank you."

Too overcome to speak, Elizabeth only nodded.

It was not long before Bennet began to squirm as though he

might wake. William leaned down to take the child from Marianne, then began to swing him slowly side to side. Quickly Bennet was lulled back to sleep, so he laid him in the cradle.

"How did you know to do that?" Marianne asked.

"My mother taught me when your aunt Georgiana was an infant."

William returned to Elizabeth's side. "Our son may want to be fed soon, so you must try to sleep, sweetheart. For my part, I intend to sleep on the chaise tonight, so I will be nearby if you need me or if the baby wakes."

"I should retire, too," Marianne said. Walking around to the other side of the bed, she leaned down to place a kiss on Elizabeth's forehead. "Mother, I am so excited I do not know if I will be able to sleep at all."

"I think we all feel the same way," Elizabeth said, giving her daughter's hand a squeeze. "Still, we must all try, else none of us will be of any use tomorrow."

After Marianne exited the room, William began straightening the pillows behind his wife's head. "Is there anything that you need or that I may get for you before you sleep?"

"There is one thing."

"Anything."

"I cannot sleep without you beside me. Instead of sleeping on the chaise, will you lie next to me?"

Unable to refuse, William stripped to his drawers and shirt and slid into bed next to Elizabeth. Carefully sliding his arms around her, it was not long until the whole family was asleep.

Since the Cowans and the Gardiners left their children in Town with Randall and his wife, they returned to London a mere three days after Bennet's birth. Though not happy to see her family leave, Elizabeth extracted a promise that they would return with all the children in the autumn. There was little time to mourn her family's departure, however, for Richard and his family were scheduled to arrive soon to meet the new heir of Pemberley.

Almost a week later

According to Dr. Porter's instructions, Elizabeth was still supposed to have been abed when William's cousins were expected; however, she had begun bending the rules almost immediately by spending part of the day sitting in a chair in her bedroom or on the balcony, most often with Bennet in her arms. That was where she was when the Fitzwilliams arrived.

Ellen and her sisters rushed onto the balcony, followed closely by William and Richard, who held six-month-old Edward. Marjorie, Marianne and Isabelle trailed only slightly behind. Lady Matlock admonished her youngest girls to slow down, and whilst her younger sisters halted immediately, Ellen went straight to Elizabeth.

Peering at the baby lying in Elizabeth's lap, Ellen's expression changed to disbelief. "I cannot believe he has hair!"

Elizabeth smiled. "It is unusual for a new-born babe to have this much."

"I was certain he would resemble Edward," Ellen replied, glancing to her flaxen-haired brother. "Even after all this time my brother has almost no hair!"

"Perhaps it is merely hard to see Edward's hair because it is so light."

"No," Ellen argued. "He just does not have much."

By then Richard, Marjorie, Isabelle and the younger children had surrounded the chaise to get a glimpse of Bennet.

"He is certainly a beautiful baby," Isabelle said.

"Rarely have I seen a babe so young resemble his father so strongly," Richard remarked.

"Did you just say I was beautiful?" William teased.

"Certainly not!" Richard cried. "I merely said that he looked like you."

"William insists Bennet favours me," Elizabeth said.

"You are mistaken, Darcy," Isabelle declared. "He will be your twin when he is grown. Just wait and see."

"I care not whom Bennet favours, as long as he is healthy," William interjected.

"Naturally," Richard said. Then he addressed Elizabeth. "I never thought I would live to see this day. I am extremely happy for you and for my cousin."

"We owe you our heartfelt gratitude," Elizabeth said. "Without your help, we might not have become a family."

"I like to think you would have reunited eventually," Richard said, smiling wryly. "Though I shall say that listening to my advice made it come to pass more expeditiously."

"When Elizabeth and I met again, I was too stubborn to let myself dream of such happiness. Your tenacity is responsible for my present joy," William said. "How can I adequately thank you?"

"I will settle for dismissing the two pounds I lost to you in billiards."

"Done!" William declared, chuckling.

"Now that we have that settled, I imagine you would like to change clothes and relax after your journey," Elizabeth said. "Tea will be served in less than an hour. Shall all of us, including the children, meet in the drawing room on this floor when tea is announced? I shall have Cook send up a tray of sandwiches and other refreshments. You must be hungry, and dinner will not be served for quite some time."

"That sounds wonderful," Isabelle said. "Come, everyone, off to your rooms! Your maids are waiting to help you change."

"I shall go with Marjorie, Mother," Marianne announced over the commotion.

Once alone on the balcony, a satisfied sense of completeness washed over William as he watched Elizabeth resettle Bennet into her lap. Sitting down on the edge of the chaise, he leaned in to give her a tender kiss.

"You have no idea what joy I derive from seeing my wife holding my child in her arms."

"There you would be wrong, William, for I feel the same way whenever I see you with Bennet."

As though the sound of his name demanded a response, Bennet began to stir.

"I know your arms must be tired, sweetheart," William said. "Let me hold him."

Elizabeth passed the baby to him and, placing the child on his shoulder, William stood and walked to the railing around the balcony. After kissing his son's forehead, he began speaking to him just as he had done since his birth.

"According to the ledgers our ancestors have been keeping for centuries, Bennet, last year's crops set a new record. Therefore, I do not anticipate having to purchase foodstuff to fill Pemberley's pantries or buy additional hay for the animals. Moreover, there were more foals and lambs born this spring than in all the years I have been master. I hope by the time you assume my duties, Son, we will have doubled the number of tenants, which will help to alleviate..."

As her husband continued to speak of Pemberley, Elizabeth was no longer listening. Instead, she was considering how blessed she had been as a young maiden to have met and captured the heart of a man as honourable as Fitzwilliam Darcy in a village called Meryton a long time ago.

Epilogue

They had wasted too many years being estranged, so William and Elizabeth were determined to make the most of every day left to them. To this end, when Bennet was fifteen months old, he was joined by a sister, Elizabeth Jane. To William's delight, she was the image of her mother.

Marianne adored her siblings and quickly became adept at caring for them. By the time she reached her majority, she had learned by good example what marriage and a family of her own would entail. At one and twenty, she became engaged to Viscount Durham of Dunbarton Hall in Hertfordshire, whose father, Lord Marshall, had finished Cambridge two years after William.

It was during preparations for Marianne's December wedding that Elizabeth discovered she was with child once more at the age of nine and thirty.

Wishing to be at home for the birth, Marianne postponed her wedding from December to March and was present when Anthony Fitzwilliam Thomas Darcy was born on Christmas Day. Anthony also favoured his father except his eyes were brown like Elizabeth's. Bennet, then four years of age, was especially overjoyed to have a brother. Dr. Porter pronounced Elizabeth in excellent health after her second son's birth, which was a great relief to her husband.

Marianne married the following spring and moved to Hertfordshire, residing not far from her Aunt Kitty. She would give birth to three children: two daughters and a son.

Georgiana and Gregory moved to London after his family opened a shipping office there. William and Elizabeth were delighted to see his sister and her family more often, and the Langston children shared in the easy camaraderie amongst the cousins. Several times a year the former Bennet girls and their families found time to get together with the Matlocks, Langstons and Gardiners either in London or at Pemberley to share holidays and other special events.

Richard's eldest, Marjorie, married the newly titled Earl of Glenaire the year before Marianne married and took up residence at his estate in Coventry. The only child of the Matlocks to remain in Derbyshire, besides the heir, was Ellen, who married the heir of Locklear Manor after Lord and Lady Blakely died. Edward, Viscount Sele, was Richard and Isabelle's youngest child, and he proved just as amiable as his father. Shortly after finishing Cambridge, Edward took Lady Honora Frampton, daughter of the Earl of Tattershall as his bride.

As William and Elizabeth's younger children began to reach adulthood, they were encouraged to wait until they were certain of their hearts' desire before embarking on anything as serious as marriage. Consequently, Elizabeth Jane became a writer and did not marry until she accepted an offer from Lord Seymour of Seymour Park in Liverpool when she was four and twenty. Afterwards, she gave birth to a son and two daughters.

Bennet, who, just as his cousin Isabelle had predicted, bore an uncanny likeness to his father by the time he was eighteen, became a favourite of the ladies of the *ton*. Nevertheless, he declared he would not marry until he had finished Cambridge and taken a tour of the Continent, and he kept to his word. At the age of six and twenty, he fell in love with Lady Sophie, the twenty-year-old daughter of Lord Beauford, the former Viscount Righton. Sophie looked very much like Elizabeth had at that age, a fact that was not lost on William. Both he and Elizabeth adored their new daughter, who gave Bennet two sons and three daughters.

Graduating from Cambridge with a degree in Natural Sciences[7], which included everything from physical sciences to biology which was taught alongside the history and philosophy of science, Anthony Darcy spent his life becoming an expert on the subject of anaesthesia and alleviating pain. In his thirtieth year, he married the daughter of one of his fellow researchers, Miss Catherine Devereux. He and Catherine were the parents of four children—two sons and two daughters.

Life held abundant blessings for the Darcys and all their relations. And, though each family suffered the sorrows and disappointments that life presents, each setback was met with the strength and resilience which can be found when one is part of a loving and compassionate family.

In generations to come, the Darcys that followed William and Elizabeth would delight in reading their journals and getting lost in stories written by two people so obviously in love, marvelling at how much the couple had accomplished. They had raised four admirable children who had filled Pemberley's halls with laughter and left a legacy of love for their grandchildren: Love for Pemberley, love for their family and love for each other.

Finis

---

7   The **Natural Sciences Tripos** (**NST**), begun in 1851, is the framework within which most of the science at the University of Cambridge is taught. The tripos includes a wide range of Natural Sciences from physical sciences to biology which are taught alongside the history and philosophy of science. The tripos covers several courses which form the University of Cambridge system of Tripos. https://en.wikipedia.org/wiki/Natural_Sciences_(Cambridge)

THANK YOU FOR READING!

I hope you enjoyed *Taking Another Chance – A Pride and Prejudice Variation.* I enjoyed writing this love story of an older Darcy and Elizabeth. To those who remember, I promised to write the sequel to *Proof of Love – A Pemberley Tale* and though I have several chapters written, I wished to get this shorter tale out first. The sequel will be my next novel.

As always, I would love to hear from you. You can send me an email at DarcyandLizzy@earthlink.net or you can always find me on my forum DarcyandLizzy.com/forum. If you join the forum, you'll find stories posted by a host of JAFF writers whose names I'm sure you'll recognize. Prior to publishing, I always post my latest book there.

If you would like notifications when my books are published or when I begin posting them on the forum, please send an email to this address and tell me you wish to be added to the 'Notifications' email list: Brendabigbee@earthlink.net. I will never share your information, and I promise you will not be inundated with emails.

Finally, if you are so inclined, I would appreciate it very much if you would review this book. You, the reader, have the power to make a book more visible by leaving a review.

Again, thank you so much for reading *Taking Another Chance – A Pride and Prejudice Variation.*

With gratitude,
Brenda Webb

Printed in Great Britain
by Amazon